SWIMMING HOME

SWIMMING HOME

Deborah Levy

Introduced by Tom McCarthy

ANANSI
INTERNATIONAL

First published in 2011 in Great Britain by And Other Stories.

This edition published in 2012 by
House of Anansi Press Inc.
110 Spadina Avenue, Suite 801
Toronto, ON, M5V 2K4
Tel. 416-363-4343
Fax 416-363-1017
www.houseofanansi.com

Distributed in Canada by
HarperCollins Canada Ltd.
1995 Markham Road
Scarborough, ON, M1B 5M8
Toll free tel. 1-800-387-0117

House of Anansi Press is committed to protecting our natural environment. As part of our efforts, the interior of this book is printed on paper that contains 100% post-consumer recycled fibres, is acid-free, and is processed chlorine-free.

This book is a work of fiction. Names, characters, businesses, organizations, places, and events are either the product of the author's imagination or are used fictitiously. Any resemblance to actual persons, living or dead, events or locales is entirely coincidental.

16 15 14 13 12 1 2 3 4 5

Library and Archives Canada Cataloguing in Publication

Levy, Deborah
Swimming home / Deborah Levy.

Also issued in electronic format.
ISBN: 978-1-77089-332-0

I. Title.

PR6062.E823S95 2012   823'.914   C2012-905592-1

Text design and typesetting: Charles Boyle

We acknowledge for their financial support of our publishing program the Canada Council for the Arts, the Ontario Arts Council, and the Government of Canada through the Canada Book Fund.

Printed and bound in Canada

To Sadie and Leila, so dear, always

INTRODUCTION

Entering the Whirlpool:
commerce, politics, marriage and hearth

If, as a young aspirant writer in the early to mid 1990s, you raised your head and took a look around the British literary landscape, one figure stood out from all the others: Deborah Levy. Read two pages of her work, and it was instantly apparent that she was a writer as much at home within the fields of visual and conceptual art, philosophy and performance as within that of the printed word. She'd read her Lacan and Deleuze, her Barthes, Marguerite Duras, Gertrude Stein, and Ballard, not to mention Kafka and Robbe-Grillet – and was putting all these characters to work in new, exhilarating ways. Like the emotional and cerebral choreographies of Pina Bausch, her fiction seemed less concerned about the stories it narrated than about the interzone (to borrow Burroughs's term) it set up in which desire and speculation, fantasy and symbols circulated. Even commonplace objects took on eerie, intense dimensions, like Duchampian readymades or objects in dreams for Freud.

If the setting and plot of *Swimming Home* are borrowed, almost ironically, from the staid English-middle-class-on-holiday novel, all similarities end there. The book's real drama plays out through blue sugar mice who scuttle from candy stalls into nightmares; or stones with holes in that turn into voyeuristic (or myopic) telescopes, then lethal weights, then, simply, holes. What holds this kaleidoscopic narrative together, even as it tears its characters apart, is – in classical Freudian fashion – desire: desire and its inseparable flip side, the death drive. This comes embodied – nakedly, almost primordially, floating in the water to which it will return – in the figure of Kitty Finch, half doomed and daddy-obsessed Sylvia Plath, half post-breakdown Edie Sedgwick out of *Ciao! Manhattan*: volatile, imploding around a swimming pool. Lured towards her, and the vortex or whirlpool she mermaids at the side of, are the worlds of commerce, politics, marriage and hearth, and literature itself, as represented by two exotica traders, a war correspondent and a celebrated poet, all uneasily coupled. And, at the spectrum's far end, the teenage girl who will emerge as the novel's real protagonist, inheritor of its historical traumas.

Tom McCarthy
June 2011

'Each morning in every family, men, women and children, *if they have nothing better to do*, tell each other their dreams. We are all at the mercy of the dream and we owe it to ourselves to submit its power to the waking state.'

– *La Révolution surréaliste*, No. 1, December 1924

SWIMMING HOME

ALPES-MARITIMES, FRANCE

July 1994

A Mountain Road. Midnight.

When Kitty Finch took her hand off the steering wheel and told him she loved him, he no longer knew if she was threatening him or having a conversation. Her silk dress was falling off her shoulders as she bent over the steering wheel. A rabbit ran across the road and the car swerved. He heard himself say, 'Why don't you pack a rucksack and see the poppy fields in Pakistan like you said you wanted to?'

'Yes,' she said.

He could smell petrol. Her hands swooped over the steering wheel like the seagulls they had counted from their room in the Hotel Negresco two hours ago.

She asked him to open his window so she could hear the insects calling to each other in the forest. He wound down the window and asked her, gently, to keep her eyes on the road.

'Yes,' she said again, her eyes now back on the road. And then she told him the nights were always 'soft' in the French Riviera. The days were hard and smelt of money.

He leaned his head out of the window and felt the cold mountain air sting his lips. Early humans had once lived in this forest that was now a road. They knew the past lived in rocks and trees and they knew desire made them awkward, mad, mysterious, messed up.

To have been so intimate with Kitty Finch had been a pleasure, a pain, a shock, an experiment, but most of all it had been a mistake. He asked her again to please, please, please drive him safely home to his wife and daughter.

'Yes,' she said. 'Life is only worth living because we hope it will get better and we'll all get home safely.'

SATURDAY

Wild Life

The swimming pool in the grounds of the tourist villa was more like a pond than the languid blue pools in holiday brochures. A pond in the shape of a rectangle, carved from stone by a family of Italian stonecutters living in Antibes. The body was floating near the deep end, where a line of pine trees kept the water cool in their shade.

'Is it a bear?' Joe Jacobs waved his hand vaguely in the direction of the water. He could feel the sun burning into the shirt his Hindu tailor had made for him from a roll of raw silk. His back was on fire. Even the roads were melting in the July heatwave.

His daughter, Nina Jacobs, fourteen years old, standing at the edge of the pool in her new cherry-print bikini, glanced anxiously at her mother. Isabel Jacobs was unzipping her jeans as if she was about to dive in. At the same time she could see Mitchell and Laura, the two family friends sharing the villa with them for the summer, put down their mugs of tea and walk towards the stone steps that led to the shallow end. Laura, a slender giantess at six foot three, kicked off her sandals and waded in up to her knees. A battered yellow lilo knocked against the mossy sides, scattering the bees that were in various stages of dying in the water.

'What do you think it is, Isabel?'

Nina could see from where she was standing that it was a woman swimming naked under the water. She was on her stomach, both arms stretched out like a starfish, her long hair floating like seaweed at the sides of her body.

'Jozef thinks she's a bear,' Isabel Jacobs replied in her detached war-correspondent voice.

'If it's a bear I'm going to have to shoot it.' Mitchell had recently purchased two antique Persian handguns at the flea market in Nice and shooting things was on his mind.

Yesterday they had all been discussing a newspaper article about a ninety-four-kilo bear that had walked down from the mountains in Los Angeles and taken a dip in a Hollywood actor's pool. The bear was on heat, according to the Los Angeles Animal Services. The actor had called the authorities. The bear was shot with a tranquilliser gun and then released in the nearby mountains. Joe Jacobs had wondered out loud what it was like to be tranquillised and then have to stumble home. Did it ever get home? Did it get dizzy and forgetful and start to hallucinate? Perhaps the barbiturate inserted inside the dart, also known as 'chemical capture', had made the bear's legs shake and jerk? Had the tranquilliser helped the bear cope with life's stressful events, calming its agitated mind so that it now pleaded with the authorities to throw it small prey injected with barbiturate syrups? Joe had only stopped this riff when Mitchell stood on his toe. As far as Mitchell was concerned it was very, very hard to get the arsehole poet known to his readers as JHJ (Joe to every one else except his wife) to shut the fuck up.

Nina watched her mother dive into the murky green water and swim towards the woman. Saving the lives of bloated bodies floating in rivers was probably the sort of thing her mother did all the time. Apparently television ratings always went up when she was on the news. Her mother disappeared to Northern Ireland and Lebanon and Kuwait and then she came back as if she'd just nipped down the road to buy a pint of milk. Isabel Jacobs' hand was about to clasp the ankle of whoever it was floating in the pool. A sudden violent splash made Nina run to her father, who grasped her sunburnt shoulder, making her scream out loud. When a head emerged from the water, its mouth open and gasping for breath, for one panicked second she thought it was roaring like a bear.

A woman with dripping waist-length hair climbed out of the pool and ran to one of the plastic recliners. She looked like she might be in her early twenties, but it was hard to tell because she was frantically skipping from one chair to another, searching for her dress. It had fallen on to the paving stones but no one helped her because they were staring at her naked body. Nina felt light-headed in the fierce heat. The bittersweet smell of lavender drifted towards her, suffocating her as the sound of the woman's panting breath mingled with the drone of the bees in the wilting flowers. It occurred to her she might be sun-sick, because she felt as if she was going to faint. In a blur she could see the woman's breasts were surprisingly full and round for someone so thin. Her long thighs were joined to the jutting hinges of her hips like the legs of the dolls she used to bend and twist as a child. The only thing that seemed real about the woman was the triangle of golden pubic hair glinting in the sun. The sight of it made Nina fold her arms across her chest and hunch her back in an effort to make her own body disappear.

'Your dress is over there.' Joe Jacobs pointed to the pile of crumpled blue cotton lying under the recliner. They had all been staring at her for an embarrassingly long time. The woman grabbed it and deftly slipped the flimsy dress over her head.

'Thanks. I'm Kitty Finch by the way.'

What she actually said was I'm Kah Kah Kah and stammered on for ever until she got to Kitty Finch. Everyone couldn't wait for her to finish saying who she was.

Nina realised her mother was still in the pool. When she climbed up the stone steps, her wet swimming costume was covered in silver pine needles.

'I'm Isabel. My husband thought you were a bear.'

Joe Jacobs twisted his lips in an effort not to laugh.

'Of course I didn't think she was a bear.'

Kitty Finch's eyes were grey like the tinted windows of Mitchell's hire car, a Mercedes, parked on the gravel at the front of the villa.

'I hope you don't mind me using the pool. I've just

arrived and it's sooo hot. There's been a mistake with the rental dates.'

'What sort of mistake?' Laura glared at the young woman as if she had just been handed a parking ticket.

'Well, I thought I was staying here from this Saturday for a fortnight. But the caretaker . . .'

'If you can call a lazy stoned bastard like Jurgen a caretaker.' Just mentioning Jurgen's name brought Mitchell out in a disgusted sweat.

'Yeah. Jurgen says I've got the dates all wrong and now I'm going to lose my deposit.'

Jurgen was a German hippy who was never exact about anything. He described himself as 'a nature man' and always had his nose buried in *Siddhartha* by Hermann Hesse.

Mitchell wagged his finger at her. 'There are worse things than losing your deposit. We were about to have you sedated and driven up to the mountains.'

Kitty Finch lifted up the sole of her left foot and slowly pulled out a thorn. Her grey eyes searched for Nina, who was still hiding behind her father. And then she smiled.

'I like your bikini.' Her front teeth were crooked, snarled into each other, and her hair was drying into copper-coloured curls. 'What's your name?'

'Nina.'

'Do you think I look like a bear, Nina?' She clenched her right hand as if it was a paw and jabbed it at the cloudless blue sky. Her fingernails were painted dark green.

Nina shook her head and then swallowed her spit the wrong way and started to cough. Everyone sat down. Mitchell on the ugly blue chair because he was the fattest and it was the biggest, Laura on the pink wicker chair, Isabel and Joe on the two white plastic recliners. Nina perched on the edge of her father's chair and fiddled with the five silver toe-rings Jurgen had given her that morning. They all had a place in the shade except Kitty Finch, who was crouching awkwardly on the burning paving stones.

'You haven't anywhere to sit. I'll find you a chair.' Isabel wrung the ends of her wet black hair. Drops of water glistened on her shoulders and then ran down her arm like a snake.

Kitty shook her head and blushed. 'Oh, don't bother. Pah pah please. I'm just waiting for Jurgen to come back with the name of a hotel for me and I'll be off.'

'Of course you must sit down.'

Laura, puzzled and uneasy, watched Isabel lug a heavy wooden chair covered in dust and cobwebs towards the pool. There were things in the way. A red bucket. A broken plant pot. Two canvas umbrellas wedged into lumps of concrete. No one helped her because they weren't quite sure what she was doing. Isabel, who had somehow managed to pin up her wet hair with a clip in the shape of a lily, was actually placing the wooden chair between her recliner and her husband's.

Kitty Finch glanced nervously at Isabel and then at Joe, as if she couldn't work out if she was being offered the chair or being forced to sit in it. She wiped away the cobwebs with the skirt of her dress for much too long and then finally sat down. Laura folded her hands in her lap as if preparing to interview an applicant for a job.

'Have you been here before?'

'Yes. I've been coming here for years.'

'Do you work?' Mitchell spat an olive pip into a bowl.

'I sort of work. I'm a botanist.'

Joe stroked the small shaving cut on his chin and smiled at her. 'There are some nice peculiar words in your profession.'

His voice was surprisingly gentle, as if he intuited Kitty Finch was offended by the way Laura and Mitchell were interrogating her.

'Yeah. Joe likes pe-cu-li-ar words cos he's a poet.' Mitchell said 'peculiar' as if imitating an aristocrat in a stupor.

Joe leaned back in his chair and closed his eyes. 'Ignore him, Kitty.' He sounded as if he had been wounded in some inexplicable way. 'Everything is pe-cu-li-ar to Mitchell. Strangely enough, this makes him feel superior.'

Mitchell stuffed five olives into his mouth one after the other and then spat out the pips in Joe's direction as if they were little bullets from one of his minor guns.

'So in the meantime ' – Joe leaned forward now – 'perhaps you could tell us what you know about cotyledons?'

'Right.' Kitty's right eye winked at Nina when she said 'right'. 'Cotyledons are the first leaves on a seedling.' Her stammer seemed to have disappeared.

'Correct. And now for my favourite word . . . how would you describe a leaf?'

'Kitty,' Laura said sternly, 'there are lots of hotels, so you'd better go and find one.'

When Jurgen finally made his way through the gate, his silver dreadlocks tied back in a ponytail, he told them every hotel in the village was full until Thursday.

'Then you must stay until Thursday.' Isabel said this vaguely, as if she didn't quite believe it. 'I think there's a spare room at the back of the house.'

Kitty frowned and leaned back in her new chair.

'Well, yeah. Thanks. Is that OK with everyone else? Please say if you mind.'

It seemed to Nina that she was asking them to mind. Kitty Finch was blushing and clenching her toes at the same time. Nina felt her own heart racing. It had gone hysterical, thumping in her chest. She glanced at Laura and saw she was actually wringing her hands. Laura was about to say she did mind. She and Mitchell had shut their shop in Euston for the entire summer, knowing the windows that had been smashed by thieves and drug addicts at least three times that year would be smashed again when their holiday was over. They had come to the Alpes-Maritimes to escape from the futility of mending broken glass. She found herself struggling for words. The young woman was a window waiting to be climbed through. A window that she guessed was a little broken anyway. She couldn't be sure of this, but it seemed to her that Joe Jacobs had already wedged his foot into the crack and his wife had helped him. She cleared her throat and was about to speak her mind, but what was on her mind was so unutterable the hippy caretaker got there first.

'So, Kitty Ket, shall I carry your valises to your room?'

Everyone looked to where Jurgen was pointing with his nicotine-stained finger. Two blue canvas bags lay to the right of the French doors of the villa.

'Thanks, Jurgen.' Kitty dismissed him as if he was her personal valet.

He bent down and picked up the bags.

'What are the weeds?' He lifted up a tangle of flowering plants that had been stuffed into the second blue bag.

'Oh, I found those in the churchyard next to Claude's café.'

Jurgen looked impressed.

'You'll have to call them the Kitty Ket plant. It is a historical fact. Plant hunters often named the plants they found after themselves.'

'Yeah.' She stared past him in to Joe Jacobs' dark eyes as if to say, 'Jurgen's special name for me is Kitty Ket.'

Isabel walked to the edge of the pool and dived in. As she swam low under the water, her arms stretched out in front of her head, she saw her watch lying on the bottom of the pool. She flipped over and scooped it up from the green tiles. When she surfaced she saw the old English woman who lived next door waving from her balcony. She waved back and then realised Madeleine Sheridan was waving to Mitchell, who was calling out her name.

Interpreting a Smile

'Madel-eeene!'

It was the fat man who liked guns calling up to her. Madeleine Sheridan lifted up her arthritic arm and waved with two limp fingers from her straw chair. Her body had become a sum of flawed parts. At medical school she had learned she had twenty-seven bones in each hand, eight in the wrist alone, five in the palm. Her fingers were rich in nerve endings but now even moving two fingers was an effort.

She wanted to remind Jurgen, whom she could see carrying Kitty Finch's bags into the villa, that it was her birthday in six days' time, but she was reluctant to appear so begging of his company in front of the English tourists. Perhaps she was dead already and had been watching the drama of the young woman's arrival from the Other Side? Four months ago, in March, when Kitty Finch was staying alone at the tourist villa (apparently to study mountain plants), she had informed Madeleine Sheridan that a breeze would help her tomatoes grow stronger stems and offered to thin the leaves for her. This she proceeded to do, but she was whispering to herself all the while, pah pah pah, kah kah kah, consonants that made hard sounds on her lips. Madeleine Sheridan, who believed human beings had to suffer real hardships before they agreed to lose their minds, told her in a steely voice to stop making that noise. To stop it. To stop it right now. Today was Saturday and the noise had come back to France to haunt her. It had even been offered a room in the villa.

•

'Madel-eeene, I'm cooking beef tonight. Why don't you join us for supper?'

She could just make out the pink dome of Mitchell's balding head as she squinted at him in the sun. Madeleine Sheridan, who was quite partial to beef and often lonely in the evenings, wondered if she had it in herself to decline Mitchell's invitation. She thought she did. When couples offer shelter or a meal to strays and loners, they do not really take them in. They play with them. Perform for them. And when they are done they tell their stranded guest in all sorts of sly ways she is now required to leave. Couples were always keen to return to the task of trying to destroy their lifelong partners while pretending to have their best interests at heart. A single guest was a mere distraction from this task.

'Madel-eeene.'

Mitchell seemed more anxious than usual. Yesterday he told her he had spotted Keith Richards drinking Pepsi in Villefranche-sur-Mer and was desperate to ask for his autograph. In the end he didn't because, in his own words, 'The arsehole poet was with me and threatened to headbutt me for being normal.'

Mitchell with his flabby, prawn-pink arms amused her when he gloomily observed that Joe Jacobs was not the sort of poet who gazed at the moon and had no muscle tone. He could probably lift a wardrobe with his teeth. Especially if it had a beautiful woman inside it. When the English tourists arrived two weeks ago, Joe Jacobs (JHJ on his books but she'd never heard of him) knocked on her door to borrow some salt. He was wearing a winter suit on the hottest day of the year and when she pointed this out, he told her it was his sister's birthday and he always wore a suit to show his respect.

This bemused her, because her own birthday was much on her mind. His suit seemed more appropriate for a funeral but he was so charming and attentive she asked him if he would like to try the Andalucían almond soup she had made earlier. When he muttered, 'How kind, my dear,' she poured a generous amount into one of her favourite ceramic bowls and invited him to drink it on her balcony. Something terrible happened. He took a sip and felt something tangle with his teeth, only to discover it was her hair. A small clump of silver hair had somehow found its way into the bowl. He was mortified beyond her comprehension, even though she apologised, unable to fathom how it had got there. His hands were actually shaking and he pushed the bowl away with such force the soup spilt all over his ridiculous pinstriped suit, its jacket lined with dandyish pink silk. She thought a poet might have done better than that. He could have said, 'Your soup was like drinking a cloud.'

'Madel-eeene.'

Mitchell couldn't even say her name properly. Possibly because he had such a ridiculous name himself. The prospect of having to live with Kitty Finch had obviously got him into a panic and she wasn't surprised. She squeezed her eyes into slits, enjoying the view of her ugly bare feet. It was such a pleasure not to wear socks and shoes. Even after fifteen years living in

France, wrenched as she was from her country of birth and her first language, it was the pleasure of naked feet she was most grateful for. She could live without a slice of Mitchell's succulent beef. And she would be insanely brave to risk an evening in the company of Kitty Finch, who was pretending not to have seen her. Right now she was scooping pine cones out of the pool with Nina Jacobs as if her life depended on it. There was no way Madeleine Sheridan, six days away from turning eighty, would perform like a dignified old woman at the dinner table in the tourist villa. The same table Jurgen had bought at the flea market and polished with beeswax and paraffin. What's more, he had polished it in his underpants because of the heatwave. She had had to avert her eyes at the sight of him sweating in what she delicately called his 'undergarments'.

An eagle was hovering in the sky. It had seen the mice that ran through the uncut grass in the orchard.

She called down her excuses to Mitchell, but he seemed not to have heard her. He was watching Joe Jacobs disappear inside the villa to find a hat. Kitty Finch was apparently going to take the English poet for a walk and show him some flowers. Madeleine Sheridan couldn't be sure of this, but she thought the mad girl with her halo of red hair shining in the sun might be smiling at her.

To use the language of a war correspondent, which was, she knew, what Isabel Jacobs happened to be, she would have to say that Kitty Finch was smiling at her with hostile intent.

The Botany Lesson

There were signs everywhere saying the orchard was private property, but Kitty insisted she knew the farmer and no one was going to set the dogs on them. For the last twenty minutes she had been pointing out trees that, in her view, 'were not doing too well'.

'Do you only notice trees that suffer?' Joe Jacobs shaded his eyes with his hands, which were covered in mosquito bites, and stared into her bright grey eyes.

'Yes, I suppose I do.'

He was convinced he could hear an animal growling in the grass and told her it sounded like a dog.

'Don't worry about the dogs. The farmer owns 2,000 olive trees in the Grasse area. He's too busy to set his dogs on us.'

'Well, I suppose that many olive trees would keep him busy,' Joe mumbled.

His black hair now fading into silver curls fell in a mess around his ears and the battered straw hat kept slipping off his head. Kitty had to run behind him to pick it up.

'Oh, 2,000 . . . that's not a lot of trees . . . not at all.'

She stooped down to peer at wild flowers growing between the long white grasses that came up to her knees.

'These are *Bellis perennis*.' She scooped up what looked like daisy petals and stuffed them in her mouth. 'Plants are always from some sort of family.'

She buried her face in the flowers she was clutching and named them for him in Latin. He was impressed by the tender way she held the plants in her fingers and spoke about them with easy intimacy, as if indeed they were a family with various problems and unusual qualities. And then she told him what she wanted most in life was to see the poppy fields in Pakistan.

'Actually,' she confessed nervously, 'I've written a poem about that.'

Joe stopped walking. So that was why she was here.

Young women who followed him about and wanted him to read their poetry, and he was now convinced she was one of them, always started by telling him they'd written a poem about something extraordinary. They walked side by side, flattening a path through the long grass. He waited for her to speak, to make her request, to say how influenced by his books she was, to explain how she'd managed to track him down, and then she would ask would he mind, did he have time, would he be so kind as to please, please read her small effort inspired by himself.

'So you've read all my books and now you've followed me to France,' he said sharply.

A new wave of blush crashed over her cheeks and long neck.

'Yes. Rita Dwighter, who owns the villa, is a friend of my mother. Rita told me you had booked it for the whole summer. She lets me stay in her house for free off-season. I couldn't stay because YOU hah hah hah hah hogged it.'

'But it's not off-season, Kitty. July is what they call the high season, isn't it?'

She had a north London accent. Her front teeth were

crooked. When she wasn't stammering and blushing she looked like she'd been sculpted from wax in a dark workshop in Venice. If she was a botanist she obviously did not spend much time outside. Whoever had made her was clever. She could swim and cry and blush and say things like 'hogged it'.

'Let's sit in the shade.'

He pointed to a large tree surrounded by small rocks. A plump brown pigeon perched comically on a thin branch that looked like it was about to snap under its weight.

'All right. That's a haaaah hazelnut tree by the way.'

He charged ahead before she finished her sentence and sat down, leaning his back against the tree trunk. When she seemed reluctant to join him he patted the space next to him, brushing away the twigs and leaves until she sat down by his side, smoothing her faded blue cotton dress over her knees. He could not so much hear her heart as feel it beating under her thin dress.

'When I write poems I always think you can hear them.'

A bell tinkled in the distance. It sounded like a goat grazing somewhere in the orchard, moving around in the long grass.

'Why are you shaking?' He could smell chlorine in her hair.

'Yeah. I've stopped taking my pills so my hands are a bit shaky.'

Kitty moved a little nearer him. He wasn't too sure what to make of this until he saw she was avoiding a line of red ants crawling under her calves.

'Why do you take pills?'

'Oh, I've decided not to for a while. You know . . . it's quite a relief to feel miserable again. I don't feel anything when I take my pills.'

She slapped at the ants crawling over her ankles.

'I wrote about that too . . . it's called "Picking Roses on Seroxat".'

Joe fumbled for a scrap of green silk in his pocket and blew his nose. 'What's Seroxat?'

'You know what it is.'

His nose was buried in the silk handkerchief.

'Tell me anyway,' he snuffled.

'Seroxat is a really strong antidepressant. I've been on it for years.'

Kitty stared at the sky smashing against the mountains. He found himself reaching for her cold shaking hand and held it tight in his lap. She was right to be indignant at his question. Clasping her hand was a silent acknowledgement that he knew she had read him because he had told his readers all about his teenage years on medication. When he was fifteen he had very lightly grazed his left wrist with a razor blade. Nothing serious. Just an experiment. The blade was cool and sharp. His wrist was warm and soft. They were not supposed to be paired together but it was a teenage game of Snap. He had snapped. The doctor, an old Hungarian man with hair in his ears, had not agreed this pairing was an everyday error. He had asked questions. Biography is what the Hungarian doctor wanted.

Names and places and dates. The names of his mother, his father, his sister. The languages they spoke and how old was he when he last saw them? Joe Jacobs had replied by fainting in the consulting room and so his teenage years had been tranquillised into a one-season pharmaceutical mist. Or as he had suggested in his most famous poem, now translated into twenty-three languages: a bad fairy made a deal with me, 'give me your history and I will give you something to take it away'.

When he turned to look at her face, now drained of its blush, her cheeks were wet.

'Why are you crying?'

'I'm OK.' Her voice was matter of fact.

'I'm pleased to save money and not spend it on a hotel, but I didn't expect your wife to offer me the spare room.'

Three black flies settled on his forehead, but he did not let go of her hand to flick them away. He passed her the scrap of silk he kept as a handkerchief.

'Mop yourself up.'

'I don't want your handkerchief.' She threw the scrap of silk back into his lap. 'And I hate it when people say mop yourself up. Like I'm a dirty floor.'

He couldn't be sure of it, but he thought that was a line from one of his poems too. Not quite as it was written but near enough. He noticed a scratch running across her left ankle and she told him it was where his wife had grabbed her foot in the pool.

The goat was getting nearer. Every time it moved the bell rang. When it was still the bell stopped. It made him feel uneasy. He brushed a small green cricket off his shoulder and placed it in her open palm.

'I think you've written something you'd like me to read. Is that right?'

'Yes. It's just one poem.' Again her voice was matter of fact. She set the cricket free, watching it jump into the grass and disappear. 'It's a conversation with you, really.'

Joe picked up a twig that had fallen from the tree. The brown pigeon above his head was chancing its luck. There were stronger branches it could move to but it refused to budge. He told her he would read her poem that evening and waited for her to thank him.

He waited. For her thank-yous. For his time. For his attention. For his generosity. For defending her against Mitchell. For his company and for his words, the poetry that had made her more or less stalk him on a family holiday. Her thank-yous did not arrive.

'By the way' – he stared at her pale shins covered in crushed ants – 'the fact I know that you um take medication and all that . . . is confidential.'

She shrugged. 'Well, actually, Jurgen and Dr Sheridan and everyone in the village know already. And I've stopped taking it anyway.'

'Is Madeleine Sheridan a doctor?'

'Yeah.' She clenched her toes. 'She's got friends at the hospital in Grasse, so you'd better pretend to be happy and have a grip.'

He laughed and then to make him laugh some more, so he would appear to be happy and to have a grip, she advised him that nothing, NOTHING AT ALL, was confidential when it was told to Jurgen. 'Like all indiscreet people, he puts his hand on his heart and assures his confidant that his lips are sealed. Jurgen's lips are never sealed, because they always have a giant spliff between them.'

Joe Jacobs knew he should ask her more questions. Like his journalist wife. The why the how the when the who and all the other words he was supposed to ask to make life more coherent. But she had given him a little information. On the way to the orchard she told him she had given up her job clearing leaves and cutting grass in Victoria Park in Hackney. A gang of boys had pulled a knife on her because when she was on medication it made her legs twitch so she was easy prey.

They heard the bell again.

'What is it?' Kitty stood up and peered into the long grass.

Joe could see the vertebrae of her spine under her dress. When he dropped his hat once again, she picked it up and dusted it with the tips of her green fingernails, holding it out to him.

'Oh!'

Kitty shouted 'Oh' because at that moment the long grass moved and they saw flashes of pink and silver glinting through the blades. Something was making its way towards them. The grass seemed to open and Nina stood in front of them, barefoot in her cherry-print bikini. On her toes were Jurgen's gift of the five silver rings from India with little bells attached to them.

'I came to find you.' She gazed at her father, who seemed to be holding Kitty's Finch's hand. 'Mum's gone to Nice. She said she had to take her shoes to get mended.'

24

Kitty looked at the watch on her thin wrist.

'But the cobblers are shut in Nice now.'

Three growling dogs sprang out of the grass and circled them. When the farmer appeared and told the sweating English poet that he was trespassing on his land, the beautiful English girl ripped the scarf off the hat she was wearing and passed it to the frowning poet.

'Mop yourself up,' she said, and told the farmer in French to call the dogs off them.

When they got back to the villa, Joe walked through the cypress trees to the garden, where he had set up a table and chair to write in the shade. For the last two weeks he had referred to it as his study and it was understood he must not be disturbed, even when he fell asleep on the chair. Through the gaps in the branches of the cypress trees he saw Laura sitting on the faded wicker chair by the pool. Mitchell was carrying a bowl of strawberries towards her.

He glanced drowsily at Laura and Mitchell eating their strawberries in the sunshine and found himself about to fall asleep. It was an odd sensation, 'to find himself' about to fall into sleep. As if he could find himself anywhere at any time. Best to make the anywhere a good place to be, then, a place without anguish or impending threat; sitting at a table under the shade of an old tree with his family; taking photographs in a gondola moving across the canals of Venice; watching a film in an empty cinema with a can of lager between his knees. In a car on a mountain road at midnight after making love to Kitty Finch.

A Mountain Road. Midnight.

It was getting dark and she told him the brakes on the hire car were fucked, she couldn't see a thing, she couldn't even see her hands.

Her silk dress was falling off her shoulders as she bent over the steering wheel. A rabbit ran across the road and the car swerved. He told her to keep her eyes on the road, to just do that, and while he was speaking she was kissing him and driving at the same time. And then she asked him to open his window so she could hear the insects calling to each other in the forest. He wound down the window and told her, again, to keep her eyes on the road. He leaned his head out of the window and felt the cold mountain air sting his lips. Early humans had once lived in this mountain forest. They knew the past lived in rocks and trees and they knew desire made them awkward, mad, mysterious, messed up.

'Yes,' Kitty Finch said, her eyes now back on the road. 'I know what you're thinking. Life is only worth living because we hope it will get better and we'll all get home safely. But you tried and you did not get home safely. You did not get home at all. That is why I am here, Jozef. I have come to France to save you from your thoughts.'

Imitations of Life

Isabel Jacobs was not sure why she had lied about taking her shoes to be mended. It was just one more thing she was not sure of. After Kitty Finch's arrival all she could do to get through the day was to imitate someone she used to be, but who that was, who she used to be, no longer seemed to be a person worth imitating. The world had become increasingly mysterious. And so had she. She was not sure what she felt about anything any more, or how she felt it, or why she had offered a stranger the spare room. By the time she had driven down the mountains, found change for the toll, got lost in Vence and tried to turn back in the traffic that choked the coast road to Nice, enraged drivers jerked their hands at her, pressed their horns, rolled down their windows and shouted at her. In the back seats of their cars, groomed little dogs stared at her mockingly, as if not knowing where you were going in a one-way system was something they despised too.

She parked opposite the beach called Opéra Plage and walked towards the pink dome of the Hotel Negresco, which she recognised from the map stapled on to the 'fact sheet' that came with the villa. The fact sheet was full of information about the Hotel Negresco, the oldest and grandest belle époque hotel on the Promenade des Anglais. Apparently it was built in 1912 by Henri Negresco, a Hungarian immigrant who designed it to attract to Nice 'the very top of the upper crust'.

A breeze was blowing across the two lanes of traffic that separated her from the crowded beaches. This blast of dirty city life felt better, far better than the clean sharp mountain air that only seemed to make sorrow sharper too. Here in Nice, France's fifth biggest city, she could disappear into the crowds of holidaymakers as if she had nothing on her mind except to complain about the cost of hiring a sun lounger on the Riviera.

A woman with a helmet of permed, hennaed hair stopped her to ask if she knew the way to Rue François Aune. The lenses of her big sunglasses were smeared with what looked like dried milk. She spoke in English with an accent that Isabel thought might be Russian. The woman pointed a finger laden with rings at a mechanic in oily navy overalls lying under a motorbike, as if to suggest Isabel ask him for directions on her behalf. For a moment she couldn't work out why this was demanded of her, but then she realised the woman was blind and could hear the mechanic revving his bike nearby.

When Isabel knelt down on the pavement and showed him the scrap of paper the woman had pushed into her hand, he jerked his thumb at the apartment block across the road. The blind woman was standing in the street she was looking for. 'You are here.' Isabel took her arm and led her through the gate towards the affluent mansion block, every window framed with newly painted green shutters. Three sprinklers watered the palm trees planted in neat lines in the communal gardens.

'But I want the port, Madame. I am looking for Dr Ortega.'

The blind Russian woman sounded indignant, as if she

had been taken to the wrong place against her will. Isabel gazed at the names of residents carved on to brass plaques by the door and read them out loud: 'Perez, Orsi, Bergel, Dr Ortega.' There was his name. This was where he lived, even though the woman disagreed.

She pressed the bell for Dr Ortega and ignored the Russian woman, who was now fumbling urgently in her crocodile-skin handbag for what turned out to be a grubby portable dictionary.

The voice that came out of the polished brass speaker of the door entry system was a soft Spanish voice asking her, in French, to say who she was.

'My name is Isabel. Your visitor is waiting for you downstairs.'

A police siren drowned her out and she had to start again.

'Did you say your name is Isabel?' It was a simple enough question but it made her anxious, as if she was indeed pretending to be someone she was not.

The entry system made a whining sound and she pushed open the glass door framed in heavy dark wood that led into the marble foyer. The Russian woman in her stained dark glasses did not want to move and instead kept repeating her request to be taken to the port.

'Are you still there, Isabel?'

Why did the doctor not walk down the stairs and collect the blind woman himself?

'Could you come down and get your patient?' She heard him laugh.

'*Señora, soy doctor en filosofía*. She is not my patient. She is my student.'

He was laughing again. The dark rumbling laugh of a smoker. She heard his voice through the holes in the speaker and moved closer to it.

'My student wants the port because she wishes to go back to St Petersburg. She does not want to arrive for her Spanish lesson and therefore does not believe she is here. *Ella no quiere estar aquí.*'

He was playful and flirtatious, a man who had time to speak in riddles from the safety of the door entry system. She wished she could be more like him and fool around and play with whatever the day brought in. What had led her to where she was now? Where was she now? As usual she was running away from Jozef. This thought made her eyes sting with tears she resented. No, not again, not Jozef, not again. She turned away and left the Russian woman groping the banisters of the marble stairway, still insisting she was in the wrong place and the port was her final destination.

The sky had darkened and she could smell the sea somewhere close. Seagulls screeched above her head. The sweet yeasty smell of the *boulangerie* across the road wafted over the parked cars. Families were returning from the beach carrying plastic balls and chairs and colourful towels. The *boulangerie* was suddenly full of teenage boys buying slices of pizza. Across the road the mechanic was revving his motorbike triumphantly. She was not ready to go home and start imitating someone she used to be. Instead she walked for what seemed like an hour along the Promenade des Anglais and stopped at one of the restaurants set up on the beach near the airport.

The planes taking off flew low over the black sea. A party of students was drinking beer on the slopes of the pebbles. They were opinionated, flirtatious, shouting at each other, enjoying a summer night on the city beach. Things were starting in their lives. New jobs. New ideas. New friendships. New love affairs. She was in the middle of her life, she was nearly fifty years old and had witnessed countless massacres and conflicts in the work that pressed her up close to the suffering world. She had not been posted to cover the genocide in Rwanda, as two of her shattered colleagues had been. They had told her it was impossible to believe the scale of the human demolition, their own eyes dazed as they took in the dazed eyes of the orphans. Starved dogs had become accustomed to eating human flesh. They had seen dogs roam the fields with bits of people between their teeth. Yet even without witnessing first-hand the terrors of Rwanda, she had gone too far into the unhappiness of the world to start all over again. If she could choose to unlearn everything that was supposed to have made her wise, she would start all over again. Ignorant and hopeful, she would marry all over again and have a child all over again and drink beer with her handsome young husband on this city beach at night. They would be enchanted beginners all over again, kissing under the bright stars. That was the best thing to be in life.

A large extended family of women and their children sat at three tables pushed together. They all had the same wiry brown hair and high cheekbones and they were eating elaborate swirls of ice cream piled into pint-sized glasses. The waiter lit the sparklers he had stuck into the chantilly and they oohed and aahed and clapped their hands. She was cold in her halter-neck dress, too naked for this time of night. The women feeding their children with long silver teaspoons glanced curiously at the silent brooding woman with bare shoulders. Like the waiter, they seemed offended by her solitude. She had to tell him twice she was not expecting anyone to join her. When he slammed her espresso on the empty table set for two, most of it spilled into the saucer.

She watched the waves crash on the pebbles. The ocean folding into itself the plastic bags left on the beach that day. While she tried to make what was left of her coffee last long enough to earn her place at a table set for two, the thoughts she tried to push away kept returning like the waves on the stones.

She was a kind of ghost in her London home. When she returned to it from various war zones and found that in her absence the shoe polish or light bulbs had been put in a different place, somewhere similar but not quite where they were before, she learned that she too had a transient place in the family home. To do the things she had chosen to do in the world, she risked forfeiting her place as a wife and mother, a bewildering place haunted by all that had been imagined for her if she chose to sit in it. She had attempted to be someone she didn't really understand. A powerful but fragile female character. If she knew that to be forceful was not the same as being powerful and to be gentle was not the same as being fragile, she did not know how to use this knowledge in her own life or what it added up to, or even how it made sitting alone at a table laid for two on a Saturday night feel better. When she arrived in London from Africa or Ireland or Kuwait it was Laura who sometimes offered her a bed in the storeroom above their shop in Euston. It was a kind of convalescence. She lay on it in the daytime and Laura brought her cups of tea when the shop was quiet. They had nothing in common except they had known each other for a long time. The time that had passed between them counted for something. They did not have to explain anything or be polite or fill in the gaps in conversation.

She invited Laura to share the villa with them for the summer and was surprised at how quickly her friend accepted. Laura and Mitchell usually needed more notice to shut up the shop and get their affairs in order.

The sparklers were spluttering to an end in the ice creams. One of the mothers suddenly shouted at her five-year-old son, who had dropped his glass on the floor. It was a cry of incandescent rage. Isabel could see she was exhausted. The woman had become fierce, neither unhappy nor happy. She was now on her hands and knees, wiping the ice cream on the floor with the napkins the clan were holding out to her. She felt the disapproval of the women staring at her as she sat alone, but she was grateful to them. She would bring Nina to this restaurant and buy her daughter an ice cream with a sparkler in it. The women had planned something lovely for their children, something she would imitate.

Walls That Open and Close

Nina watched Kitty Finch press the palms of her hands against the walls of the spare bedroom as if she was testing how solid they were. It was a small room looking over the back of the villa, the yellow curtains drawn tight across the only window. It made the room hot and dark, but Kitty said she liked it that way. Upstairs in the kitchen they could hear Mitchell singing an Abba song out of tune. Kitty told Nina she was checking the walls because the foundations of the villa were shaky. Three years ago a gang of cowboy builders from Menton had been paid to patch the whole house together. There were cracks everywhere but they had been hastily covered up with the wrong sort of plaster.

Nina couldn't get over how much Kitty knew about everything. What was the right sort of plaster, then? Did Kitty Finch work in the construction industry? How did she manage to tuck all her hair into a hard hat?

It was as if Kitty had read her thoughts, because she said, 'Yeah, well, the right sort of plaster has limestone in it,' and then she knelt down on the floor and examined the plants she had collected in the churchyard earlier that morning.

Her green fingernails stroked the triangular leaves and clusters of white flowers that, she insisted, wrinkling her nose, smelt of mice. She was collecting the seeds from the plants because she wanted to study them and Nina could help her if she wanted to.

'What sort of plant is it?'

'It's called *Conium maculatum*. It comes from the same family as fennel, parsnips and carrot. I was really surprised to see it growing by the church. The leaves look like parsley, don't they?'

Nina didn't really know.

'This is hemlock. Your father knew that, of course. In the old days children used to make whistles from the stems and it sometimes poisoned them. But the Greeks thought it cured tumours.'

Kitty seemed to have a lot to do. After she'd hung up her summer dresses in the wardrobe and lined up a few tattered well-thumbed books on the shelf, she ran upstairs to look at the pool again, even though it was now dark outside.

When she came back she explained that the pool now had underwater lighting. 'It didn't last year.'

She took a brown A4 envelope out of the blue canvas bag and studied it. 'This,' she said, waving it at Nina, 'is the poem your father has promised to read tonight.' She chewed at her top lip. 'He said to put it on the table outside his bedroom. Will you come with me?'

Nina led Kitty Finch to the room where her parents slept. Their bedroom was the largest in the villa, with an even larger bathroom attached to it. It had gold taps and a power shower and a button to turn the bath into a jacuzzi. She pointed to a small table pushed against the wall outside their bedroom. A bowl stood in the centre of the table, a muddle of swimming goggles, dried flowers, old felt-tips, postcards and keys.

'Oh, those are the keys to the pump room.' Kitty sounded

excited. 'The pump room stores all the machinery that makes the swimming pool work. I'll put the envelope under the bowl.'

She frowned at the brown envelope and kept taking deep breaths, shaking her curls as if something was caught in her hair.

'Actually, I think I'll slip it under the door. That way he'll trip over it and have to read it immediately.'

Nina was about to tell her that it wasn't his bedroom, her mother slept there too, but she stopped herself because Kitty Finch was saying weird things.

'You have to take a chance, don't you? It's like crossing a road with your eyes shut . . . you don't know what's going to happen next.' And then she threw back her head and laughed. 'Remind me to drive you to Nice tomorrow for the best ice cream you'll ever taste in your life.'

Standing next to Kitty Finch was like being near a cork that had just popped out of a bottle. The first pop when gasses seem to escape and everything is sprinkled for one second with something intoxicating.

Mitchell was calling them for supper.

Manners

'My wife is having her shoes mended in Nice,' Joe Jacobs announced theatrically to everyone at the dinner table.

His tone suggested he was merely giving information and required no reply from the audience assembled for dinner. They concurred. It was not mentioned.

Mitchell, always the self-appointed chef, had spent the afternoon roasting the hunk of beef Joe had insisted on paying for in the market that morning. He sliced it gleefully, pink blood oozing from its centre.

'None for me, thank you,' Kitty said politely.

'Oh, just a morsel.' A thin slice of bloody meat dropped from his fork and landed on her plate.

'Morsel is Mitchell's favourite word.' Joe picked up his napkin and tucked it into his shirt collar.

Laura poured the wine. She was wearing an ornate African necklace, a thick band of plaited gold fastened with seven pearls around her neck.

'You look like a bride,' Kitty said admiringly.

'Strangely enough,' Laura replied, 'this actually is a bridal necklace from our shop. It's from Kenya.'

Kitty's eyes were watering from the horseradish, which she spooned into her mouth as if it was sugar. 'So what do you and Mitchell sell at your "Cash and Carry"?'

'"Emporium",' Laura corrected her. 'We sell primitive Persian, Turkish and Hindu weapons. And expensive African jewellery.'

'We are small-time arms dealers,' Mitchell said effusively. 'And in between we sell furniture made from ostriches.'

Joe rolled a slice of meat with his fingers and dipped it into the bowl of horseradish. 'Furniture is made from ostriches and horseradish is made from horses,' he chanted.

Nina flung down her knife. 'Shut the fuck up.'

Mitchell grimaced. 'Girls of your age shouldn't use such ugly words.'

Her father nodded as if he entirely agreed. Nina stared at him furiously as he polished his spoon with the end of the tablecloth. She knew her father had a lot of time for what Mitchell called 'ugly' words. When she told him, as she regularly did, that she was sick of wearing totally sad shoes to school with the wrong colour tights, her father the poet corrected her choice of words: 'Next time say totally sad *fucking* crap shoes. It will give your case more emphasis.'

'Ugly words are for ugly thoughts.' Mitchell briskly tapped the side of his bald head and then licked a smear of horseradish off his thumb. 'I never would have sworn in front of my father when I was your age.'

Joe shot his daughter a look. 'Yes, my child. Please don't swear like that and offend the fuckers at this table. Especially Mitchell. He's dangerous. He's got weapons. Swords and ivory revolvers.'

'Ac-tu-ally' – Mitchell wagged his finger – 'what I really need is a mousetrap, because there are rodents in this kitchen.'

He glanced at Kitty Finch when he said 'rodents'.

Kitty dropped her slice of beef on the floor and leaned towards Nina. 'Horseradish is not made out of horses. It's related to the mustard family. It's a root and your father probably eats so much of it because it's good for his rheumatism.'

Joe raised his thick eyebrows. 'Whaat? I haven't got rheumatism!'

'You probably have,' Kitty replied. 'You're a bit stiff when you walk.'

'That's because he's old enough to be your father,' Laura smiled nastily. She was still puzzled why Isabel had been so insistent that a young woman, who swam naked and obviously wanted her middle-aged husband's attention should stay with them. Her friend was supposed to be the betrayed partner in their marriage. Hurt by his infidelities. Burdened by his past. Betrayed and lied to.

'Laura congratulates herself on seeing through people and talking straight,' Joe declared to the table. He squeezed the tip of his nose between his finger and thumb, a secret code between himself and his daughter, of what he wasn't sure, perhaps of enduring love despite his flaws and foolishness and their mutual irritations with each other.

Kitty smiled nervously at Laura. 'Thank you all so much for letting me stay.'

Nina watched her nibble on a slice of cucumber and then push it to the side of her plate.

'You should thank Isabel,' Laura corrected her. 'She is very kind-hearted.'

'I wouldn't say Isabel is kind, would you, Nina?'

Joe rolled another slice of bloody beef and pushed it into his mouth.

This was the cue for Nina to say something critical

about her mother to please her father, something like, 'My mother doesn't know me at all.' In fact she was tempted to say, 'My mother doesn't know I know my father will sleep with Kitty Finch. She doesn't even know I know what anorexic means.'

Instead she said, 'Kitty thinks walls can open and close.'

When Mitchell whirled his left forefinger in circles around his ear as if to say, crazeee she's crazeee, Joe reached over and violently slapped down Mitchell's teasing pink finger with his tight brown fist.

'It's rude to be so normal, Mitchell. Even you must have been a child once. Even you might have thought there were monsters lurking under your bed. Now that you are such an impeccably normal adult you probably take a discreet look under the bed and tell yourself, well, maybe the monster is invisible!'

Mitchell rolled his eyes and stared at the ceiling as if pleading with it for help and advice. 'Has anyone ever actually told you how up yourself you are?

The telephone was ringing. A fax was sliding and grinding its way on to the plastic tray next to the villa's fact file. Nina stood up and walked over to pick it up. She glanced at it and brought it to her father.

'It's for you. About your reading in Poland.'

'Thank you.' He kissed her hand with his wine-stained lips and told her to read the fax out loud to him.

SATURDAY

LUNCH ON ARRIVAL.
TWO MENUS. White borscht with boiled egg and sausage.
Traditional hunter's stew with mash potatoes. Soft drink.
OR
Traditional Polish cucumber soup. Cabbage leaves stuffed
with meat and mash potatoes. Soft drink.
KINDLY FAX YOUR CHOICE.

Laura coughed. 'You were born in Poland, weren't you, Joe?'

Nina watched her father shake his head vaguely.

'I don't remember.'

Mitchell raised his eyebrows in what he imagined was disbelief. 'You got to be a bit forgetful not to remember where you were born. You're Jewish, aren't you, sir?'

Joe looked startled. Nina wondered if it was because her father had been called sir. Kitty was frowning too. She sat up straighter in her chair and addressed the table as if she was Joe's biographer.

'Of course he was born in Poland. It's on all his book jackets. Jozef Nowogrodzki was born in western Poland in 1937. He arrived in Whitechapel, east London, when he was five years old.'

'Right.' Mitchell looked confused again. 'So how come you're Joe Jacobs, then?'

Kitty once again took charge. She might as well have pinged her wine glass three times to create an expectant silence. 'The teachers at his boarding school changed his name so they could spell it.'

41

The spoon Joe had been polishing all through supper was now silver and shiny. When he held it up as if to inspect his hard work, Nina could see Kitty's distorted reflection floating on the back of it.

'Boarding school? Where were your parents, then?'

Mitchell noticed that Laura was squirming in her chair. Whatever it was he was supposed to know about Joe had totally gone from his mind. Laura had told him of course, but it hadn't sunk in. He was relieved Kitty Finch did not take it upon herself to answer his question and sort of wished he hadn't gone there.

'Well, you're more or less English, then, aren't you, Joe?'

Joe nodded. 'Yes, I am. I'm nearly as English as you are.'

'Well, I wouldn't go along all the way with that, Joe,' Mitchell asserted in the tone of a convivial customs official, 'but, as I always say to Laura, it's what we feel inside that counts.'

'You're right,' Joe agreed.

Mitchell thought he was on to something because Joe was being polite for a change.

'So what do you feel inside, Joe?'

Joe peered at the spoon in his hand as if it was a jewel or a small triumph over cloudy cutlery.

'I've got an FFF inside.'

'What's that, sir?'

'A fucking funny feeling.'

Mitchell, who was now drunk, slapped him on the back to confirm their new solidarity.

'I'll second that, Jozef whatever your surname is. I've got an FFF right here.' He tapped his head. 'I've got three of those.'

Laura shuffled her long feet under the table and announced she had made a trifle for pudding. It was a recipe she had taken from Delia Smith's *Complete Cookery Course* and she hoped the custard had set and the cream hadn't curdled.

SUNDAY

Hemlock Thief

The beginning of birdsong. The sound of pine cones falling into the stillness of the pool. The harsh scent of rosemary growing in wooden crates on the window ledge. When Kitty Finch woke up she felt someone breathing on her face. At first she thought the window had blown open in the night, but then she saw him and had to shove her hair into her mouth to stop herself screaming out loud. A black-haired boy was standing by her bed and he was waving to her. She guessed he was fifteen years old and he was holding a notebook in the hand that was not waving. The notebook was yellow. He was wearing a school blazer and his tie was stuffed in his pocket. Eventually he disappeared into the wall, but she could still feel the breeze of his invisible waving hand.

He was inside her. He had trance-journeyed into her mind. She was receiving his thoughts and feelings and his intentions. She dug her fingernails into her cheeks and, when she was sure she was awake, she walked towards the French

45

doors and climbed into the pool. A wasp stung her wrist as she swam to the half-deflated lilo and pulled it to the shallow end. She wasn't sure if the spectral vision was a ghost or a dream or a hallucination. Whatever it was, he had been in her mind for a long time. She plunged her head under the water and started to count to ten.

Someone was in the pool with her.

Kitty could just make out the magnified tips of Isabel Jacobs' fingers scooping up insects that were always dying in the deep end. When she surfaced, Isabel's strong arms were now slicing through the cold green water, the insects writhing in a pile on the paving stone nearest the pool's edge. The journalist wife, so silent and superior, apparently disappeared to Nice at mealtimes and no one talked about it. Least of all her husband, who, Kitty hoped, had read her poem by now. That's what he said he was going to do after the endless supper last night. He was going to lie on his bed and read her words.

'You're shivering, Kitty.'

Isabel swam towards her until the two women stood shoulder-to-shoulder, watching the early-morning mist rise from the mountains. She told Isabel she had earache and she was feeling dizzy. It was the only way she could talk about what she had seen that morning.

'You probably have an ear infection. It's not surprising you're unsteady on your feet.'

Isabel was trying to sound like she was in control of everything. Kitty had seen her on the television about three years ago. Isabel Jacobs standing in the desert near a camel skeleton in Kuwait. She was leaning on a burnt-out army tank, pointing to a charred pair of soldier's boots lying underneath it. Elegant and groomed, Isabel Jacobs was meaner than she looked. When she had dived into the pool yesterday and grabbed Kitty's ankle, she had twisted it hard enough to give her a Chinese burn. Her foot still hurt from that. Isabel had hurt her deliberately, but Kitty couldn't say anything because the next thing she did was offer her the spare room. No one dared say they minded, because the war correspondent was controlling them all. Like she had the final word or was daring them to contradict her. The truth was her husband had the final word because he wrote words and then he put full stops at the end of them. She knew this, but what did his wife know?

Kitty leapt out of the water and walked to the edge of the pool, picking bay leaves off a small tree that grew in a pot by the shallow end. Isabel got out too and sat on the edge of a white recliner. The journalist wife was lighting a cigarette absent-mindedly, as if she was thinking about something more important than what was happening now. She must have seen the battered A4 envelope Kitty had left propped against the bedroom door.

Swimming Home
by
Kitty Finch

She did not tell Isabel that she was feeling hot and her vision was blurred. Her skin was itching and she thought her tongue might be swollen too. Nor did she tell her about the spectral boy who had walked out of the wall to greet her when she woke up. He had stolen some of her plants, because when he walked back into the wall he had a bundle of them in his arms. She thought he might be searching for ways to die. The words she heard him say were words she heard in her head and not with her ears. He was waving as if to greet her, but now she thought he might have been saying goodbye.

'So did you come here because you're a fan of Jozef's poetry?'

Kitty chewed slowly on a silver bay leaf until she could mask the anxiety in her voice. 'I suppose I am a fan. Though I don't see it like that.'

She paused, waiting for her voice to steady itself. 'Joe's poetry is more like a conversation with me than anything else. He writes about things I often think. We are in nerve contact.'

She turned round to see Isabel stub out her cigarette with her bare foot. Kitty gasped.

'Didn't that hurt?'

If Isabel had burned herself she seemed not to care.

'What does "nerve contact" with Jozef mean?'

'It doesn't mean anything. I just thought of it now.'

Kitty noticed how Isabel Jacobs always used her husband's full name. As if she alone owned the part of him that was secret and mysterious, the part of him that wrote things. How could she tell her that she and Joe were transmitting messages to each other when she didn't understand it herself? This was something she would discuss with Jurgen. He would explain that she had extra senses because she was a poet and then he would say words to her in German that she knew were love words. It was always tricky to get away from him at night, so she was grateful to have the spare room to escape to. Yes, in a way she was grateful to Isabel for saving her from Jurgen's love.

'What's your poem about?'

Kitty studied the bay leaf, her fingertips tracing the outline of its silver veins.

'I can't remember.'

Isabel laughed. This was offensive. Kitty was offended. No longer grateful, she glared at the woman who had offered her the spare room but had not bothered to provide sheets or pillows or notice the windows did not open and the floor was covered in mouse droppings. The journalist was asking her questions as if she was about to file her copy. She was curvaceous and tall, her black hair dark as an Indian woman's, and she wore a gold band on her left hand to show she was married. Her fingers were long and smooth, like she'd never scrubbed a pot clean or poked her fingers into the earth. She had not even bothered to offer her guest a few clothes hangers. Nina had had to bring down an armful from her own cupboard. Nevertheless Isabel Jacobs was still asking questions, because she wanted to be in control.

'You said you know the owner of this villa?'

'Yeah. She's a shrink called Rita Dwighter and she's a friend of my mother's. She's got houses everywhere. In fact she's got twelve properties in London alone worth about two million each. She probably asks her patients if they've got a mortgage.'

Isabel laughed and this time Kitty laughed too.

'Thank you for letting me stay, by the way.'

Isabel nodded dismissively and said something about going inside to make toast and honey. Kitty watched her run through the glass doors, bumping into Laura, who was now sitting at the kitchen table, a pair of earphones clamped on her head and a tangle of wires around her neck. Laura was learning some sort of African language, her thin lips mouthing the words out loud.

Kitty sat naked and shivering at the end of the pool, listening to the tall blonde woman with scared blue eyes repeat singsong sentences from another continent. She could hear the church bells ringing in the village and she could hear someone sighing. When she looked up she had to stop herself from losing it for the second time that morning. Madeleine Sheridan was sitting on her balcony as usual, staring at her as if she was scanning the ocean for a shark. That was too much. Kitty jumped up and shook her fist at the shadowy figure drinking her morning tea.

'Don't fucking watch me all the time. I'm still waiting for you to get my shoes, Dr Sheridan. Have you got them yet?'

SUNDAY

Homesick Aliens

Jurgen was dragging an inflatable three-foot rubber alien with a wrinkled neck into the kitchen of Claude's café. He had bought it at the flea market on Saturday and he and Claude were having three conversations at once. Claude, who had only just turned twenty-three and knew he looked like Mick Jagger, owned the only café in the village and was planning to sell it to Parisian property developers next year. What Claude wanted to know was why the tourists had offered Kitty Finch a room.

Jurgen scratched his scalp and swung his dreadlocks to get an angle on the question. The effort was exhausting him and he could not find an answer. Claude, whose silky shoulder-length hair was expensively cut to make it look as if he never bothered with it, reckoned Kitty must secretly be repulsed by the dreadlocks Jurgen cultivated, because she knew she could stay with him whenever she wanted. At the same time they were both jeering at Mitchell, who was sitting on the terrace stuffing himself with baguettes and jam while he waited for the grocery store to open. The fat man with his collection of old guns was running up a tab at the café *and* the grocery store, which was run by Claude's mother. Mitchell was going to bankrupt Claude's entire family. Meanwhile Jurgen was explaining the plot of the film *ET* while Claude peeled potatoes. Jurgen whipped the cigarette butt out of his friend's thick lips and sucked on it while he tried to remember the film he'd seen in Monaco three years ago.

'ET is this baby alien who finds himself lost on earth,

51

three million light years away from home. He makes friends with a ten-year-old boy and they start to have a very special connection with each other.'

Claude gave the little alien in his kitchen a leering wink. 'What sort of connection?'

Jurgen swung his dreadlocks over a freshly baked pear tart cooling under the kitchen window as if to summon a plot he had long forgotten.

'So . . . if ET gets sick the earth boy gets sick, if ET is hungry earth boy gets hungry, if ET is tired or sad then earth boy suffers with him. The alien and his friend are in touch with each other's thoughts. They are mentally connected.'

Claude grimaced, because he was being called by Mitchell for another basket of bread and a slice of the pear tart, newly written into the menu. Claude told Jurgen he couldn't work out why the fat man never had any money on him despite staying in the luxurious villa. His tab had gone off the scale. 'So anyway how does *ET* end?'

Jurgen, who was usually too stoned to remember anything, had just spotted Joe Jacobs in the distance, walking among the sheep grazing in the mountains. For some reason he could remember every line the baby alien uttered in the film. He thought this was because he was also an alien, a German nature boy living in France. He explained that ET has to disconnect himself from the boy because he fears he will make him too sick and he doesn't want to harm him. And then he finds a way of getting home to his own planet.

Jurgen nudged Claude and pointed to the English poet in the distance. He looked like he was saluting something invisible, because his fingers were touching his forehead. Claude quite liked the poet, because he always left big tips and had somehow managed to produce a gorgeous, long-legged teenage daughter whom Claude had personally invited to the café for an aperitif. So far she had not taken him up on his offer, but he lived in hope because, as he told Jurgen, what else was there to live in?

'He is superstitious, he's just seen a magpie. He is famous. Do you want to be famous?'

Jurgen nodded. And then shook his head and helped himself to a swig from a bottle of green liquid leaning against the cooking oil.

'Yes. Sometimes I think it would be nice to no longer be a caretaker and everyone wants to kiss my arse. But there is one problem. I don't have the energy to be famous. I have too much to do.'

Claude pointed to the poet, who looked like he was still saluting magpies.

'Perhaps he is homesick. He wants to go home to his planet.'

Jurgen gargled with the green drink that Claude knew was mint syrup. Jurgen was more or less addicted to it in the same way some people are addicted to absinthe, which had the same fairy green colour.

'No. He is just avoiding Kitty Ket. He has not read Ket's thing and he is avoiding her. The Ket is like ET. She thinks she has a mental connection with the poet. He has not read her thing and she will be sad and her blood pressure will go up and she will murder them all with the fat man's guns.'

MONDAY

The Trapper

Mitchell lay on his back sweating. It was three a.m. and he had just had a nightmare about a centipede. He had hacked it with a carving knife but it split in two and started to grow again. The more he hacked at it the more centipedes there were. They writhed at his feet. He was up to his ears in centipedes and the blade of his knife was covered in slime. They were crawling into his nostrils and trying to get into his mouth. When he woke up he wondered if he should tell Laura his heart was pounding so hard and fast he thought he might be about to have a heart attack. Laura was sleeping peacefully on her side, her feet poking out of the bed. There was no bed in the world that was long enough for Laura. Their bed in London had been specially designed for her height and his width by a Danish shipbuilder. It took up the whole room and resembled a galleon beached on a pond in a civic park. Something was crawling towards him along the whitewashed wall. He screamed.

'What is it, Mitch?' Laura sat up and put her hand on her husband's heaving chest.

He pointed to the thing on the wall.

'It's a moth, Mitchell.'

Sure enough it spread its grey wings and flew out of the window.

'I had a nightmare,' he grunted. 'A terrible, terrible nightmare.'

She squeezed his hot clammy hand. 'Go back to sleep. You'll feel better in the morning.' She tugged the sheet over her shoulder and lay down again.

There was no way he could sleep. Mitchell got up and walked upstairs to the kitchen, where he felt most safe. He opened the fridge and reached for a bottle of water. As he put the bottle to his lips and thirstily gulped down the iced water, he felt in bits and pieces like the centipede. When he lifted up his aching head, he noticed something lying on the kitchen floor. It was the trap he had set for the rat. He had caught something. He swallowed hard and made his way towards it.

A small animal was lying on its side with its back to him, but it was not a rat. He recognised the creature. It was Nina's brown nylon rabbit, its long floppy ear stapled under the wire. He could see its worn white ball of a tail and the grubby label sewn inside its leg. The green satin ribbon around its neck had somehow got tangled in the wires too. He found himself sweating as he bent down to free it from the wire and then noticed a shadow on the floor. Someone was there with him. Someone had broken into the villa and he didn't have his

guns with him. Even his ancient ebony weapon from Persia
would see off whoever was there.

'Hello, Mitchell.'

Kitty Finch was leaning naked against the wall, watching him struggle not to catch his fingers in his own trap. She
was nibbling the chocolate he had left for the rat, her arms
folded across her breasts.

'I call you the trapper now, but I've warned all the owls
about you.'

He pressed his hand on his pounding heart and stared
at her pale, righteous face. He would shoot her. If he had
his weapons with him he would do it. He would aim for
her stomach. He imagined how he would hold the gun and
timed the moment he would snap the trigger. She would fall
to the ground, her glassy grey eyes wide open, a bloody hole
gouged in her belly. He blinked and saw she was still standing against the wall, taunting him with the chocolate he had
placed so carefully in the wires. She looked thin and pathetic
and he realised he had scared her.

'Sorry I was so abrupt.'

'Yeah.' She nodded as if they were suddenly best friends.
'You gave me a fright, but I was frightened anyway.'

He was terrified too. For a moment he seriously considered telling her about his nightmare.

'Why do you kill animals and birds, Mitchell?'

She was almost pretty, with her narrow waist and long
hair glowing in the dark, but ragged too, not far off someone
begging outside a train station holding up a homeless and
hungry sign.

'It takes my mind off things,' he found himself saying as if he meant it, which he did.

'What sorts of things?'

Again he considered telling her about some of the worries that weighed heavily on his mind but stopped himself just in time. He couldn't go shooting his mouth off to someone crazy like her.

'You're a complete fuck-up, Mitchell. Stop killing things and you'll feel better.'

'Haven't you got a home to go to?' He thought he had meant this quite kindly, but even to his own ears it sounded like an insult.

'Yeah, I live with my mother at the moment, but it's not my home.'

As she knelt down to help him untangle the grubby toy rabbit that made a mockery of his trap, he couldn't work out why he thought someone as sad as she was might be dangerous.

'You know what?' This time Mitchell thought he genuinely meant this kindly. 'If you wore clothes more often instead of walking around in your birthday suit, you'd look more normal.'

MONDAY

Spirited Away

Nina's disappearance was only discovered at seven a.m. after Joe called for her because he had lost his special ink pen. His daughter was the person who always found it for him, whatever the time, a drama Laura had heard at least twelve times that holiday. Whenever Nina returned the pen victoriously to her loud, forlorn father he wrapped her in his arms and bellowed melodramatically, 'Thank you thank you thank you.' Often in a number of languages: Polish, Portuguese, Italian. Yesterday it was, 'Danke danke danke.'

No one could believe Joe was actually shouting for his daughter to find his pen so early in the morning, but that was what he did and Nina did not answer. Isabel walked into her daughter's bedroom and saw the doors to her balcony were wide open. She whipped off the duvet, expecting to see her hiding under the covers. Nina wasn't there and the sheet was stained with blood. When Laura heard Isabel sobbing, she ran into the room to find her friend pointing to the bed, strange choking sounds coming out of her mouth. She was pale, deathly white, uttering words that sounded to Laura like 'bone' or 'hair' or 'she isn't there'; it was hard to make sense of what she was saying.

Laura suggested they go together to look for Nina in the garden and steered her out of the room. Small birds swooped down to drink from the still, green water of the pool. A box of cherry chocolates from the day before lay melting on Mitchell's big blue chair, covered in ants. Two damp towels were

59

draped on the canvas recliners and in the middle of them, like an interrupted conversation, was the wooden chair Isabel had dragged out for Kitty Finch. Under it was Joe's black ink pen.

This was the rearranged space of yesterday. They walked through the cypress trees and into the parched garden. It had not rained for months and Jurgen had forgotten to water the plants. The honeysuckle was dying, the soil beneath the brown grass cracked and hard. Under the tallest pine tree, Laura saw Nina's wet bikini lying on the pine needles. When she bent down to pick it up, even she could not help thinking the cherry print on the material looked like splashes of blood. Her fingers started to fumble in her pocket for the little stainless-steel calculator she and Mitchell had brought with them to do their accounts.

'Nina's OK, Isabel.' She ran her fingers over the calculator as if the numbers and symbols she knew were there, the m+ and m–, the x and the decimal point, would somehow end in Nina's appearance. 'She's probably gone for a walk. I mean, she's fourteen you know, she really has not been' – she was about to say 'slaughtered' but changed her mind and said 'spirited away' instead.

She didn't finish her sentence because Isabel was running through the cypress trees so fast and with such force the trees were shaking for minutes afterwards. Laura watched the momentary chaos of the trees. It was as if they had been pushed off balance and did not quite know how to find their former shape.

Mothers and Daughters

The spare room was dark and hot because the windows were closed and the curtains drawn. A pair of grubby flip-flops lay on top of the tangle of drying weeds lying on the floor. Kitty's red hair streamed over a lumpy stained pillow, her freckled arms wrapped around Nina, who was clutching the nylon fur rabbit that was her last embarrassed link with childhood. Isabel knew Nina was awake and that she was pretending to be asleep under what seemed to be a starched white tablecloth. It looked like a shroud.

'Nina, get up.' Isabel's voice was sharper than she meant it to be.

Kitty opened her grey eyes and whispered, 'Nina started her period in the night so she got into bed with me.'

The girls were drowsy and content in each other's arms. Isabel noticed the tattered books Kitty had put on the shelves, about six of them, were all her husband's books. Two pink rosebuds stood in a glass of water next to them. Roses that could only have been picked from Madeleine Sheridan's front garden, her attempt to create a memory of England in France.

She remembered Kitty's strange comment yesterday morning, after their swim together: 'Joe's poetry is a more like a conversation with me than anything else.' What sort of conversation was Kitty Finch having with her husband? Should she insist her daughter get out of bed and leave this room that was as hot as a greenhouse? Kitty was obviously trapping energy to heat her plants. She had made a small, hot, chaotic world, full of books and fruit and flowers, a sub-state in the country of the tourist villa with its Matisse and Picasso prints clumsily framed and hanging on the walls. Two plump bumblebees crawled down the yellow curtains, searching for an open window. The cupboard was open and Isabel glimpsed a short white feather cape hanging in the corner. Slim and pretty in her flip-flops and ragged summer dresses, it would seem Kitty Finch could make herself at home anywhere. Should she insist that Nina get up and return to her clean lonely room upstairs? Tearing her away from Kitty's arms felt like a violent thing to do. She bent down and kissed her daughter's dark eyebrow, which was twitching slightly.

'Come and say hello when you're awake.'

Nina's eyes were shut extra tight. Isabel closed the door.

When she walked into the kitchen she told Jozef and Laura that Nina was sleeping with Kitty.

'Ah. Thought as much.' Her husband scratched the back of his neck and disappeared into the garden to get his pen, which, Laura informed him, was 'under Kitty's chair'. He had covered his bare shoulders with a white pillowcase and looked like a self-ordained holy man. He did this to stop his shoulders burning when he wrote in the sun, but it infuriated Laura all the same. When she looked at him again he was examining the gold nib as if it had been damaged in some way. She opened the fridge. Mitchell wanted a piece of stale cheese to trap the brown rat he had seen scuttling about in the kitchen at night. It had gnawed through the salami hung on a hook above the sink and he'd had to throw it away. Mitchell was not so much squeamish as outraged by the vermin who devoured the morsels he bought with his hard-earned money. He took it personally, as if slowly but surely the rats were gnawing through his wallet.

Fathers and Daughters

So his lost daughter was asleep in Kitty's bed. Joe sat in the garden at his makeshift desk, waiting for the panic that had made his fingers tear the back of his neck to calm as he watched his wife talking to Laura inside the villa. His breathing was all over the place, he was fighting to breathe. Did he think Kitty Finch, who had stopped taking Seroxat and must be suffering, had lost her grip and murdered his daughter? His wife was now walking towards him through the gaps in the cypress trees. He shifted his legs as if part of him wanted to run away from her or perhaps run towards her. He truly did not know which way to go. He could try to tell Isabel something, but he wasn't sure how to begin because he wasn't sure how it would end. There were times he thought she could barely look at him without hiding her face in her hair. And he could not look at her either, because he had betrayed her so often. Perhaps now he should at least try and tell her that when she abandoned her young daughter to lie in a tent crawling with scorpions, he understood it made more sense of her life to be shot at in war zones than lied to by him in the safety of her own home. All the same, he knew his daughter had cried for her in the early years, and then later learned not to because it didn't bring her back. In turn (this subject turned and turned and turned regularly in his mind), his daughter's distress brought to him, her father, feelings he could not handle with dignity. He had told his readers how he was sent to boarding school by his guardians and how he used to watch the parents of his school friends leave on visiting day (Sundays), and if his own parents had visited him too, he would have stood for ever in the tyre marks their car had made in the dust. His mother and father were night visitors, not afternoon visitors. They appeared to him in dreams he instantly forgot, but he reckoned they were trying to find him. What had worried him most was he thought they might not have enough English words between them to make themselves understood. Is Jozef my son here? We have been looking for him all over the world. He had cried for them and then later learned not to because it didn't bring them back. He looked at his clever tanned wife with her dark hair hiding her face. This was the conversation that might start something or end something, but it came out wrong, just too random and fucked. He heard himself ask her if she liked honey.

'Yes. Why?'

'Because I know so little about you, Isabel.'

He would poke his paw inside every hollow of every tree to scoop up the honeycomb and lay it at her feet if he thought she might stay a little longer with him and their cub. She looked hostile and lonely and he understood it. He obviously disgusted her. She even preferred Mitchell's company to his.

He heard her say, 'The main thing to do for the rest of the summer is to make sure Nina is all right.'

'Of course Nina is all right,' he snapped. 'I've looked after her since she was three years old and she's bloody all right, isn't she?'

And then he took out his notebook and the black ink pen

that had disappeared that morning, knowing that Isabel was defeated every time he appeared to be writing and every time he talked about their daughter. These were his weapons to silence his wife and keep her in his life, to keep his family intact, flawed and hostile but still a family. His daughter was his main triumph, in their marriage, the one thing he had done right.

    – yes yes yes she said yes yes yes she likes honey – his pen scratched these words aggressively across the page while he watched a white butterfly hover above the pool. It was like breath. It was a miracle. A wonder. He and his wife knew things it was impossible to know. They had both seen life snuffed out. Isabel recorded and witnessed catastrophes to try and make people remember. He tried to make himself forget.

Collecting Stones

'It has a hole in the middle.'

Kitty held up a pebble the size of her hand and gave it to Nina to look through. They were sitting on one of the public beaches in Nice below the Promenade des Anglais. Kitty said on the private beaches they had to pay a fortune for sun-loungers and umbrellas. Everyone looked like patients on hospital beds and gave her the creeps. The sun was burning pink blotches in her waxy pale face.

Nina obediently looked through the hole. She saw a young woman smiling, a purple jewel drilled into her front tooth. When she turned the pebble round the woman was unpacking a carrier bag of food. There was another woman there too, sitting on a low striped canvas chair, and she was holding a large white dog by the lead with her right hand. The dog looked like a snow wolf. A husky with blue eyes. Nina stared into its blue eyes from the hole in the pebble. She couldn't be sure of this but she thought the snow wolf was undoing the shoelaces of the woman with the jewel in her tooth. Nina saw all of this in fragments through the hole in the pebble. When she looked again she saw the woman in the black T-shirt only had one arm. She turned the pebble lengthways and peered through it, squeezing her eye half shut. An electric wheelchair decorated with shells was parked near the canvas chair. Now the women were kissing. Like lovers. Watching them lean into each other, Nina heard her own breath get louder. She had been thinking all holiday about what she would do if she ever found herself alone with Claude. He had invited her to come to his café for what he described as an aperitif. She wasn't sure what that was and anyway something had happened that changed everything.

Last night when she woke up she discovered she was menstruating for the first time. She had dared herself to put on her bikini because it was the only thing she could find and knock on Kitty's door to tell her the news. Kitty was lying awake under an old tablecloth and she had rolled up one of her dresses to make a pillow.

'I've started.'

At first Kitty didn't know what she meant. And then she grabbed Nina's hand and they ran into the garden. Nina could see her own shadow in the pool and in the sky at the same time. She was tall and long, there was no end to her and no beginning, her body stretched out and vast. She wanted to swim and when Kitty insisted it didn't matter about the blood, she dared herself to take off her bikini and be naked, watching her twin shadow untie the straps more bravely than the real-sized Nina actually felt. She finally jumped into the pool and hid herself in the blanket of leaves that floated in the water, not sure what to do with her new body because it was morphing into something alien and perplexing to her.

Kitty swam over and pointed to the silver snails on the paving stones. She said the stars laid their dust over everything. There were bits of broken stars on the snails. And then she blinked.

blah blah blah blah blah blinked

Standing naked in the water, Nina pretended she had a serious speech impediment and made stammering sounds in her head. She felt like someone else. Like someone who had started. Someone who wasn't her. She felt unbearably happy and plunged her head into the water to celebrate the miracle of Kitty Finch's arrival. She was not alone with Laura and Mitchell and her mother and father who she wasn't sure liked each other never mind loved each other.

Nina threw the pebble into the sea, which seemed to annoy Kitty. She stood up and yanked Nina up too.

'I need to collect more pebbles. That one you threw away was perfect.'

'Why do you want them?'

'To study them.'

Nina was hobbling because her trainers were rubbing up against the blisters on the back of her heels. 'They're too heavy to carry,' she groaned. 'I want to go now.'

Kitty was sweating and her breath smelt sweet.

'Yeah, well, sorry to waste your time. Have you ever cleaned a floor, Nina? Ever got down on your hands and knees with a rag while your mother screams at you to clean the corners? Have you ever hoovered the stairs and taken out the bin bags?'

The pampered girl in her pricey shorts (she had seen the label) and all her split ends trimmed had obviously got to fourteen years old without lifting a finger.

'You need some real problems to take back to your posh house in London with you.'

She flung down the rucksack full of pebbles and marched into the sea in the butter-coloured dress she said made her feel extra cheerful. Nina watched her dive into a wave. The house in London Kitty referred to wasn't exactly cosy. Her father always in his study. Her mother away, her shoes and dresses lined up in the wardrobe like someone who had died. When she was seven and always had nits in her hair the house had smelt of the magic potions she used to make from her mother's face creams and her father's shaving foam. The big house in west London smelt of other things too. Of her father's girlfriends and their various shampoos. And of her father's perfume, made for him by a Swiss woman from Zurich who married a man who owned two show horses in Bulgaria. He said her perfumes 'opened his mind', especially his favourite, which was called Hungary Water. The posh house smelt of his special status and of the sheets he always put in the washing machine after his girlfriends left in the morning. And of the apricot jam he spooned into his mouth straight from the jar. He said the jam changed the weather inside him, but she didn't know what the weather was in the first place.

She did sort of know. Sometimes when she walked into his study she thought he looked a sorry sight stooped in his dressing gown, silent and still as if he'd been pinned down by something. She'd got used to the days he was sunk in his chair and refused to look at her or even get up for nights on end. She'd close the door of his study and bring him mugs of tea he never touched, because they were still there when she talked to him from behind the door (a slimy beige skin grown over the tea) and asked him for lunch money or to sign a letter giving his permission for a school trip. In the end she signed them herself with his ink pen, which is why she always knew where it was, usually under her bed or upside down in the bathroom with the toothbrushes. She had designed a signature she could always replicate, J.H.J with a full stop between the letters and a flourish on the last J. After a while he usually cheered up and took her to the Angus Steak House, where they sat on the same faded red velvet banquette they always sat on. They never talked about his own childhood or his girlfriends. This was not so much an unspoken secret pact between them, more like having a tiny splinter of glass in the sole of her foot, always there, slightly painful, but she could live with it.

When Kitty came back, her dress dripping wet, she was saying something but the husky was barking at a seagull. Nina could just see Kitty's lips moving and she knew, with an aching feeling inside her, that she was still angry or something was wrong. As they walked to the car Kitty said, 'I'm meeting your father at Claude's café tomorrow. He's going to talk to me about my poem. Nina, I am so nervous. I should have got a summer job in a pub in London and not bothered. I don't know what's going to happen.'

Nina wasn't listening. She had just seen a boy in silver shorts roller-skating down the esplanade with a bag of lemons tucked under his tanned arm. He looked a bit like Claude but he wasn't. When she heard a bird screeching in what she thought sounded like agony, she dared not look back at the beach. She thought the husky or snow wolf might have caught the seagull after all. Maybe it wasn't happening and anyway she had just spotted the old lady who lived next door walking on the promenade. She was talking to Jurgen, who was wearing purple sunglasses in the shape of hearts. Nina called out and waved.

'That's Madeleine Sheridan, our neighbour.'

Kitty gazed up. 'Yes, I know. The evil old witch.'

'Is she?'

'Yes. She calls me Katherine and she nearly killed me.'

After she said that, Kitty did something so spooky that Nina told herself she hadn't seen it properly. She leaned backwards so that her copper hair rippled down the back of her knees and shook her head from side to side very fast while her hands jerked and flailed above her head. Nina could see the fillings in her teeth. And then she lifted her head up and gave Madeleine Sheridan the finger.

Kitty Finch was mental.

Medical Help from Odessa

Madeleine Sheridan was trying to pay for a scoop of caramel-
ised nuts she had bought from the Mexican vendor on the
esplanade. The smell of burnt sugar made her greedy for the
nuts that would at last, she hoped, choke her to death. Her
nails were crumbling, her bones weakening, her hair thin-
ning, her waist gone for ever. She had turned into a toad in
old age and if anyone dared to kiss her she would not turn
back into a princess because she had never been a princess in
the first place.

'These damn coins. What's this one, Jurgen?' Before
Jurgen could answer she whispered, 'Did you see Kitty Finch
doing *that thing* to me?'

He shrugged. 'Sure. Kitty Ket has something to say to
you. But now she has some new friends to make her happy. I
have to book the horse-riding for Nina. The Ket will take her.'

She let him take her arm and steer her (a little too fast)
into one of the bars on the beach. He was the only person she
talked to in any detail about her life in England and her escape from her marriage. She appreciated his stupor, it made
him non-judgemental. Despite the difference in their age she
enjoyed his company. Having nothing to do in life but live off
other people and his wits, he always made her feel dignified
rather than a sad case, probably because he wasn't listening.

Today she was barely listening to him. The arrival of Kitty
Finch was bad news. This is what she was thinking as she

stared at a motorboat making white frothy scars on the chalky-blue sea. When he found a table in the shade and helped her into a chair that was much too small for a toad, he seemed not to realise she would have to twist her body into positions that made her ache. It was thoughtless of him, but she was too disorientated by the sight of Kitty Finch to care.

She tried to calm herself by insisting Jurgen take off his sunglasses.

'It's like looking into two black holes, Jurgen.'

It was her birthday in four days' time and right now she was thirsty in the heat, almost crazed with thirst. She had been looking forward to their lunch appointment for weeks. That morning she had telephoned her favourite restaurant to find out what was on the menu, where their table was positioned and to request the maître d' save her a parking space right outside the door in return for a healthy tip. She screamed at a waiter for a whisky and a Pepsi for Jurgen, who disliked alcohol for spiritual reasons. It was hard for an old woman to get a waiter's attention when he was busy serving topless women sunbathing in thongs. She had read about yogic *siddhas* who mastered human invisibility through a combination of concentration and meditation. Somehow she had managed to make her body imperceptible to the waiter without any of the training. She lifted both her arms and waved at him as if she were flagging down an aeroplane on a desert island. Jurgen pointed to the accordion player from Marseilles perched on a wooden box by the flashing pinball machine. The musician was sweating in a black suit three sizes too large for him.

'He's playing at a wedding this afternoon. The beekeeper from Valbonne told me. If I got married I would ask him to play at my wedding too.'

Madeleine Sheridan, sipping her hard-won whisky, was surprised at how his voice was suddenly so high-pitched.

'Marriage is not a good idea, Jurgen.'

Not at all. She began to tell him (again) how the two biggest departures in her life were leaving her family to study medicine and leaving her husband to live in France. She had come to the conclusion that she was not satiated with love for Peter Sheridan and exchanged a respectable life of unhappiness for the unrespectable unhappiness of being a woman who had cut her ties with love. Now it seemed, staring at her companion, whose voice was shaking all over the place, that in his damaged heart (too many cigarettes) he wanted to tie the knot, to close the circle of his life alone, which frankly was an affront.

It reminded her of the time they were walking on the beach in Villefranche and saw a wedding taking place in the harbour. The bridesmaids were dressed in yellow taffeta and the bride in cream and yellow satin. She had scoffed out loud, but what did the hippy Jurgen say?

'Give them a chance.'

This was the same man who only a few months before had told his girlfriend that nothing had taught him marriage was a good idea. She didn't believe him and took him to an Argentinian barbecue to propose to him. Great piles of scented wood. Hunks of beef from the pampas thrown on to the fire. His girlfriend ate her way through the red meat until she noticed Jurgen was not eating and remembered he was a militant vegetarian. Perhaps she had laughed too loudly when he told her that.

'I think Kitty Finch wants to harm me.'

'*Ach, nein.*' Jurgen frowned as if he was in pain. 'The Ket she only harms herself. Claude asked me why Madame Jacobs insisted she stay. But I have no idea why.'

She gazed at her friend with her cloudy, short-sighted eyes. 'I believe she wants the beautiful mad girl to distract her husband so she can finally leave him.'

Jurgen suddenly wanted to buy the accordion player a drink. He called the waiter and told him to offer the man in the big suit a beer. Madeleine watched the waiter whisper in the musician's ear and tried to forget how she came across Kitty Finch in the tunnel by the flower market in Cours Saleya four months ago. Their encounter was one more thing she wanted to add to the long list of things she wanted to forget.

She had found the flame-haired English girl on a cool spring morning on her way to buy two slabs of Marseilles soap, one made from palm oil, the other from olive oil, both mixed with sea plants from the Mediterranean by the local soap master. Kitty was naked and talking to herself on a box of rotten plums the farmers had thrown out at the end of the day. The homeless men who slept in the tunnel were laughing at her, making lewd remarks about her naked body. When Madeleine Sheridan asked her what had happened to her clothes, she said they were on the beach. Madeleine offered to drive to the beach and get her clothes for her. Kitty could stay exactly where she was and wait for her. And then she'd drive her back to the tourist villa where she was staying to study mountain plants. She often stayed there when Rita Dwighter had not let it out to retired hedge-fund managers because Kitty's mother used to clean for her. Mrs Finch was Rita Dwighter's right-hand woman, her secretary and cook but mostly her cleaner, because her right hand always had a mop in it.

Kitty Finch insisted she go away or she would shout for the police. Madeleine Sheridan could have left her there, but she did not do that. Kitty was too young to be talking to herself among the dead-eyed men staring at her breasts. To her surprise, the crazy girl suddenly changed her mind. Apparently she had left her jeans and a T-shirt and a pair of shoes, her favourite red polka-dot shoes, on the beach opposite the Hotel Negresco. Kitty leaned towards her and whispered in her ear, 'Fanks. I'll wait here while you get them.' Madeleine Sheridan had walked round the corner and when she thought Kitty could no longer see her she called an ambulance.

In her view Katherine Finch was suffering from psychic anxiety, loss of weight, reduced sleep, agitation, suicidal thoughts, pessimism about the future, impaired concentration.

The musician raised his glass of beer in a thank-you gesture to the snake-hipped man sitting with the old woman.

Kitty Finch had survived her summary. Her mother took her home to Britain and she spent two months in a hospital in Kent, the Garden of England. Apparently the nurses were from Lithuania, Odessa and Kiev. In their white uniforms they looked like snowdrops on the mown green lawns of the hospital. That was what Kitty Finch told her mother and what Mrs Finch told Madeleine, who was astonished to learn that the nurses all chain-smoked in their lunch break.

Jurgen nudged her with his elbow. The accordion player from Marseilles was playing a tune for her. She felt too agitated to listen. Kitty had survived and now she had come to punish her. Perhaps even kill her. Why else was she here? She did not think Kitty was a safe person to drive Nina to the beach and up dangerous mountain roads. She should tell Isabel Jacobs that but somehow she couldn't bring herself to have that conversation. If she had been on her way to buy soap and ended up calling an ambulance, Transport Sanitaire in French, she did not feel her hands were entirely clean. All the same, to be naked in a public place, to be jumping forwards and then backwards while chanting something incoherent, this had made her frightened for the wretched young woman. It was impossible to believe that someone did not want to be saved from their incoherence.

When the accordion player nodded at Jurgen, the caretaker knew he was in luck. He would buy some hashish and he and Claude would smoke it and get out of the Riviera while all the tourists wanted to get into it. He put his purple sunglasses on again and told Madeleine Sheridan that he was very, very happy today but he was also a little tight in the bowels. He thought his colon was blocked and this was because he had not lived his dream. What was his dream? He took a sip of Pepsi and noticed the English doctor had dressed up for lunch. She had put lipstick on and her hair, what was left of it, had been washed and curled. He could not tell her his dream was to win the lotto and marry Kitty Ket.

TUESDAY

Reading and Writing

Joe Jacobs lay on his back in the master bedroom, as it was described in the villa's fact sheet, longing for a curry. The place he most wanted to be at this moment was in his Hindu tailor's workshop in Bethnal Green. Surrounded by silk. Drinking sweet tea. What he was missing in the Alpes-Maritimes was dhal. Rice. Yoghurt. And buses. He missed the top deck of buses. And newspapers. And weather forecasts. Sometimes he sat in his study in west London with the radio on and listened intently to what the weather was going to be like in Scotland, Ireland and Wales. If the sun was shining in west London, it comforted him to know it would be snowing in Scotland and raining in Wales. Now he was going to have to sit up and not lie down. Worse, he was going to have to stand up and search the master bedroom for Kitty Finch's poem. In the distance he could hear Mitchell shooting rabbits in the orchard. He knelt on the floor and grabbed the envelope he had kicked under the bed. He held the battered envelope in his hands and found himself staring at the title written in the neat scientific handwriting of a botanist used to making precise drawings of plants and labelling them.

Swimming Home
by
Kitty Finch

When he finally prised out the sheet of paper inside it, he was surprised to feel his hand trembling in the way his father's hand might have trembled if he had lived long enough to mend kettles in his old age. He held the page closer to his eyes and forced himself to read the words floating on the page. And then he moved the page further away from his eyes and read it again. There was no angle that made it easier to comprehend. Her words were all over the place, swimming round the edges of the rectangle of paper, sometimes disappearing altogether but coming back to the centre of the lined page with its sad and final message. What did she hope he might say to her after he had read it? He was mystified. A fish van had pulled up outside the villa. The voice bellowing through a loudspeaker was shouting out the names of fish. Some were *grand*, some were *petit*. Some were six francs and some were thirteen francs. None of them had swum home. They were all caught on the way. The Sellotape that had sealed the lip of the envelope reminded him of a plaster on a graze. He took a deep breath and exhaled slowly. He was going to have to busk it at lunch with her. He checked the inside of his jacket pocket to make sure his wallet was there and kicked the envelope under the bed, telling himself once again how much he hated Tuesdays. And Wednesdays, Thursdays, Fridays, etc.

et cetera

A Latin expression meaning 'and other things' or 'so forth' or 'the rest of such things'. The poem, 'Swimming Home', was mostly made up of etcs; he had counted seven of them in one half of the page alone. What kind of language was this?

> My mother says I'm the only jewel in her crown
> But I've made her tired with all my etc,
> So now she walks with sticks

To accept her language was to accept that she held him, her reader, in great esteem. He was being asked to make something of it and what he made of it was that every etc concealed some thing that could not be said.

Kitty was waiting for him on the terrace of Claude's café. To his displeasure he noticed that Jurgen was sitting at the table opposite her. He seemed to be playing with a piece of string, weaving it between his fingers to make a spider's web. It was becoming clear to him that Jurgen was a sort of guard dog to Kitty Finch, not exactly baring his teeth at all intruders but he was protective and possessive all the same. He seemed to have forgotten that it was she who was the intruder. All the same Jurgen was obviously there to make sure anyone who came near her was a welcome visitor and not a trespasser. He did not seem to elicit much affection from her. It was as if she knew he must never be patted and cuddled and made to feel anything less than alert on her behalf.

'Hi, Joe.' Kitty smiled. Her forehead looked as if she had pressed it against a hot iron. She was a redhead and the sun had been brutal to her pale skin.

He nodded, jangling the coins in his jacket pocket as he sat down. 'You should use sun block, Kitty,' he said paternally.

Claude, who knew he looked more like Mick Jagger every day and worked quite hard on this happy genetic accident, strutted to their table carrying a large bottle of mineral water and two glasses. Joe saw this as an opportunity to pass some time and avoid talking about the poem he had kicked under his bed with the cockroaches, etc.

He turned to Kitty. 'Did you order this?'

She shook her head and made a glum face at Claude. Joe heard himself bellowing at the pouting waiter.

'What's wrong with tap water?'

Claude stared at him with blatant dislike. 'Tap water is full of hormones.'

'No, it's not. Bottled water is a trick to get more money from tourists.'

Joe could hear Claude laughing. The only other sound was the birds. And the nervous hum inside Kitty Finch, who was a bird or something fairyish anyway. He couldn't look at her. Instead he fixed his eyes on Claude.

'Tell me, sir. Is your country incapable of processing water that is safe to drink?'

Claude, with the flourish of a low-rent pimp showing off his new diamond cufflinks, unscrewed the cap on the ice-cold bottle of water and walked towards his dogs, who were sleeping under the chestnut tree. He winked at Jurgen as he poured the water into the chipped ceramic bowls that lay by their paws. The dogs lapped at the water indifferently and then gave up. Claude patted their heads and strutted back into the café. When he came out again he was holding a glass of warm cloudy tap water, which he handed to the English poet.

Joe held the glass up to the sun. 'I assume,' he shouted to the caretaker, who was still untangling his string, 'that this glass of water comes from a putrid swamp.' He gulped the water down in one go and pointed to the empty glass. 'This is water. It can be found in oceans and polar ice caps . . . It can be found in clouds and rivers . . . it will . . .'

Claude snapped his fingers under the poet's nose. 'Thank you, monsieur, for the geography lesson. But what we want to know is have you read the poetry of our friend here?' He pointed to Kitty. 'Because she tells us you are a very respected poet and she says you have so kindly offered to give her an opinion.'

Joe had to finally look at Kitty Finch. Her grey eyes that were sometimes green seemed to shine with extra radiance in her sunburnt face. She did not seem in the least embarrassed by Claude's intervention on her behalf. In fact she appeared to be amused, even grateful. Joe reckoned this was the worst day of his holiday so far. He was too old, too busy to have to endure a village full of idiots more fascinated with him than he was with them.

'That is a private conversation between two writers,' he said quietly to no one in particular.

Kitty blushed and stared at her feet. 'Do you think I'm a writer?'

Joe frowned. 'Yeah, I think you probably are.'

He stared nervously at Jurgen, who appeared to be lost in the puzzle of his string. The dogs were now lapping up the expensive bottled water in their bowls. Claude danced into the café, where he had pinned up a poster of Charlie Chaplin standing white-faced in a circle of light, his walking stick between his legs. Underneath it were the words *Les Temps modernes*. Next to it stood the new rubber model of ET, his baby alien neck garlanded with a string of fake plastic ivy. He started to fry yesterday's potatoes in duck fat, peering out of the window to see what the poet and Kitty Ket were up to.

Kitty leaned forward and touched Joe's shoulder with her hand. It was a strange gesture. As if she were testing that he was there.

'I've got all your books in my room.'

She sounded vaguely threatening. As if by owning his books, he in turn owed her something. The copper curls of her long unbrushed hair falling over her shoulders resembled a marvellous dream he might have invented to cheer himself up. How had she managed to hog so much beauty? She smelt of roses. She was soft and slender and supple. She was interesting and lovely. She loved plants. She had green fingers. And more literally, green fingernails. She admired him, wanted his attention and intrigued him, but he need not have bothered to read her poem because he understood it already.

Claude, with new humility and even-handedness, placed a bowl of green salad and fried potatoes on their table. Joe picked up a potato and dipped it in mustard.

'I've been thinking about your title, "Swimming Home".'

His tone was offhand, more nonchalant than he felt. He did not tell her how he had been thinking about her title. The rectangular swimming pool that had been carved from stone in the grounds of the villa reminded him of a coffin. A floating open coffin lit with the underwater lights Jurgen swore at when he fiddled with the incandescent light bulbs he'd had to change twice since they arrived. A swimming pool was just a hole in the ground. A grave filled with water.

Two paragliders drifted on yellow silk between the mountains. The narrow cobbled streets of the village were deserted. The paragliders were landing near the river instead of the usual base five kilometres away.

Kitty stuffed her mouth with lettuce leaves. A thin cat purred against her ankles as she threw her potato chips under the table. She leaned forward.

'Something happened to me this year. I've forgotten things.' She frowned and he saw that the burn on her forehead was beginning to blister.

'What sort of things?'

'I can't rah rah rah rah rah.'

She was not a poet. She was a poem. She was about to

snap in half. He thought his own poetry had made her la la la la love him. It was unbearable. He could not bear it. She was still trying to remember how to say remember.

If he couldn't talk about her poem what good was he? He might as well move to the countryside and run the tombola stand at the church fête. He might as well take up writing stories set in the declining years of empire featuring a dusty black Humber V8 Snipe with an aged loyal driver.

She was an astute reader and she was troubled and she had suicidal thoughts, but then what did he want his readers to be like? Were they required to eat all their vegetables, have a regular monthly salary and pension fund with yearly gym membership and a loyalty card to their favourite supermarket?

Her gaze, the adrenalin of it was like a stain, the etcs in her poem a bright light, a high noise. And if all this wasn't terrifying enough, her attention to the detail of every day was even more so, to pollen and struggling trees and the instincts of animals, to the difficulties of pretending to be relentlessly sane, to the way he walked (he had kept the rheumatism that aged him a secret from his family), to the nuance of mood and feeling in them all. Yesterday he had watched her free some bees trapped in the glass of a lantern as if it were she who was held captive. She was as receptive as it was possible to be, an explorer, an adventurer, a nightmare. Every moment with her was a kind of emergency, her words always too direct, too raw, too truthful.

There was nothing for it but to lie.

'I'm sorry, Kitty, but I haven't read your poem yet. AND I have a deadline with my publisher. AND I have to give a reading in Kraków in three weeks. AND I promised to take Nina fishing this afternoon.'

'Right.' She bit her lip and looked away. 'Right,' she said again, but her voice was breaking. Jurgen seemed to have disappeared and Kitty was biting her fingers.

'Why don't you give it to Jurgen to read?' As soon as he said it he wished he hadn't. She was literally changing colour in front of him. It was not so much a blush as a fuse. An electrical cable wire starting to melt. She fixed him with a glare of such intense hostility he wondered what it was he had actually done that was so bad.

'My poem is a conversation with you and no one else.'

It shouldn't be happening, his search for love in her, but it was. He would go to the ends of the earth to find love. He was trying not to, but the more he tried not to search, the more there was to find. He could see her on a British beach with a Thermos of tea in her bag, dodging the cold waves, tracing her name in the sand, looking out at the nuclear power stations built in the distance. This was more her landscape, a catastrophic poem in itself. He had touched her with his words, but he knew he must not touch her in any other sort of way, in a more literal way, with his lips for example. That would be taking advantage. He had to fight it all the way. The way to where? He didn't know, but he would fight it to the very end. If he were religious he would get down on his knees and pray. Father, take all this away. Away. Let all this fade away. He knew it was as much a plea or a wish or a chant to his own father, the sombre bearded patriarch, the shadow he had chased all his life, etc. His father said goodbye, etc. His mother said goodbye, etc. He hid in a dark forest in western Poland, etc.

Kitty stood up and fumbled with her purse. He told her not to worry. Please. He wanted to buy her lunch. She insisted she would pay her share. He saw her purse was flat, empty, there was nothing in it but she was searching for coins all the same. He insisted. It meant nothing to him. Please would she leave the bill for him to sort out? She was shouting too while her fingers frantically searched inside the purse, shouting at him to shut up shut up shut up, who did he think she was, what was he thinking she was? Blushing and furious, she at last found what she had been looking for, a grubby twenty-franc note folded in two as if it had been saved for something. She unfolded it carefully, her hands shaking as she slid it under a saucer, and then she ran down one of the cobbled streets. He could hear her coughing. And then he heard Jurgen's voice talking to her and realised the caretaker must have been waiting for her. She was asking him in French why the pool was so cloudy and he was asking her why she was crying. He heard Jurgen say forget forget, the sun is shining, Kitty Ket. It was a sort of song: forget forget Kitty Ket forget forget Kitty Ket.

Joe searched for his silk handkerchief and buried his face in it. Silk was used to make early bulletproof vests. It was a second skin and he needed it. What was he supposed to do? What was he supposed to do with her poem? He was not her doctor. She didn't want him to shine a light in her eyes. Should he tell Isabel the young woman she had invited to stay had threatened to do something?

He would be in Poland soon. Performing in an old palace in Kraków. His translator and guide would talk him through tram routes and menus. She would take him to rest in the Tatra Mountains and show him the wooden dachas built in the forest. Women in headscarves would tend their geese and invite him to taste their jams and cheeses. When he finally departed from Warsaw airport and customs asked him if he was taking any caviar out of the country, he would say, 'No caviar. I'm taking my black oily past out of the country and it belongs to us both. It goes like this. My father said goodbye, etc. My mother said goodbye, etc. They hid me in a dark forest in western Poland, etc.'

Someone was patting his shoulder. To his surprise, Claude had placed a glass of cold lager on his table. What had brought on this kind fraternal gesture from the Mick Jagger of Wurzelshire? Joe drank it down in one long thirsty gulp. He picked up the note Kitty had left under the saucer and poked it into his shirt pocket before Claude swept it up to pay his hair stylist. He would find a way of returning it to her. She was going in two days' time, thank God. It would be over. To his dismay, just as he was beginning to feel elated at being on his own, he saw his daughter walking down the hill towards the café.

Nina was carrying a fishing net and a bucket. Oh no. Bloody hell. He began to moan to himself. Here she is. My daughter is wearing mascara to go fishing. And earrings. Big gold hoops that will be caught on the branches of trees. Now he would have to hike with her all the way to the river in the afternoon heat as he had promised her. Two kilometres.

No one seemed to understand he was fifty-seven years old. He would have to scramble down the slope of the river bank and try not to slip on the stones. He waved unenthusiastically and his daughter shook the fishing net in his direction. When she finally slumped down on the chair opposite him, he took her hand and squeezed it. 'Congratulations. Your mother told me you've started your period at last.'

'Shut the fuck up.' Nina rolled her eyes and stared in rapt fascination at the bucket.

'OK, I will. Why don't we cancel fishing and just sit here and drink lager together?'

'No way.'

Joe cleared his throat. 'Um . . . have you got everything you need . . . you know, for a girl who has just started . . .?'

'Shut up.'

'OK, I will.'

'Where's Kitty?'

'She's . . . um . . . I don't know where she's gone.'

Nina stared at her father's hair. He had actually brushed it for a change. She had to admit he was quite handsome even though he was repulsive. He had made an effort to look good for Kitty whatever he said.

'Did you like her poem?'

What was he supposed to say? Again he did what he did best, which was to lie.

'I haven't read it yet.'

Nina punched his arm as hard as she could.

'She was so nervous about you reading it she nearly crashed the car. With ME in it. She practically drove us both over the mountains. She had to summon all her courage to see you. She was SHAKING.'

'Oh, God.' Joe blew out his cheeks.

'Why "Oh, GOD"? I thought you didn't believe in God?' his daughter snarled and turned her back on him.

He banged the table and it jumped.

'Don't EVER get into a car with Kitty Finch again. Do you understand?'

Nina thought she sort of understood but didn't really know what it was she had agreed to understand. Was Kitty a bad driver or what? Her father looked furious.

'I can't stand THE DEPRESSED. It's like a job, it's the only thing they work hard at. Oh good my depression is very well today. Oh good today I have another mysterious symptom and I will have another one tomorrow. The DEPRESSED are full of hate and bile and when they are not having panic attacks they are writing poems. What do they want their poems to DO? Their depression is the most VITAL thing about them. Their poems are threats. ALWAYS threats. There is no sensation that is keener or more active than their pain. They give nothing back except their depression. It's just another utility. Like electricity and water and gas and democracy. They could not survive without it. GOD, I'M SO THIRSTY. WHERE'S CLAUDE?'

Claude poked his head round the door. He was trying

not to laugh but looked at Joe with slightly more respect than usual. In fact he was thinking about asking him in confidence if he might see his way to paying the tab Mitchell was running up in the café.

'Please, Claude, bring me some water. Any water. A bottle will do. No. I'll have another beer. A large one. Don't you do pints in this country?'

Claude nodded and disappeared inside the café, where he had switched on the television to watch the football. Nina picked up the fishing net and waved it in her father's face.

'The whole point of this afternoon is we are going fishing, so stand up and start walking, because you are boring me shitless.'

Shitless was her newest word and she said it with relish.

'I know I don't bore you "shitless",' her father growled pathetically, his voice now hoarse.

Nina did not dare say it again because every time he took her out with the net and bucket she was always excited at the horrors he somehow managed to scoop up.

Claude brought out the beer, 'a large one', in a pint glass and explained to Nina that he was taking no more orders from her father because he was watching the semi between Sweden and Brazil.

'Fair enough.' Joe threw some money on the table and when Claude whispered something in his ear, he slapped a bundle of notes into his hand and told him he would pay for anything Mitchell ordered at the café but he must not know, the fat man must not be told that his endless pastries would be paid for with the royalties of the rich arsehole poet.

Claude tapped his nose. Their plan was safe with him. He glanced at Nina and then snapped a branch of the purple bougainvillea growing up the wall. He looped the flowers into a bracelet and offered it to her with a small bow. 'For the beautiful daughter of the poet.'

Nina found herself brazenly holding out her arm so he could wrap the violet petals around it like a handcuff. Her pulse was going berserk as his fingertips touched her wrist.

'Give me the net, Nina.' Her father held out his arm. 'I can use it to poke my eyes out. Actually I would like to watch the World Cup with Claude. You need to learn to be a bit kinder to your father.'

She bit her lip in what she hoped was an appealing manner and dared herself to glance at Claude, who shrugged helplessly. They both knew he would rather just watch her.

As they walked past the church to get to the road that Joe knew led to the gate that led to the field of snorting bulls that led to the path that led to the bridge that led to the river, he felt his daughter's hand slip into his trouser pocket.

'Nearly there,' she said encouragingly.

'Shut up,' her father replied.

'I think you get depressed. Don't you, Dad?'

Joe stumbled on an uneven cobblestone.

'As you said, "We are nearly there."'

The Photograph

The group of Japanese tourists was happy. They had been smiling for what seemed an unnaturally long time. Isabel, who was sitting in the shade of a silver olive tree waiting for Laura, reckoned they had been smiling for about twenty minutes. They were taking photographs of each other outside the faded pink château of the Matisse Museum and their smiles were beginning to look pained and tormented.

The park was full of families picnicking under the olive trees. Four old men playing *boules* in the shade paused their game to talk about the heatwave that was ruining the vineyards in France. Laura was waving to her and did not realise she had walked straight into a photograph. The seven Japanese tourists standing with their arms draped around each other were still smiling, Laura in front of them, her arm raised in the air as the camera flashed.

Isabel had always been first in class to raise her hand at her grammar school in Cardiff. She had known the answers long before the other girls caught up, girls who, like her, all wore green blazers inscribed with the school motto, Let Knowledge Serve the World. Now she thought she would change the school motto to something that warned the girls that knowledge would not necessarily serve them, nor would it make them happy. There was a chance it would instead throw light on visions they did not want to see. The new motto would have to take into account the idea that knowledge was sometimes hard to live with and once the clever young girls of Cardiff had a taste for it they would never be able to put the genie back in the bottle.

The men had resumed their game of *boules*. Voices from a radio somewhere close by were discussing the air controllers' strike. Flasks of coffee were being opened under the trees. Children fell off their bicycles. Families unpacked sandwiches and fruit. Isabel could see the sweep of white and blue belle époque hotels built on the hill and knew that somewhere nearby was the cemetery where Matisse was buried. Laura was holding a bottle of red wine in her left hand. Isabel called out to her, but Laura had seen her anyway. She was a fast walker, efficient and focused. Laura would have things to say about her inviting Kitty Finch to stay, but Isabel would insist she pay the entire summer's rent for the villa herself. Laura and Mitchell must book themselves into a country hotel near Cannes she had read about in a guidebook. A yellow ochre Provençal manor that served fine wines and sea bass in a crust of salt. This would be the right place for Mitchell, who had been hoping for an epic gastronomic summer but instead found himself unwillingly sharing his holiday with a stranger who seemed to be starving herself. Laura and Mitchell thrived on order and structure. Mitchell made five-year plans for their business in Euston, flow charts describing tasks to be done, the logic of decisions, the outcomes desired. She admired their faith in the future: the belief that it delivered outcomes that could be organised to come out in the right shape.

Laura was smiling but she did not look happy. She sat down

beside Isabel and took off her sandals. And then she pulled at tufts of the parched grass with her fingers and told her friend that the shop in Euston was closing down. She and Mitchell could no longer make ends meet. They could barely pay their mortgage. They had come to France with five credit cards between them and not very much cash. They could not even afford to buy petrol for the Mercedes Mitchell had foolishly hired at the airport. In fact Mitchell had run up debts she was only just beginning to get a grip on. He owed large sums of money all over the place. For months he had been saying something would turn up, but nothing had turned up. The shop would go into liquidation. When they returned to London they would have to sell their house.

Isabel moved closer to Laura and put her arms around her. Laura was so tall it was sometimes hard to believe she was not literally above the things that bothered everyone else. She was obviously not feeling herself, because her shoulders were pulled down too. Her friend had never adopted the stoop tall people sometimes develop to make themselves human scale, but now she looked crushed.

'Let's open the wine.' Laura had forgotten to bring a corkscrew so they used the end of Isabel's comb, plunging its long plastic spike into the cork, and found themselves drinking from the bottle, passing it to each other like teenagers on their first holiday away from family. Isabel told Laura how she had spent the morning searching shops for sanitary towels for Nina, but had no idea how to say it in French. At last the man in the pharmacy told her the words were '*serviettes hygiéniques*'. He had wrapped the pads in a brown paper bag and then in a plastic bag and then in another plastic bag as if in his mind they were already soaked in blood. And then she changed the subject. She wanted to know if Laura had a personal bank account. Laura shook her head. She and Mitchell had had a joint account ever since they set up business together. And then Laura changed the subject and asked Isabel if she thought Kitty Finch might be a little . . . she searched for the word . . . 'touched'? The word stuck in her mouth and she wished she had another language to translate what she meant, because the only words stored inside her were from the school playground of her generation, a lexicon that in no particular order started with barmy, bonkers, barking and went on to loopy, nuts, off with the fairies and then danced up the alphabet again to end with cuckoo. Laura began to tell her how much Kitty's arrival alarmed her. Just as she was leaving the villa to drive to the Matisse Museum she had seen Kitty arrange the tails of three rabbits Mitchell had shot in the orchard in a vase – as if they were flowers. The thing was, she must have actually cut the tails off the rabbits herself. With a knife. She must have sawed through the rabbits with a carving knife. Isabel did not reply because she was writing Laura a cheque. Peering over her shoulder, Laura saw it was for a considerable amount of money and was signed in Isabel's maiden name.

Isabel Rhys Jones. When they were students introducing themselves to each other in the bar, Isabel always pronounced her home city in Welsh: Caerdydd. She had had a Welsh accent to start with and then it more or less disappeared. In the second year of their studies Isabel spoke with an English accent that wasn't quite English but would become so by the time she was on television reporting from Africa. Laura, who had studied African languages, tried to not sound English when she spoke Swahili. It was a complicated business and she would have liked to think about it some more, but Isabel had put the lid back on her pen and was clearing her throat. She was saying something and she sounded quite Welsh. Laura missed the first bit of what her friend was saying but tuned in on time to hear how the North African cleaner who mopped the floors for a pittance in the villa was apparently on strike. The woman wore a headscarf and mended the European plugs for Jurgen, who had gleefully discovered she was more skilled with electrics than he was. Laura had seen her gazing at the wires and then out of the window at the silver light that apparently cured Matisse's tuberculosis. This woman had been on her mind for some reason and just as she was wondering why she had been so preoccupied by her she remembered what Isabel had said when she was writing out the cheque. It was something to do with Laura opening a separate account from the one she shared with Mitchell. She started to laugh and reminded Isabel that her maiden name was Laura Cable.

The Thing

'You shouldn't cover yourself with so much sun lotion, Mitchell.'

Kitty Finch was obviously upset about something. She had taken off all her clothes and stood naked at the edge of the pool as if no one else was there. 'It changes the chemical balance of the water.'

Mitchell put a protective hand on the dome of his stomach and groaned.

'The water is actually CLOUDY.' Kitty sounded furious. She ran around the sides of the pool staring into it from every angle. 'Jurgen has got the chemical treatment all wrong.' She stamped her bare foot on the hot paving stones. 'It's chemistry that does the fine-tuning. He's added chlorine tablets to the skimmer box and now it's too concentrated in the deep end.'

Once again Mitchell took it upon himself to tell her to fuck off. Why didn't she make herself a cheese sandwich and go and get lost in the woods? In fact he would even drive her there if she could see her way to putting some petrol in his Mercedes.

'You're so easily frightened, Mitchell.'

She jumped towards him. Two long leaps as if she was playing at being a gazelle or a deer and was taunting him to come and hunt her down. Her ribs poked out of her skin like the wires of the trap Mitchell had bought for the rat.

'It's a good thing Laura's so tall, isn't it? She can peer

over your head when you shoot animals and never have to look at the ground where they lie wounded.'

Kitty leapt into the cloudy water holding her nose. Mitchell sat up and immediately felt dizzy. The sun always made him ill. Next year he would suggest they hire a chalet on the edge of an icy fjord in Norway, as far away from the Jacobs family as possible. He would catch seals and thrash himself with birch twigs in saunas and then he'd run out into the snow and scream while Laura practised speaking Yoruba and longed for Africa.

'THE WATER IS FUCKED.'

What had got into her? Adjusting the umbrella over his pink bald head, he could see Joe limping towards the small gate that led to the back of the garden. Nina followed him through the cypress trees carrying a red bucket and a net.

'Hi, Joe.'

Kitty jumped out of the pool and started to shake water out of the copper coils of her hair. He nodded at her, relieved that despite their unpleasant meeting earlier she sounded genuinely pleased to see him. He pointed to the bucket Nina was carrying with some difficulty to the edge of the pool. ·

'Come and see what we found in the river.'

They crowded around the bucket, which was half full of muddy water. A slimy grey creature with a red stripe down its spine clung to a clump of weed. It was as thick as Mitchell's thumb and seemed to have some sort of pulse because the water trembled above it. Every now and again it curled into a ball and slowly straightened out again.

'What is it?' Mitchell couldn't believe they had bothered to lug this vile creature across the fields all the way back to the villa.

'It's a thing.' Joe smirked.

Mitchell groaned and moved away. 'Nasty.'

'Dad always finds gross things.'

Nina stared over Kitty's shoulder, making sure not to look at her breasts, which were now hanging over the bucket as she peered in. She didn't want to look at naked Kitty Finch and her father standing too near her. Nina could count the bones that ran like beads down her spine. Kitty was a starver. Her room was full of rotting food she had hidden under cushions. As far as Nina was concerned, she'd rather stare at the blotches of chewing gum on London pavement than at her father and Kitty Finch.

Kitty reached for a towel. She was all fingers and thumbs, dropping it and picking it up again until Joe finally took it from her and helped wrap it around her waist.

'What do you think it is?' Kitty stared into the bucket.

'It's a creepy-crawly,' Joe announced. 'My best find yet.'

Nina thought it might be a centipede. It had hundreds of tiny legs that were frantically waving around in the water, trying to find something to grip on to.

'What exactly is it you are looking for when you go fishing?' Kitty lowered her voice, as if the creature might hear her. 'Do you find the things you want to find?'

'What are you talking about?' Mitchell sounded like a schoolteacher irritated with a child.

'Don't talk to her like that.' Joe's arms were now clasped

around Kitty's waist, holding up the towel as if his life depended on it.

'She's asking why don't I find silver fish and pretty shells? The answer is they are there anyway.'

While he talked he poked his finger through the wet curls of Kitty's hair. Nina saw her mother and Laura walking through the white gate. Her father let go of the towel and Kitty blushed. Nina stared miserably into the cypress trees, pretending to look for the hedgehog she knew sheltered in the garden. Joe walked over to the plastic recliner and lay down. He glanced at his wife, who had walked over to the bucket. There were leaves in her hair and grass stains on her bare shins. She had not so much distanced herself from him as moved out to another neighbourhood altogether. There was new vigour in the way she stood by the bucket. Her determination not to love him seemed to have renewed her energy.

Mitchell was still peering at the creature crawling up the sides of the red plastic bucket. It was perfectly camouflaged by the red markings on its spine.

'What are you going to do with your slug?'

Everyone looked at Joe.

'Yes,' he said. 'My "thing" is freaking you all out. Let's put it on a leaf in the garden.'

'No.' Laura squirmed. 'It'll only make its way back here.'

'Or crawl through the plughole and come up in the water.' Mitchell looked truly alarmed.

Laura shuddered and then screamed, 'It's climbing out. It's nearly out.' She ran to the bucket and threw a towel over it.

'Do something to stop it, Joe.'

Joe limped to the bucket, removed the towel and flicked the creature back into the bottom of the water with his thumb.

'It is really quite tiny.' He yawned. 'It's just a strange tiny slimy thing.'

A clump of river weed trailed down his eyebrow. Everything had gone very quiet. Even the late-afternoon rasp of the cicadas seemed to have faded away. When Joe opened his eyes, everyone except Laura had disappeared into the villa. Laura was shaking but her voice was matter of fact.

'Look, I know Isabel invited Kitty to stay.' She stopped and started again. 'But you don't have to. I mean, do you? Do you have to? Do you? Do you have to keep doing it?'

Joe clenched his fists inside his pockets.

'Doing what?'

WEDNESDAY

Body Electric

Jurgen and Claude were smoking the hashish Jurgen had bought from the accordion player on the beach in Nice. He usually bought it from the driver who dropped the immigrant cleaners at the tourist villas, but they were organising a strike. What's more the news last night forecast a gale and the entire village had spent the night preparing for it. Jurgen's cottage was owned by Rita Dwighter but not yet 'restored' and he wanted to keep it that way. Sometimes he threw heavy objects at the walls in the hope that it would become unrestorable and keep its status as the ugly dysfunctional child in Rita Dwighter's family of properties.

Now he was huddled over Claude's mobile phone. Claude had recorded a cow mooing. He didn't know why, but he had to do it. He had walked into a field and held his phone as close as he dared to the cow's mouth. If Jurgen pressed the play button the cow mooed. Technology had made the cow sound familiar but uncomfortably strange as well. Every time the cow mooed they laughed hysterically, because the cow had trodden on Claude's big toe and now his toenail was deformed.

Madame Dwighter had told Jurgen to wait in for her call. Jurgen didn't mind. Waiting in made a change from being called out to change a light bulb in the 'Provençal style' villas he would never afford to buy. A pile of Picasso prints he had bought in a job lot at the flea market lay against the wall. He preferred the rubber model of ET he had found for Claude. Rita Dwighter had instructed him to frame and hang 'the Picassos' in every available space left in the three villas she owned, but he couldn't be bothered. It was more interesting hearing the cow mooing on Claude's mobile.

When Jurgen started to roll another joint he could hear a telephone ringing. Claude pointed to the telephone lying on the floor. Jurgen twisted his nose with his thumb and forefinger and eventually picked up the receiver.

Claude had to slap his hand over his mouth to stop himself from laughing as loudly as he would have liked. Jurgen didn't want to be a caretaker. Madame Dwighter was always asking him to tell her what was on his mind, but he only ever told Claude what was on his mind. There was only ever one thing on Jurgen's mind.

Kitty Finch. If pressed he would include: sex, drugs, Buddhism as a means to achieve oneness in life, no meat, no vivisection, Kitty Finch, no vaccination, no alcohol, Kitty Finch, purity of body and soul, herbal remedies, playing slide guitar, Kitty Finch, becoming what Jack Kerouac described as a Nature Boy Saint. He heard his friend telling Madame

Dwighter that yes, everything was very serene in the villa this year. Yes, the famous English poet and his family were enjoying their vacation. In fact they had a surprise visitor. Mademoiselle Finch was staying in the spare room and she was charming them all. Yes, she had very good equilibrium this year and she had written something to show the poet.

Claude unbuttoned his jeans and let them fall to his knees. Jurgen had to hold the phone away from his ear while he doubled over, making obscene gestures to Claude, who was now doing press-ups in his Calvin Klein boxer shorts on the floor. Jurgen tapped the joint against his knee and continued speaking to Rita Dwighter, who was phoning from tax exile in Spain. He would soon have to call her *Señora*.

Yes, the fact sheet was up to date. Yes, the water in the pool was perfect. Yes, the cleaners were doing a good job. Yes, he had replaced the broken window. Yes, he was feeling good in himself. Yes, the heatwave was coming to an end. Yes, there were going to be thunderstorms. Yes, everyone knew about the weather forecast. Yes, he would secure the shutters.

Claude could hear the voice of Rita Dwighter fall out of the receiver and disappear into the clouds of hashish smoke. Everyone in the village laughed at the mention of the wealthy psychoanalyst and property developer who paid Jurgen so handsomely for his lack of skill. They liked to joke that she had built a helicopter pad for businessmen to land outside her consulting room in west London. They sat on designer chairs while their pilots, usually former alcoholics struck off by the commercial airlines, smoked duty-free cigarettes in the rain. Claude had been thinking of spreading a rumour that one of her most affluent clients had managed to get his arm stuck in the blades of the propeller just as she had sorted out why he liked to dress up in a Nazi uniform and whip prostitutes. He had had to have his arm amputated and stopped seeing her, which meant she could not afford to buy the postman's cottage after all.

When Madame Dwighter came to inspect her properties, which to Jurgen's relief was not often, she always invited Claude with his Mick Jagger looks to supper. The last time he ate with her she stuck an erect pineapple stalk into a moist melting Brie and asked him to help himself.

Jurgen finally put the phone down. He stared at the Picasso prints as if he wanted to murder them. He told Claude, who had now taken off his T-shirt and was lying face down on the floor in his boxer shorts, that he'd been instructed to hang *Guernica* in the corridor to hide the jagged cracks in the plaster. Dominatrix Dwighter was obviously impressed by the techniques the great artist employed to say something about the human condition. Claude just about managed to stand up and put on one of Jurgen's battered CDs. It had been lying on top of an Indian jewellery box labelled 'Prague Muzic. Ket's Selection for Calm'.

Someone was knocking on the door. Jurgen disliked all visitors because they were always asking him to do his job. This time it was the pretty fourteen-year-old daughter of the arsehole British poet. She was wearing a short white skirt and naturally she wanted him to do something.

'My mother asked me to come over to check you'd booked the horse-riding for tomorrow.'

He nodded wisely, as if nothing else had ever been on his mind. 'Come in. Claude's here.'

When Jurgen said Claude's here, the CD seemed to jump or it got stuck or something happened. Nina heard a violin playing and under it the sound of a wolf howling and the female singer breathing a word that sounded like snowburst. She glanced at Claude, who was dancing in his boxer shorts. His back was so smooth and brown she stared at the wall instead.

'*Bonjour*, Nina. The dogs ate my jeans so now I only have my shorts. The CD is scratched but I like it for calming.'

When she looked through him pitifully, he saw himself as a snail crushed on the rope sole of her red espadrilles. Jurgen had his hands on his bony hips, his elbows pointing out in triangles. He seemed to want her opinion on his dreadlocks.

'So do you think I should cut off my hair?'

'Yeah.'

'I make my hair like this to be different from my father.'

He laughed and Claude laughed with him.

> snowburst
> drifting away
> to the dark

Jurgen was trying to get a grip on geography. 'Austria is the start of my childhood. Then I think it was Baden-Baden. My father taught me to cut timber in the old tradition.' He scratched his head. 'I think it was Austrian. Something old anyway. So what kind of music do you like?'

'Nirvana is my favourite band.'

'Ah, you are liking the Kurt Cobain with his blue eyes, yes?'

She told him she had made a shrine to Kurt Cobain in her bedroom after he had shot himself that spring. April the fifth to be precise but his body was found on April the eighth. She had played his album *In Utero* all that day.

Jurgen cocked his dreadlocks to one side. 'Has your father read Kitty Ket's poem yet?'

'No. I'm going to read it myself.'

Claude pouted and strutted towards the fridge. 'That is a good plan. Do you want a beer?'

She shrugged. Claude was so anxious to please her it was pathetic. Claude translated her shrug as an enthusiastic Yes.

'I have to bring my own beer over to Jurgen's because he only drinks carrot juice.'

Jurgen had just heard a motorbike pull up outside his cottage. It was his friend Jean-Paul, who always gave him a commission on horse-riding bookings. Jean-Paul only kept ponies, so it was not exactly going to be a horse ride, but the ponies had hooves and a nice tail all the same. When he ran out of the door to make the deal, Claude reached for his T-shirt and struggled to put it on.

Nina stared at everything that wasn't him. And then she sat cross-legged on the floor, her back leaning against the wall, while he walked over with a beer in his hand. He opened it for her and sat down so close their thighs almost touched.

'So are you enjoying your vacation?'

She took a swig of the sour-tasting beer. 'It's OK.'

'If you come to my café I'll show you the Extra Terrestrial I keep in my kitchen.'

What was he talking about? She found herself moving closer to his shoulder. And then she turned her face towards him and she made her eyes say you can kiss me kiss me kiss me and there was a second when she sensed he wasn't sure what she meant. The beer was still in her hand and she put it down on the floor.

> drifting away
> to the dark
> forest

His lips were warm and they were on hers. She was kissing Mick Jagger and he was devouring her like a wolf or something fierce but soft as well and definitely not calm. He was telling her she was so so everything. She moved even closer and then he stopped talking.

> to the dark
> forest
> where trees bleed
> snowburst

When she peeped her eyes open and saw he had his eyes

shut she shut her eyes again, but then the door opened and Jurgen was standing in the middle of the room blinking at them.

'So everything is cool with the horse-riding.'

There was a kissing coma in the atmosphere. Everything had gone dark red. Jurgen put his hands on his hips so his elbows would jut out and the vibes could flow through the triangles his elbows made.

'Please, I am asking you to read the Ket's poem so you can tell me the way to her heart.'

THURSDAY

The Plot

Nina opened the door of her parents' bedroom and skated in her socks across the tiled floor. She was wearing socks despite the heat because her left foot was swollen from a bee sting. To give her courage for the task in hand she had spent the last hour smearing her eyelids with Kitty's blue stick of kohl. When she looked in the mirror her brown eyes were glittering and certain. From the window by the bed she could see her mother and Laura talking by the pool. Her father had gone to Nice to see the Russian Orthodox Cathedral and Kitty Finch was with Jurgen as usual. They were going to collect cow dung from the fields and then spread it over Jurgen's new allotment, which she said she had 'taken over for the summer'. No one could work out why she wasn't actually living with Jurgen in his cottage next door, but her mother had implied that Kitty might not be as 'sweet' on him as he was on her. She heard a bashing noise coming from the kitchen. Mitchell had wrapped a slab of dark chocolate in a tea cloth and was hammering at it excitedly. It was hot outside but she felt cold in her parents' room, as if it was an ice rink after all. She knew what the envelope looked like but she couldn't see it anywhere. What she needed was a torch, because she must not put the lights on and attract attention. If anyone came in she would slip into the bathroom and hide behind the door. On the table by her mother's side of the bed she noticed a slab of waxy honeycomb half wrapped in a page of newspaper. It had obviously been tied with the green string that lay next to it. She walked towards it and saw it was a gift from her father, because he had written in black ink across the page,

To my sweetest with my whole love as always, Jozef.

Nina frowned at the thick golden honey oozing through the holes. If her parents quite liked each other after all it would ruin the story she had put together for herself. When she thought about her parents, which was most of the time, she was always trying to fit the pieces together. What was the plot? Her father had very gentle hands and yesterday they were all over her mother. She had seen them kissing in the hallway like something out of a film, pulled into each other while moths crashed into the light bulb above their heads. As far as she was concerned, her parents tragically couldn't stand the sight of each other and only loved her. The plot was that her mother abandoned her only daughter to go and hug orphans in Romania. Tragically (so much tragedy) Nina had taken her mother's place in the family home and become her father's most precious companion, always second-guessing his moods and needs. But things started to wobble when her mother asked her if she'd like to go to a special restaurant by the sea for an ice cream with a sparkler in it. What's more, if her parents were kissing yesterday (the sheets on their unmade bed looked a bit frantic), and if they seemed to understand each other in a way that left her out, the plot was going off track.

It was only after six minutes of urgent searching that she eventually found the envelope with Kitty's poem inside it. She had given up rummaging through the silk shirts and handkerchiefs her father always ironed so carefully and crawled on her knees to look under the bed. When she saw the envelope propped up against her father's slippers and two dead brown cockroaches lying on their backs, she lay on her stomach and swept it up with her arm. There was something else under the bed too but she did not have time to find out what it was.

The window overlooking the pool was a problem. Her mother was sitting on the steps by the shallow end eating an apple. She could hear her asking Laura why she was learning Yoruba and Laura saying, 'Why not? Over twenty million people speak it.'

She crouched on the floor where she could not be seen and tore the Sellotape off the lip of the envelope. It was empty. She peered inside it. A sheet of paper had been folded into a square the size of a matchbox and it was stuck at the bottom of the envelope like an old shoe wedged into the mud of a river. She scooped it out and began carefully to unfold it.

Swimming Home

by

Kitty Finch

After she read it Nina didn't bother to fold the paper back into its intricate squares. She shoved it inside the envelope and put it back under the bed with the cockroaches. Why hadn't her father read it? He would understand exactly what was going on in Kitty's mind.

She made her way up the stairs to the open-plan living room and poked her head through the French doors.

Her mother was dangling her feet in the warm water and she was laughing. It made Nina frown because the sound was so rare. She found Mitchell frying liver in the kitchen. He was wearing one of his most flamboyant Hawaiian shirts to cook in.

'Hello,' he snorted. 'Have you come for a morsel?'

Nina leaned her back against the fridge and folded her arms.

'What have you done to your eyes?' Mitchell peered at the blue sparkling kohl smeared over her eyelids. 'Has someone punched your lights out?'

Nina took a deep breath to stop herself from screaming.

'I think Kitty is going to drown herself in our pool.'

'Oh dear,' Mitchell grimaced. 'Why's that?'

'I just get that impression.'

She did not want to say she had opened the envelope meant for her father. Mitchell switched the blender on and watched the chestnuts and sugar whirl into a paste and splatter over the palm trees on his shirt.

'If I threw you into the pool now you would float. Even I with my big stomach would float.'

He was shouting over the noise of the blender. Nina waited for him to turn it off so she could whisper.

'Yes. She's been collecting stones. I was with her on the beach when she was looking for them.' She explained how Kitty told her she was studying the drains in the pool and had said mental things like, 'You don't want to get hair caught in the plumbing.'

Mitchell looked at the fourteen-year-old fondly. He realised she was jealous of the attention her father had been paying Kitty and probably wanted the girl to drown.

'Cheer up, Nina. Have some sweet chestnut purée on a spoon. I'm going to mix it with chocolate.' He licked his fingers. 'And I'm going to save a little square for the rat tonight.'

She knew a terrible secret no one else knew. And there were other secrets too. Yesterday when she was sitting on the bed in Kitty's room helping her nudge out the seeds from her plants, a bird was singing in the garden. Kitty Finch had put her head in her hands and sobbed like there was no tomorrow.

She must speak to her father, but he was in Nice making his way to some Russian church even though he had told her that if she was ever tempted to believe in God she might be having a nervous breakdown. Something else worried her. It was the thing under the bed, but she didn't want to think about that because it was something to do with Mitchell and anyway now her mother was calling her to go horse-riding.

Ponyland

The ponies were drinking water from a tank in the shade. Flies crawled over their swollen bellies and short legs and into their brown eyes that always seemed wet. As Nina watched the woman who hired them out brush their tails, she decided she would have to tell her mother about Kitty's drowning poem, as she now called it. Kitty was speaking in French to the pony woman and didn't look like someone who was about to drown herself. She was wearing a short blue dress and there were small white feathers in her hair, as if her pillow had burst in the night.

'We have to follow the trail. There's an orange plastic bag tied to the branches of the trees. The woman says we have to follow the orange plastic and walk either side of the pony.'

Nina, who wanted to be alone with her mother, found herself forced to choose a grey pony with long scabby ears and pretend she was having a perfect childhood.

The little pony was not in the mood to be hired out for an hour. She stopped every two minutes to graze the grass and nuzzle her head against the bark of trees. Nina was impatient. She had important things on her mind, not least the stones she had collected with Kitty on the beach, because she thought they were in the poem. She had seen the words 'The Drowning Stones' underlined in the middle of the page.

She noticed her mother was suddenly taking notice of things. When Kitty pointed out trees and different kinds of grasses, Isabel asked her to repeat their names. Kitty was saying that certain types of insects needed to drink nectar in the heatwave. Did Isabel know that honey is just spit and nectar? When bees suck nectar they mix it with their saliva and store the mixture in their honey sacs. Then they throw up their honey sacs and start all over again. Kitty was talking as if they were one big happy family, all the while holding the rope between her thumb and finger. Nina sat in silence on the pony, staring moodily at the cracks of blue sky she could see through the trees. If she turned the sky upside down the pony would have to swim through clouds and vapour. The sky would be grass. Insects would run across the sky. The trail seemed to have disappeared, because there were no more orange plastic bags tied to the branches of trees. They had come out of the pine forest into a clearing near a café. The café was opposite a lake. Nina scanned the trees for bits of ripped orange plastic and knew they were lost, but Kitty didn't care. She was waving at someone, trying to get the attention of a woman sitting alone on the terrace outside the café.

'It's Dr Sheridan. Let's go and say hello.'

She walked the pony straight off what remained of the trail and led it up the three shallow concrete steps towards Madeleine Sheridan, who had taken off her spectacles and placed them on the white plastic table next to her book.

Nina found herself stranded on the pony as Kitty led her past the bemused waitress carrying a tray of Orangina to a family at a nearby table. The old woman seemed to have frozen on her chair at the moment she was about to put a cube of sugar into her cup of coffee. It was as if the sight of a slender young woman in a short blue dress, her red hair snaking down her back, leading a grey pony on to the terrace of a café was a vision that could only be glanced at sideways. No one felt able to intervene because they did not fully know what it was they were seeing. It reminded Nina of the day she watched an eclipse through a hole in coloured paper, careful not to be blinded by the sun.

'How are you, Doctor?'

Kitty pulled at the rope and gave the pony a sugar cube. With one hand still holding the rope, she draped her arm around the old woman's shoulder.

Madeleine Sheridan's voice when she finally spoke was calm, authoritative. She was wearing a red shawl that looked like a matador's cloak with pom-poms sewn across the edge.

'Stick to the track, Kitty. You can't bring ponies in here.'

'The track has disappeared. There's no track to stick to.' She smiled. 'I'm still waiting for you to bring me back my shoes like you said you would. The nurses told me I had dirty feet.'

Nina glanced at her mother, who was now standing on the left side of the pony. Kitty's hands were shaking and she was speaking too loudly.

'I'm surprised you haven't told my new friends what you did to me.' She turned to Isabel and imitated a horror-film whisper: 'Dr Sheridan said I have a morbid predisposition.'

To Nina's dismay, her mother actually laughed as if she and Kitty were sharing a joke.

The waitress brought out a plate of sausages and green beans and thumped it in front of Madeleine Sheridan, muttering to her in French about getting the pony out of the café.

Kitty winked at Nina. First with her left eye. And then with her right eye. 'The waitress isn't used to ponies coming in for breakfast.'

On cue the pony started to lick the sausages on the plate and all the children at the next table laughed.

Kitty took a small sip of the doctor woman's untouched coffee. Her eyes had stopped winking. 'Actually ' – her knuckle suddenly turned white as she gripped the rope that was supposed to keep the pony on the trail – 'she had me locked up.' She wiped her mouth with the back of her hand. 'I EMBARRASSED HER SO SHE CALLED AN AMBULANCE.'

Kitty picked up the knife from the plate, a sharp knife, and waved it at Madeleine Sheridan's throat. All the children in the café screamed, including Nina. She heard the old woman, her voice straining, telling her mother that Kitty was sick and unpredictable. Kitty was shaking her head and shouting at her.

'You said you'd get my clothes. I waited for you. You're a LIAR. I thought you were kind but they electrocuted me because of you. They did it THREE times. The nurse wanted to shave off some of my HAIR.'

The point of her knife hovered a centimetre away from Madeleine Sheridan's milky pearl necklace.

'I want to go!' Nina shouted at her mother, trying to keep her balance as the pony, its pointed ears now alert, jerked forward to find the bowl of sugar cubes.

Isabel tried to undo the stirrups so Nina could get off the pony. The waitress was helping her with the buckles and Nina managed to swing her legs over the saddle but didn't dare jump because the pony suddenly reared up.

Someone in the café was calling the park keeper on the telephone.

'THEY BURNED MY THOUGHTS TO MAKE THEM GO AWAY.'

As she moved closer to Madeleine Sheridan, waving the knife at her stricken frozen face, two small white feathers caught in her hair drifted towards Nina, who was still struggling to get off the pony.

'The doctors PEEPED at me through a spyhole. They forced MEAT down my throat. I tried to put on face cream but my jaws HURT from the shocks. I would rather DIE than have that done to me again.'

Nina heard herself speak.

'Kitty is going to drown herself.'

It was as if she was the only person who could hear her own voice. She was saying important things but apparently not important enough.

'Katherine is going to drown herself.'

Even to her own ears it sounded like a whisper, but she thought the old woman doctor might have heard her all the same. Her mother had somehow managed to grab the knife out of Kitty's hand and Nina heard Madeleine Sheridan's wobbling voice say, 'I must telephone the police. I'm going to call her mother. I must call her straight away.' She stopped because Jurgen had suddenly arrived.

It was as if Kitty had conjured him in her mind. He was talking to the park keeper, who was shaking his head and looked flustered.

'I have witnesses.' The pom-poms on Madeleine Sheridan's red cape were jumping up and down as if they were the witnesses she referred to.

Kitty grabbed Jurgen's arm and hung on to him. 'Don't listen to Dr Sheridan. She's obsessed with me. I don't know why but she is. Ask Jurgen.'

Jurgen's sleepy eyes blinked behind his round spectacles.

'Come on, Kitty Ket, I'll take you home.' He said something to Madeleine Sheridan in French and then put his arm around Kitty's waist. They could hear his voice soothing her. 'Forget forget Kitty Ket. We are all of us sick from pollution. We must take a nature cure.'

Madeleine Sheridan's eyes were burning like coal. Blue coal. She wanted to call the police. It was an attack. An assault. She looked like a matador that had been gored by the bull. The park keeper fiddled with a ring of keys strapped to his belt. The keys were almost as big as he was. He wanted to know where the young woman lived. What was her address? If Madame wanted him to call the police they would need this information. Isabel explained that Kitty had arrived five days ago with nowhere to stay and they had given her a room in their rented villa.

He frowned over this information, tapping his keys with his tiny thumb. 'But you must have asked her questions?'

Isabel nodded. They had asked her questions. Jozef

asked her what a leaf was. And a cotyledon.

'I don't think we need bother the police. It's a private argument. Madame is shaken but not harmed.'

' Her voice was gentle and a little bit Welsh.

The keeper was gesticulating now. 'The young woman must have come from somewhere.' He paused to nod to two men in muddy boots who seemed to need his permission to cut through a log with a circular saw.

'Yes,' Madeleine Sheridan snapped, 'she came from a hospital in Kent, Great Britain.' She tapped the assaulted pearls tied in a knot near her throat and turned to Isabel Jacobs. 'I believe your husband is taking her out for a cocktail at the Negresco tomorrow.'

FRIDAY

On the Way to Where?

People stopped to look at her. To gaze and gaze again at the vision of a radiant young woman in a green silk dress who seemed to be walking on air. The left strap of her white tap-dancing shoes had come undone, as if to help lift her above the cigarette butts and chocolate wrappers on the paving stones. Kitty Finch with her wealth of hair piled on top of her head was almost as tall as Joe Jacobs. As they strolled down the Promenade des Anglais in the silver light of the late afternoon, it was snowing seagulls on every rooftop in Nice. She had casually slung the short white feather cape across her shoulders, its satin ribbons tied in a loose knot round her neck. The feathers fluttered in the wind blowing from the sea, the Mediterranean, which, Joe mused, was the same colour as the glittery blue kohl on her eyes.

In the distance they could see the pink dome of the Hotel Negresco. He had respectfully changed into a pinstriped suit and even opened the new bottle of perfume sent to him from

Zurich. His parfumier, the last alchemist living in the twentieth century, insisted the top notes were irrelevant and the deepest notes would present when he was perspiring. Kitty slipped her bare arm through his pinstriped arm, a vertical red stripe that was not unlike the centipede he had caught in the river. She did not tell him what had happened with Madeleine Sheridan (she and Jurgen had already discussed it for hours) and he did not tell her how he had found himself on his knees lighting one and then two candles at the Russian Orthodox Cathedral. The tension of waiting to meet each other again had made them do things they did not understand.

By the time they arrived at the marble entrance, the porter in his crimson jacket and white gloves respectfully swung open the door for them, NEGRESCO printed across the arch of glass in gold letters. Her feather cape flew behind her like the wings of the swan they were plucked off. She did not so much stroll as glide into the low-lit bar with its faded red velvet armchairs and tapestries on the walls.

'See those oil paintings of noblemen in their palace?'

He looked up at the portraits of what appeared to be solemn pale aristocrats posing on chairs covered in tapestry in chilly marble rooms.

'Yeah, well, my mother cleans their silver and washes their underpants.'

'Is she a cleaner?'

'Yeah. She used to clean the villa for Rita Dwighter. That's how I get to stay free sometimes.'

This confession made her blush but he had something to say in reply.

'My mother was a cleaner too. I used to steal hen's eggs for her and bring them home in my pockets.'

They sat side by side on two antique chairs. The white feathers of her cape trembled when he whispered, 'There's a note to us on the table. I think it must be from Marie Antoinette.'

Kitty reached over and picked up the white card propped against a vase of flowers.

'It says the cocktail of the month is champagne with something called Crème de Fraise des Bois.'

Joe nodded as if this information was of vital importance.

'After the revolution everyone shall have the cocktail of the month. Shall we have one now anyway?'

Kitty nodded enthusiastically.

The waiter was already at his side, taking his order as if it were a great privilege to do so. A bored musician in a stained white dinner jacket sat at the piano playing 'Eleanor Rigby' in the corner of the bar. She crossed her legs and waited for him to talk about her poem. Last night she saw something that scared her and she wanted to tell him about it. The boy was standing by her bed again. He was waving frantically like he was asking her to help him and he had two hen's eggs in his pocket. He had broken into her mind. She had started to cover mirrors in case he appeared again. She slipped her hands under the bag on her lap so he wouldn't see they were shaking.

'Tell me more about your mother. Does she look like you?'

'No, she's obese. You could make the whole of me from one of her arms.'

'You said she knows the owner of the villa?'

'Yeah. Rita Dwighter.'

'Say more about Rita and her portfolio of property and pain.'

She did not want to talk about her mother's boss. It was shrapnel in her arm, his indifference to the envelope she had pushed through his bedroom door. He kept changing the subject. She took a deep breath and smelt the clover in his perfume.

'Rita owns so much property she has become a tax exile in Spain, but that means she can only be in the UK for a certain number of days a year. My mother told her she'll be like someone on the run and Rita took offence and said her own shrink told her she must accept her greed.'

He laughed and sank his fingers into the small bowl of nuts on the table. They clinked glasses and took their first sip of the cocktail of the month.

'What is your favourite poem, Kitty?'

'Do you mean a poem I've written or someone else's?' He must know by now that he was her favourite poet. That was why she was here. His words were inside her. She understood them before she read them. But he wouldn't own up. He was always cheerful. So fucking cheerful, she thought he might be in terrible danger.

'I mean do you like Walt Whitman or Byron or Keats or Sylvia Plath?'

'Oh, right.' She took another sip of her cocktail. 'Well, there's no competition. My favourite poem is by Apollinaire.'

'What's that?'

She tipped her chair forward and grabbed the fountain pen he always clipped on to his shirt like a microphone.

'Give me your hand.'

When he placed his hand on her knee, his palm making a sweaty mark on her green silk dress, she jabbed the nib into his skin so hard he jumped. She was stronger than she looked, because she held his hand down and he couldn't or didn't want to tear it away. She was hurting him with his own pen as she inked a black tattoo of letters on his skin.

I
T
S
R
A
I
N
I
N
G

He stared at his smarting hand. 'Why do you like it so much?'

She lifted the champagne flute up to her lips and stuck her tongue inside it, licking the last dregs of strawberry pulp.

'Because it's always raining.'

'Is it?'

'Yeah. You know it is.'

'Do I?'

'It's always raining if you're feeling sad.'

The image of Kitty Finch in perpetual rain, walking in rain, sleeping in rain, shopping and swimming and collecting plants in rain, intrigued him. His hand was still on her knee. She had not put the lid back on his pen. He wanted to demand she return it to him but instead found himself offering her another cocktail. She was lost in thought. Sitting up very straight on the velvet armchair with his pen in her hand. The gold nib pointing to the ceiling. Small diamonds of sweat dripped down her long neck. He walked to the bar and leaned his elbows against the counter. Perhaps he should beg the staff to drive him home? It was impossible. It was an impossible flirtation with catastrophe, but it had already happened, it was happening. It had happened and it was happening again, but he must fight it to the end. He stared at the black rain she had inked on his hand and told himself it was there to soften his resolve to fight. She was clever. She knew what rain does. It softens hard things. He could see her searching her bag for something. She had a book in her hand, one of his own books, and she was underlining something on the page with his pen. Perhaps she was an extraordinary writer? It hadn't occurred to him. Perhaps that is what she was?

Joe ordered two more cocktails of the month. The barman told Monsieur he'd bring them over when they were ready but he did not want to walk back to his antique armchair yet. She was really quite knowledgeable about poetry. For a botanist. Why had he not told her he had read her poem? What was stopping him? Should he trust his instinct not to reveal he had read the threat she had slipped into the envelope? He carried the iced flutes over to her. This time Joe glugged back his strawberry champagne as if it was a pint of pale ale. He bent towards her lips, which were wet from the strawberry champagne, and kissed her. When she let him, he kissed her again, his black silver hair tangling with the curls of her red hair. Her pale eyelashes sooty with mascara fluttered against his cheek while he held her long neck in the palm of his hand and felt her painted green fingernails press into his knee.

'We're kissing in the rain.' Her voice was hard and soft at the same time. Like the velvet armchairs. Like the black rain inked on his hand.

Her eyes were squeezed tight shut. He was walking her towards the heavy Austrian chandelier in the lobby. Her head was spinning and she needed some water. She could hear him asking the Italian receptionist if there were vacancies for rooms. She opened her eyes. The sleek Italian pressed his fingers on the keyboard of his computer. Yes, there was a room. But it was decorated in the style of Louis XVI rather than art deco and it did not have a sea view. Joe handed over his credit card. The bellhop led them into a lift lined with mirrors. He wore white gloves on his hands. He was pressing buttons. She stared at the multiple reflections of Joe's sweating arm around her waist, the green silk of her dress trembling as they sailed silently in the lift that smelt of leather to the third floor.

Metaphors

Madeleine Sheridan formally invited Isabel to Maison Rose. She gave her a glass of sherry and told her to make herself comfortable on the uncomfortable chaise longue. She sat herself down in the armchair opposite the journalist wife and delicately removed a few strands of silver hair from her glass of whisky. Her eyes were cloudy like the pool Kitty Finch had complained about to Jurgen and she thought she might be losing her sight. This made her all the more determined to help Isabel Jacobs see things clearly. To help her understand that being threatened with a knife was a serious business and strangely enough she experienced a sharp pain across her throat even though Kitty Finch had not in reality touched her throat. She was very much Dr Sheridan and not Madeleine when she explained that she had telephoned Kitty's mother, who would be arriving early on Sunday morning. Mrs Finch would drive from the airport to the villa to collect her daughter and take her home. Isabel stared at her sandals.

'You seem convinced she is very ill, Madeleine.'

'Yes. Of course she is.'

Every time Isabel spoke, Madeleine Sheridan reckoned it was as if she was reading the news. Her mission to help the exotic Jacobs family see things as they really are was on full alert.

'Life is something she has to do but she doesn't want to do it. Nina has told us as much.'

Isabel sipped her sherry.

'But Madeleine . . . it's only a poem.'

Dr Sheridan sighed. 'The girl has always been a bit of a mess. But what a beauty, eh?'

'She is very beautiful, yes.' Isabel heard herself say this sentence awkwardly, as if she were scared of it.

'If I may ask you, Isabel . . . why did you invite a stranger into your home?'

Isabel shrugged as if the answer was entirely obvious.

'She had nowhere to stay and we have more rooms than we need. I mean, who needs five bathrooms, Madeleine?'

Madeleine Sheridan tried to look straight through Isabel Jacobs but what she saw, she had to admit, was a blur. Her own lips were moving. She was speaking to herself in French because the things she was saying were less suited to the English language. Her thoughts were making a hard noise against her lips, Kah, Kah, Kah, as if she was indeed obsessed with Kitty Finch, who, for some reason, was so adored by Jurgen and everyone else she managed to manipulate and intrigue. For the last three weeks she had observed the Jacobs family from the best seat in the theatre, the hidden chair on her balcony. Isabel Jacobs might have pushed Kitty Finch into her ridiculous husband's arms, but it was a foolhardy thing to risk because she would lose her daughter. Yes. If her husband seduced the sick girl it would be impossible to return to life as it had been before. Isabel would have to ask her husband to leave the family house. Nina Jacobs, like an assassin, would have to choose which parent she could live without. Did Isabel not understand that her daughter had already adapted to life without her mother in it? Madeleine Sheridan tried to stop her lips from moving, because they said such unpleasant things. She could just about make out Isabel shifting on the chaise longue. Crossing her legs. Uncrossing her legs. The heat outside was so fierce she had switched on the ancient air-conditioning system. It groaned above her head. Madeleine could sense (although she could not see) that Isabel was a brave woman. When she was at medical school she had observed women train as heart specialists, gynaecologists, bone cancer consultants. Then they had children and something happened. They became tired. All the time. Madeleine Sheridan wanted this groomed, enigmatic woman sitting in her living room to fade, to be exhausted, to display some sort of vulnerability, to need her and above all to value this conversation.

Instead the betrayed wife rolled her long black hair in her fingers and asked for another sherry. She was almost flirtatious.

'When did you retire, Madeleine? I have often interviewed doctors working in the most difficult situations. No stretchers, no lights, sometimes no medication.'

Madeleine Sheridan's throat hurt. She leaned towards the woman she was trying to destroy, took a shallow breath and waited for the words to come, something about her work before she retired and the difficulty of persuading patients on low incomes to give up smoking.

'It's my birthday today.'

She heard the small begging voice that came out of her mouth but it was too late to try and catch another tone. If she could have said it again it would have been light, airy, amused at being alive at all. Isabel looked genuinely taken aback.

'Happy birthday! If you'd told me I would have bought a bottle of champagne.'

'Yes. Thank you for the thought.' Madeleine Sheridan heard herself speaking in entitled middle-class English again.

'Someone has burgled my garden. My roses have been stolen and of course I know that Kitty Finch is very angry with me.'

The exotic wife of the poet was saying something about how stealing a rose was not exactly proof of insanity and anyway it was getting late and she wanted to say goodnight to her daughter. From the window opposite she saw a full moon float across the sky. What was the poet's wife doing? She was walking towards her. She was getting closer. She could smell honey.

Isabel Jacobs was wishing her happy birthday again and her lips were warm on her cheek. The kiss hurt as much as the pains in her throat.

Foreign Languages

Nina was asleep but in her dream she was awake and she found herself walking towards the spare room where Kitty lay on the bed. Her face was swollen and her lip was split. She looked like Kitty but not a lot. She heard Kitty whisper her name.

Nina crept closer. Kitty's eyelids were dusted with green eyeshadow. They looked like leaves. Nina sat on the end of the bed. Kitty was forbidden because she was dangerous. She did dangerous things. Nina swallowed hard and gave dead Kitty some information.

Your mother is coming to get you.

She placed a blue sugar mouse on the edge of Kitty's foot. It had a tiny tail made from string. Nina had found it under Kitty's bed.

And I've bought you some soap.

She had seen Kitty look for soap lots of times but there wasn't any in her bathroom and she said she'd spent all her money on the hire car.

I read your poem. I think it's brilliant. It's the best thing I've ever read in my life.

She quoted Kitty's lines to her. Not like how they were in the poem but how she remembered them.

> Jumping forwards with both feet
> Jumping backwards with both feet
> Thinking of ways to live

FRIDAY

Kitty's eyelids trembled and Nina knew she had got the poem all wrong and hadn't remembered it properly. And then she asked Kitty to stick out her tongue, but Kitty was speaking to her in Yiddish or it might have been German and she was saying, 'Get up!', which is what made Nina wake up.

Money is Hard

He slipped his hands around her neck and untied the white satin ribbon of her feather cape. The four-poster bed draped in heavy gold curtains resembled a cave. She heard a car alarm go off while seagulls screamed on the window ledge and her eyes were fixed on the wallpaper. The white feathers of her cape lay scattered on the sheet as if it had been attacked by a fox. She had bought it in a flea market in Athens but had never worn it until now. A swan was a symbol of the dying year in autumn, she had read that somewhere. It had stuck in her head and made her think of the way swans stick their heads in the water and turn themselves upside down. She had been saving the cape for something, perhaps for this; it was hard to know what she had had in mind when she exchanged money for the feathers that had insulated this water-bird from the cold and were also made from quills that were once used as pens. He was inside her now but he was inside her anyway, that was what she couldn't tell him but she had told him in her poem which he had not read and now the car alarm had stopped and she could hear voices outside the window. A thief must have broken into a car, because someone was sweeping up broken glass.

After a while he ran her a bath.

They walked down to reception and she stood under the blinding Austrian crystals of the chandelier while Joe signed something with his pen. The Italian receptionist gave him back his credit card and the porter opened the glass doors for them. Everything was like it was before but a little bit different. The pianist was still playing 'Eleanor Rigby' in the bar they had left two hours ago, except now he was singing the words. The palm trees planted along the two lanes of traffic were lit up with golden fairy lights. Kitty jangled the car keys in her hand and told Joe to wait while she bought herself a sugar mouse from the candy stall on the esplanade. The mice were lined up on a silver tray. Pink white yellow blue. She pushed in front of a Vietnamese woman buying strawberry marshmallows and examined the tiny tails made from string. She eventually chose a blue mouse, dropping the car keys as she searched her bag for coins. When they got to the car she told him she was hungry. Her stutter had returned to torment them both. Would he mind if she stopped somewhere for a pah pah pah? Of course, he said, I'd like a pizza too, and they found a restaurant with tables outside in the warm night next to a church. It was the first time he had seen her eat. She devoured the thin pizza with anchovies and he bought her another one with capers and they drank red wine as if they were indeed the lovers they were not supposed to be. She played with the night-lights burning on the table, making prints of her finger-tips from the wax, and when he requested she give him one to keep for ever she told him her fingerprints were all over his body anyway. And then she told him about the hospital in Kent and how the nurses from Odessa compared their love bites in the lunch break. She had written about that too but she was not asking him to read it – she was just telling him it would be part of her first collection of poetry. He helped her to salad and spooned artichokes on to her plate and watched her long fingers mop up the oil with bread. They clinked glasses and she told him how after the shock treatment when she lay damaged on the white sheets she knew the English doctors had not erased the thoughts inside her head, etc, but he would know all about that and why go into it now because the night was soft here in the alleyways of old Nice in contrast to the day when it was hard and smelt of money. To all of this he nodded and though he asked her no questions he knew that in a way they were talking about her poem. Two hours later, when they were halfway up the mountain road, Kitty hunched over the steering wheel as she manoeuvred the car around perilous bends, he glanced at his watch. She was a skilled driver. He admired her firm hands with their waxy fingertips on the steering wheel as she pulled the car round the mountain bends. Kitty beeped the horn as a rabbit ran across the road and the car swerved.

She asked him to open his window so she could hear the animals calling to each other in the dark. He wound down the window and told her to keep her eyes on the road. 'Yes,' she said again, her eyes now back on the road. Her silk dress was falling off her shoulders as she bent over the steering wheel. He had something to ask her. A delicate request which he hoped she would understand.

'It would be better for Isabel if she does not know what happened tonight.'

Kitty laughed and the blue mouse bounced in her lap.

'Isabel already knows.'

'Knows what?' He told her he was feeling dizzy. Would she slow down?

'That's why she invited me to stay. She wants to leave you.'

He needed the car to move slowly. He had vertigo and could feel himself falling although he knew he was sitting in the passenger seat of a hire car. Was it true that Isabel had started the beginning of the end of their marriage and invited Kitty Finch to be the last betrayal? He dared not look down at the waterfalls roaring against the rocks or the up-rooted shrubs that clung to the sides of the mountain.

He heard himself say, 'Why don't you pack a rucksack and see the poppy fields in Pakistan like you said you wanted to?'

'Yes,' she said. 'Will you come with me?'

He lifted his arm that had been resting on her shoulders and gazed at the words she had written on his hand. He had been branded as cattle are branded to show whom they belong to. The cold mountain air stung his lips. She was driving too fast on this road that had once been a forest. Early humans had lived in it. They studied fire and the movement of the sun. They read the clouds and the moon and tried to understand the human mind. His father had tried to melt him into a Polish forest when he was five years old. He knew he must leave no trace or trail of his existence because he must never find his way home. That was what his father had told him. You cannot come home. This was not something possible to know but he had to know it all the same.

•

'Why haven't you read my pah pah pah?'

'My sweetheart' is what she heard him say as she pressed her white shoe on the brakes. The car lurched towards the edge of the mountain. His voice was truly tender when he said 'My sweetheart'. Something had changed in his voice. Her head was buzzing as if she had knocked back fifteen espressos one after the other. And then eaten twelve lumps of sugar. She turned the engine off, pulled the handbrake up and leaned back in her seat. At last. At last he was talking to her.

'It is dishonest to give me a poem and pretend to want my opinion when what you really want are reasons to live. Or reasons not to die.'

'You want reasons to live too.'

He leaned towards her and kissed her eyes. First the left and then the right, as if she was already a corpse.

'I'm not the right reader for your poem. You know that.'

She thought about this while she sucked on her blue mouse.

'The important thing is not the dying. It's making the decision to die that matters.'

He took out his handkerchief to hide his own eyes. He had vowed never to show the dread and worthlessness and panic in his own eyes to his wife and daughter. He loved them, his dark-haired wife and child, he loved them and he could never tell them what it was that had been on his mind for a long time. The unwelcome tears continued to pour out of him just as they had poured out of Kitty Finch in the orchard full of suffering trees and invisible growling dogs. He must apologise for not stamping on his own desires, for not fighting it all the way.

'I'm sorry about what happened in the Negresco.'

'What happened in the Negresco that you're sorry about?'

Her voice was soft, confident and reasonable.

'I know you like silk so I wore a silk dress.'

He felt her fingers tap his wet cheek and he could smell his perfume in her hair. To have been so intimate with her had brought him to the edge of something truthful and dangerous. To the edge of all the bridges he had stood on in European cities. The Thames flowing east across southern England and emptying into the North Sea. The Danube that started in the Black Forest of Germany and ended in the Black Sea. The Rhine that ended in the North Sea. Sex with her had brought him to the edge of the yellow line on the platforms of tube and train stations where he had stood thinking about it. Paddington. South Kensington. Waterloo. Once in the Metro in Paris. Twice in Berlin. Death had been on his mind for a long time. The thought, the throwing of himself into rivers and into trains lasted two seconds, a tremor, a twitch, a blink and a step forwards but, so far, a step backwards again. A step back to five beers for the price of four, back to roasting a chicken for Nina, back to tea, Yorkshire or Tetley's, never Earl Grey, back to Isabel, who was always somewhere else.

He was the wrong reader for her to ask if she should live or die because he was barely here himself. He wondered what kind of catastrophe lived inside Kitty Finch. She told him she had forgotten what she remembered. He wanted to close down like Mitchell and Laura's shop in Euston. Every-thing that was open must close. His eyes. His mouth. His nostrils. His ears that could still hear things. He told Kitty Finch he had read her poem and that it been ringing inside him ever since. She was a writer of immeasurable power and more than anything he hoped she would do the things she wanted to do. She must travel to the Great Wall in China, to the vitality and dream that is India, and she must not forget the mysterious luminous lakes closer to home in Cumbria. These were all things to look forward to.

It was getting dark and she told him the brakes on the hire car were fucked, she couldn't see a thing, she couldn't even see her hands.

He told her to keep her eyes on the road, to just do that, and while he was speaking she was kissing him and driving at the same time.

'I know what you're thinking. Life is only worth living because we hope it will get better and we'll all get home safe-ly. But you tried and you did not get home safely. You did not get home at all. That is why I am here, Jozef. I have come to France to save you from your thoughts.'

SATURDAY

Nina Ekaterina

When Nina woke up just after dawn on Saturday morning she knew immediately everything had changed. The doors of her balcony were wide open as if someone had been there in the night. When she saw a yellow square of paper rolled up like a scroll on her pillow she knew she would be wiser to go back to sleep and hide all day. The words on the yellow paper were written in shaky handwriting by someone who was in a hurry and who obviously liked writing things down. She finished reading the note and crept downstairs to the French doors that led to the pool. They were already open, as she thought they would be. She knew what she was going to see.

Something was floating in the pool and that did not surprise her. At a second glance she saw that Kitty's body was not so much floating as submerged vertically in the water. She was wrapped in a tartan dressing gown but the gown had slipped. The yellow lilo bounced against the edges of the pool and floated towards the body. She heard herself call out.

'Kitty?'

The head was low in the water, tilted back with its mouth open. And then she saw the eyes. The eyes were glassy and open and they were not Kitty's eyes.

'Dad?'

Her father did not reply. She thought he was playing a joke on her. Any second he would rise from the water and roar at her.

'Dad?'

His body was so big and silent. All the noise that was her father, all the words and spluttering and utterances inside him, had disappeared into the water. All she knew was that she was screaming and then suddenly doors were banging and her mother had dived into the pool. Mitchell jumped in too. Together they steered the body around the lilo and with difficulty were trying to lift it out of the pool. Nina heard her mother shout something to Laura. She watched Mitchell lay the body down on the paving stones and press his hands up and down on it. She could hear the sound of water splashing as her mother heaved the dressing gown out of the water. She did not understand why it was so heavy but then she saw her mother pull something out of the pockets. It was a pebble the size of her hand and it had a hole in the middle of it. Nina could see her struggling with three more of the pebbles she had collected on the beach with Kitty and she thought it must have got later and the sun was rising over the pool because the water had changed colour. She shivered and searched for the sun in the sky but she could not see it.

Mitchell stuck his fingers in her father's mouth. And then he pinched his nose. Mitchell was panting and actually kissing her father over and over again.

'I don't know. I don't know.'

Laura ran into the villa shouting something about the fact sheet. Where was Jurgen? Everyone was shouting for Jurgen. Nina felt someone touch her head. Kitty Finch was stroking her hair. And then Kitty pushed her through the French doors and told her to sit down on the sofa while she helped Laura look for the fact sheet. That's all she heard for the next five minutes. Where was the fact sheet? Had anyone seen the fact sheet? Although Nina was still not sure whether it was her father or Kitty who was alive or dead she sat obediently on the sofa and stared at the Picasso prints on the wall. A fish bone. A blue vase. A lemon. It was only when she heard Laura shouting, 'It's yellow. The fact sheet is a yellow piece of paper,' that she realised she was holding a yellow sheet of paper in her hand and waved it at Laura. Laura looked startled and then grabbed it from her and ran to the telephone. Nina watched her peer at the numbers.

'I don't know, Kitty. I don't know which one to call.'

Kitty was saying something in a detached flat voice.

'The hospital is in Grasse on the Chemin de Clavary.'

It began to rain. Nina heard herself sobbing. She was standing outside herself looking at herself as she stood by the glass doors.

The ambulance and the police were arriving. Madeleine Sheridan was there too. She was shouting at Mitchell.

'Tilt his head upwards, hold his nose!' and Nina could see

her fingers press into her father's neck as she felt for a pulse.

'Do not put him in the recovery position, Mitchell. I think he has a spinal injury.'

And then she heard the old woman cry out, 'There it is . . .'

Nina started to sob in the rain because she was still not sure what had happened. As she ran towards her mother she heard that she was a very loud crier. It sounded a bit like laughing but it wasn't. Her teeth were showing and she could feel little jabs in her diaphragm. She was frowning and the more she cried the more she frowned. She could feel her mother holding her in her arms, stroking her neck. Her mother was wearing a nightdress and it was wet and cold and she smelt of expensive creams. As a child she had played a morbid game in which she dared herself to have to choose which one of her parents she would rather die. She had tormented herself with this game and now she buried her face in her mother's stomach because she knew she had betrayed her.

Its softness against her cheek made her cry all the more and she thought her mother knew what she thinking because she heard her whisper in her ear, her words barely there, like an autumn leaf turning in the wind, 'Never mind, never mind.'

Her father was being laid out on a stretcher. The police had started to drain the pool. Jurgen was there too. He had a broom in his hand and was energetically sweeping around the plant pots. He had even managed to put on navy overalls that made him look like a caretaker.

The News

Isabel walked towards the paramedics and took Jozef's hand in her own. At first she thought a row of ants was crawling in a military line towards his knuckles. And then she saw the fading black inked vowels and consonants running into each other.

I
  T
    S
       R
         A
        I
       N
         I
        N
       G

She could hear the drone of the bees nearby and she heard herself insisting that what her husband required was an air ambulance, but what she was mostly saying was his name.

Jozef. Please Jozef. Jozef. Jozef please.

Why did he hack into his hand like that? Where did he do it and how could he bear it and what did it mean? She squeezed his fingers and asked him to explain himself. She promised that in turn she would explain herself. She would do that right now. She told him she would have liked to feel his love fall upon her like rain. That was the kind of rain she most longed for in their long unconventional marriage. The paramedics told her to get out of the way but she did not move because she had always got out of his way. Loving him had been the greatest risk in her life. The thing, the threat was lurking there in all his words. She had known that from the beginning. She had always known that. He had buried unexploded shells and grenades across the roads and tracks of all his books, they were under every poem, but if he died now her daughter would walk through a world that was always damaged and she was as angry as it was possible to be.

Jozef. Please Jozef. Jozef. Jozef. Please.

She suddenly understood that someone was pushing her out of the way and that she could smell blood.

A large man with a shaven head and a revolver strapped to his belt was asking her questions. To every question he asked she did not have a straightforward answer. What was her husband's name?

Jozef Nowogrodzki in his passport. Joe Harold Jacobs on all other ID. In fact she didn't think his name was Nowogrodzki but that was the name his parents had written in his passport anyway. Nor did she tell him her husband had many other names: JHJ, Joe, Jozef, the famous poet, the British poet, the arsehole poet, the Jewish poet, the atheist poet, the modernist poet, the post-Holocaust poet, the philandering poet. So where was Monsieur Nowogrodzki's place of birth? Poland. Łódź. 1937. Łódź in English is pronounced Wodge but she didn't know how to say it in French. His parents' names?

She wasn't sure how to spell them. Did he have brothers and sisters? Yes. No. He had a sister. Her name was Friga.

The inspector looked baffled. Isabel did what she did best.

She told him the news except it was a bit out of date. Her husband was five years old when he was smuggled into Britain in 1942, half starved and with forged documents. Three days after he arrived his mother and father were deported along with his two-year-old sister to the Chelmno death camp in western Poland. The inspector, who did not understand much English, put his hand up in front of his face as if he was stopping the traffic on a busy road. He told the wife of the Jewish poet that it was unfortunate the Germans occupied Poland in 1939 but he had to point out he was now engaged in a murder inquiry in the Alpes-Maritimes in 1994. Would she agree that Monsieur Nowogrodzki or was it Monsieur Jacobs had left his daughter a final note? Or was it a poem? Or was it evidence? Whatever it might be it was addressed to Nina Ekaterina. He slipped the yellow fact sheet into a plastic folder. On one side were instructions for how to work the dishwasher. On the other side were five lines written in black ink. These were apparently instructions for his daughter.

It was not yet six am but the whole village had already heard the news. When Claude arrived at the villa with a bag full of bread, Mitchell, who for once was not interested in a morsel, sent him away, his eyes still smarting from the chlorine in the cloudy water. The paramedics shouted instructions to each other and Isabel told Nina she would be in the ambulance too. They were going to put tubes up her father's nose and pump his stomach on the way to the hospital. The ambulance began its journey down the mountain road. Nina felt herself being led by Claude to Madeleine Sheridan's house, which was called Maison Rose even though it was painted blue. On the way she saw Jurgen with his arms around Kitty Finch and when she heard Mitchell shout, 'Piss off and don't come back,' everyone heard what Kitty said next. She was whispering but she might as well have been screaming, because what she said was the thing everyone knew anyway.

'He shot himself with one of your guns, Mitchell.'

Mitchell's big body was bent over double. Something was happening to his eyes, nostrils, mouth. Tears and snot and saliva were pouring out of the holes in his face. Without a shot being fired his face had five holes in it. Holes for breathing, looking, eating. Everyone was gazing in his direction but what he saw was a blur. They were a mob full of holes just like him. How was he going to protect himself from the mob when they pointed the finger? He would tell the police the truth. When the ebony Persian weapon disappeared, he thought the mental girl had stolen it to punish him for hunting animals. The telephone was ringing and then it stopped ringing and he could hear Laura wailing. His muscles ached from dragging the body out of the water. It was so heavy. It was as heavy as a bear.

NINA JACOBS

London, 2011

Whenever I dream my twentieth-century dream about my father, I wake up and immediately forget my passwords for EasyJet and Amazon. It is as if they have disappeared from my head into his head and somewhere in the twenty-first century he is sitting with me on a bus crossing London Bridge watching the rain fall on the chimney of Tate Modern. The conversations I have with him do not belong to this century at all, but all the same I ask him why he never really told me about his childhood? He replies that he hopes my own childhood wasn't too bad and do I remember the kittens?

Our family kittens (Agnieska and Alicja) always smelt a bit feral and my childhood pleasure was to groom them with my father's hairbrush. They lay on my lap and I combed out their fur while they purred and patted my hand with their soft paws. When I got near their bottoms the fur was stuck together and tangled because they were still too young to lick themselves clean. Sometimes I left the fur balls on the sofa and my father pretended to swallow them. He'd open his mouth very wide and make out he'd gulped one down and that it was stuck in his throat and he was choking. My father spent his life trying to work out why people had frogs in their throat, butterflies in their stomach, pins and needles in their legs, a thorn in their side, a chip on their shoulder and indeed if they had coughed up fur balls he would have studied them too.

No, he says. I would not have studied the fur balls.

We agree that he and I learned to muddle along together. He washed my vests and tights and T-shirts, sewed buttons on my cardigans, searched for missing socks and insisted I should never be afraid of people talking to themselves on buses.

Yes, my father says. That's what you are doing now.

No, I reply, that's not what I am doing now. I am not saying what I'm thinking out loud. That would be mad. No one on this bus can hear me talking to you.

Yes, he says, but it wouldn't matter anyway because everybody's talking out loud on their phones.

I still have the beach towel he bought me in a souvenir shop in Nice. The words *Côte d'Azur Nice Baie des Anges* fly across a big blue sky in a sunny yellow font. Tourists on the beach are rendered in black dots and just behind it is a road lined with palm trees. On the right is the pink dome of the Hotel Negresco with a French flag flying into the towelly blue sky. What it's missing is Kitty Finch with her copper hair rippling down her waist waiting for my father to read her poem. If she was named after a bird it's possible she was making a strange call, perhaps an emergency call to my father, but I cannot think about her, or the pebbles we collected together, without wanting to fall through their holes out of the world. So I will replace her with my father walking through France's fifth biggest city on his way past its monuments and statues to buy a wedge of honeycomb for my mother. The year is 1994 but my father (who has an ice cream in his hand and not a phone) is having a conversation with himself and it's probably something sad and serious to do with the past. I have never got a grip on when the past begins or where it ends, but if cities map the past with statues made from bronze forever frozen in one dignified position, as much as I try to make the past keep still and mind its manners, it moves and murmurs with me through every day.

The next time I'm sitting on a bus crossing London Bridge and the rain is falling on the chimney of Tate Modern I must tell my father that when I read biographies of famous people, I only get interested when they escape from their family and spend the rest of their life getting over them. That is why when I kiss my daughter goodnight and wish her sweet dreams, she understands my wish for her is kind, but she knows, as all children do, that it's impossible to be told by our parents what our dreams are supposed to be like. They know they have to dream themselves out of life and back into it, because life must always win us back. All the same, I always say it.

I say it every night, especially when it rains.

DEBORAH LEVY writes fiction, plays, and poetry. Her work has been staged by the Royal Shakespeare Company, and she is the author of highly praised novels, including *Beautiful Mutants*, *Swallowing Geography*, and *Billy and Girl*. *Swimming Home*, her most recent novel, was serialized on BBC Radio 4 as a Book at Bedtime and was a finalist for the Man Booker Prize. She lives in London, England.

the **NO-NONSENSE** guide to

ISLAM

Ziauddin Sardar and Merryl Wyn Davies

'Publishers hav_____ lists of short books
that discuss the _____stions that your average
[electoral] candidate will only ever touch if
armed with a slogan and a soundbite. Together
[such books] hint at a resurgence of the grand
educational tradition... Closest to the hot
headline issues are *The No-Nonsense Guides*.
These target those topics that a large army of
voters care about, but that politicos evade.
Arguments, figures and documents combine to
prove that good journalism is far too important
to be left to (most) journalists.'

Boyd Tonkin,
The Independent,
London

ISBN 81-7033-943-X
© New Internationalist Publication Ltd., 2004

This edition of The No-Nonsense Guide to Islam
first published in 2005 by arrangement with
New Internationalist Publication Ltd., Oxford, UK

First Indian Edition, 2005

For sale in India only.

Published by
Prem Rawat for **Rawat Publications**
Satyam Apts., Sector 3, Jawahar Nagar, Jaipur - 302 004 (India)
Phone: 0141-265 1748/7006 Fax: 0141-265 1748
E-mail: info@rawatbooks.com
Website: rawatbooks.com

Delhi Office
4858/24, Ansari Road, Daryaganj, New Delhi 110 002
Phone: 011-23263290

Also at Bangalore and Mumbai

Printed at Chaman Enterprises, New Delhi

the **NO-NONSENSE** guide to

ISLAM

Ziauddin Sardar and Merryl Wyn Davies

RAWAT PUBLICATIONS

Jaipur • New Delhi • Bangalore • Mumbai

About the authors
Merryl Wyn Davies is a writer and anthropologist and a former producer of religious programs for the BBC. She is the author of *Introducing Anthropology* and *Knowing One Another: shaping an Islamic anthropology*.

Ziauddin Sardar is a writer, broadcaster and cultural critic. He is the author of *Postmodernism and the Other*, *Orientalism*, and *Islam, Postmodernism and Other Futures*, *The Ziauddin Sardar Reader* and numerous other books.

Davies and Sardar are co-authors of the bestseller *Why do People Hate America?*

Foreword

HARDLY A DAY goes by without Islam being in the news. But it is almost always bad news. People around the world watching television or reading newspapers can be forgiven for thinking that Muslims have little to do except engage in acts of terrorism, oppress women and minorities, and engage in mindless and fundamentalist rhetoric.

Yet, as most Muslims believe and the history of Islam shows, Islam emerged as a force for justice, equality, human dignity and the rule of law. It created a fraternity across all cultural and tribal and racial divides. It gave honor and respect to the marginalized in society. It practised, albeit briefly, a system of elections against the prevalent norm of the hereditary right to rule. During the formative phase of its development it also followed a practice of open debate to arrive at a consensus before deciding on issues affecting the community. It emphasized knowledge, learning and human creativity. And produced a civilization noted for its learning and humility as well as tolerance, justice and concern for public interest.

None of this history seems to have any relevance for the Muslim world today. That Islam once produced a 'Golden Age' is only of historic interest. A people rise when they excel in creating ideas and decline when others are able to create better or more powerful ideas. Muslims are no exception to this general rule. The process of decline, which some scholars have traced back to 13th century, began when Muslims assumed that they had solved all human problems that needed to be solved had closed the doors of creative endeavors. Muslim societies have paid a very heavy price for this myopia. The mediocrity, intolerance and despotism that is prevalent throughout the Muslim world can all be traced back to this crucial historic upturn. Just how far Muslims have drifted from Islam's emphasis on thought, education and reasoning can be seen from a single statistic: in Pakistan, some 60 per cent of children get their basic education from the *madrassa* (school) where there is nothing but rote learning and where they learn little except bigotry and fanaticism!

The choices before Islam are stark. If Islam is to have any relevance today it must prove that it can produce a more just, tolerant and peaceful society. The orthodox, as well as various reformist movements, must realize that the goal of recreating the 'Madina of the Prophet' and implementing an 8th century 'Islamic Law' is a recipe for further disasters. Muslims need to understand that implementing the *sharia* (Islamic law) would not empower people but creating a civil society and a just order for humanity might.

The No-Nonsense Guide to Islam is a warts-and-all guide to the complex world of Islam. It is a lucid and concise survey of the rich history and the multifaceted diversity of Islam as well as the trials and tribulations of Muslim people. Sardar and Davies show what Islam has achieved; and what it is capable of achieving. But they also delineate what went wrong and what could still go wrong. And, most importantly, they suggest how both Islam and the West can transform themselves to see each other as fully human and capable of laying the foundation for a just world order. That's just how Muslims should think and write.

Dr Ghayasuddin Siddiqui
Director, The Muslim Institute
London, UK

the NO-NONSENSE guide to

ISLAM

CONTENTS

the **NO-NONSENSE** guide to

ISLAM

AS MUSLIM WRITERS, we constantly find ourselves
caught in a pincer movement. Our Western friends
associate Islam largely with violence and bigotry, despotism and suppression, obstinacy and chaos. Our
Muslim friends, on the other hand, emphasize that
the very term Islam means peace; they conceive of
Islam as a religion that by its very essence is about
peace and justice. They look to the example of
Prophet Muhammad as a model of love, gentleness,
fairness, equality and brotherhood.

The association of Islam with aggression has not
been hard to find in recent times.

With the terrorist attacks of 11 September 2001 in
New York and Washington this association has
reached new heights, or more properly, depths. Our
Western friends repeatedly asked: Why are Muslims so
violent? How can Islam justify the terrorism of al-
Qaeda, the suicide bombers in Palestine, the whip-
pings and beheadings under Islamic Law in Saudi
Arabia, or stoning to death of adulterers in Nigeria?
From these headlines other more general questions
arise. Why do Muslims doggedly ignore human and
women's rights? Why is democracy in the Muslim
world conspicuous by its general absence? Why are
Muslims still living in the Middle Ages? And the all
round favorite: Is there a clash of civilizations? Have
the Muslims declared *jihad* (righteous struggle)
against 'Western infidels'? These are highly pertinent
questions. Yet, on the whole, Muslims tend to ignore,

evade or side step such issues with various forms of apologia. They concentrate on representing the ideals Islam seeks to implement. For example, the famous Muslim scholar Muhammad Asad, a German convert to Islam who produced one of the most respected commentaries on the Qur'an, describes Islam as the 'middle way', the way of balance and tolerance; and of 'liberalism' founded on 'the conception that man's original nature is essentially good'.[1] 'At a fundamental level,' writes Omid Safi, a self-declared 'progressive' Muslim scholar, 'Islamic tradition offers a path to peace, both in the hearts of the individual and the world at large. The actions of these terrorists do not represent real Islam.'

But what is 'real Islam'? When confronted with the reality of terrorist attacks, or the authoritarianism so evident in Muslim states such as Saudi Arabia or the Sudan, or the oppression of women in places like Afghanistan and Pakistan, Muslims have tended, conventionally, to point towards history. 'Just look at our glorious history to see what real Islam is all about,' they say. Indeed, Muslim history, which begins in 610 AD when Prophet Muhammad commenced his career as a prophet in the city of Mecca, in modern-day Saudi Arabia, does present a different picture of Islam. Classical Muslim civilization was progressive. The initial rapid expansion of Islam beyond Arabia was one of the most amazing sequences of events in human history. The emergence of a series of empires in Muslim lands is also a record of the growth of a culture of cities which produced a flowering in arts and sciences that played a major role in the heritage of human ideas. From the 8th to 16th centuries, cities like Baghdad, Damascus, Cairo, Samarkand and Timbuktu were renowned for extensive and elaborate networks of libraries, bookshops, public baths, and hospitals. Experimental method, and thus science as we know it today, was born here. Philosophy was rescued from oblivion, critiqued, extended and expanded. And in

Introduction

Muslim Spain a genuine multicultural society emerged, where Muslims, Christians and Jews participated in a *convivencia* (the Spanish term for living side by side in harmony).

The trouble is that all this is history. It is far temporally and in temperament from contemporary Islam. How do we reconcile the theoretical ideals of Islam and the progressive glories of history with the situation of the contemporary Muslim world? This question is as important for Muslims as non-Muslims. The Muslim world today is beset by acute problems. It is composed of zones of devastation: large sections of the world's Muslims are among the world's poorest people. It is checkered with zones of conflict where civil war, inter-ethnic fighting, insurgency and terrorism contribute to and compound poverty while ensuring most of the world's refugees are Muslims. There are zones of plenty, oil-rich states where abundance manages to secure continued dependence on Western expertise rather than sponsor self-reliance or generate a new flowering of culture and future possibilities. Across the Muslim world there is populist clamor for Islam, but a dearth of pragmatic thinking and search for solutions derived from the ethos and worldview of Islam. Islam is offered as an antidote to the plethora of problems, but signally fails to galvanize Muslims to solve their own problems. Where there is need or conflict, as much as where there is plenty, Muslims have little confidence in their own polities, nor are their low expectations disappointed. It is a common reflex to blame the West for the genesis of their troubles while at the same time turning to the West in the expectation that solutions to home-grown afflictions will nevertheless be forthcoming.

Contemporary Islam, it has to be said, is not one thing. Its diversity is legendary – not only are there numerous and varied Islamic cultures, but there are also abundant (and competing) interpretations, Schools of Thought, sects and political, apolitical and mystical groups. The term 'Islamic' can be applied to, and is employed by, a vast complex that extends from spiritual practices, mosques and minarets to styles of dress, forms of human behavior, economic practices, political ideas, modes of resistance, philosophy and literature as well as a diversity of social and political movements that exist and affect the affairs of the world today. On one hand this diversity prevents Muslims co-operating and co-ordinating efforts to resolve the evident problems afflicting their societies.

And yet on the other hand populist clamor for Islam, the clarion calls and rhetoric of radical Islamic movements, even earnest debates among well-intentioned concerned Muslim intellectuals all concentrate on the idea there is a unitary, even uniform Islam that should be applied to all situations, circumstances and problems. Resort to this imagined uniformity operates by denying the diversity of Muslim history and the complexity of contemporary life and ends by compounding existing problems.

For Muslims, Islam matters; faith continues to be meaningful. The difficulty is in debating and expressing this faithful confidence as a balanced approach to unity-in-diversity, and as a practical remedy for the multiple problems and multiplicity of problems faced by Muslims.

What we can say with certainty is that Islam today is in need of urgent reforms. And this is important not just for Muslims but for non-Muslims as well. Islam is the world's second largest religion with an estimated 1.3 billion adherents. Every fifth person on the planet is a Muslim. Islam is also a complex of geography and culture, a world civilization. The Muslim world extends from Morocco to Indonesia and from Kazakhstan in Central Asia to the coastal regions of Kenya and Tanzania in Africa. There are substantial Muslim minorities in Europe, Australia and North America. So what the Muslims say and do, how they attempt to solve their problems, how they reform or do not reform Islam, has a direct bearing on all of us.

Thus, what happens to Islam and within Islam will not only affect Muslims, it will shape all our futures. The ability to reform Islam, to expand current debates, to find new approaches and turn away from pathological tendencies confronts everyone with the challenge of understanding how Islam is to make visible the scope and potential Muslims have to make a better future.

Ziauddin Sardar and *Merryl Wyn Davies*

1 M Asad, 'The Sprit of Islam' in *Islam: Its Meaning and Message* edited by Khurshid Ahmad (Islamic Foundation, Leicester, 1975, p 51).

1 Islam: the Qur'an and Sirah

Islam is one of the great religions of the world with some 1.3 billion adherents. But it is also a tradition and culture, a civilization with a long and distinguished history. And it is a worldview – a way of looking at and shaping the world. To see Islam as only one of these components is to miss the whole picture.

HISTORICALLY, ISLAM BEGINS with the Qur'an, the written record of the Revelation made to Prophet Muhammad over a 23-year period from 610 to 632 AD. The Qur'an is the sacred book of Islam. Knowing it is the basis of being a Muslim; it is the direct revelation of God to Prophet Muhammad who lived his entire life in the shadow of the Qur'an. Together with the *Sirah* (the story of his life) the two texts – one written, one lived – constitute the fundamental sources of Islam. Reciting the opening verse, the *Fatihah*, and at least one other is the basis of each cycle in the five daily prayers offered by Muslims.

The language of the Qur'an is itself taken as proof of its divine origin. It uses a distinctive heightened form of Arabic unlike any other Arabic text. Even for native speakers of Arabic reading the Qur'an is a challenge and the majority of Muslims around the world are not native Arabic speakers. The majesty of the use of language in the Qur'an has great beauty and power to move listeners. Indeed, converts to Islam during the time of the Prophet Muhammad were often influenced directly by the language of the Qur'an. Yet the use, structure and expression of language also make it relatively easy to memorize: millions of people around the world, known as *hafiz*, have committed the entire Qur'an to memory. Today, Qur'anic recitation competitions are held all over the Muslim world; public readings, records and tapes of noted recitations are popular with Muslims everywhere.

Wrestling with the meaning of the words of the Qur'an has been a basic part of Muslim scholarship and teaching from the outset. Maintaining and preserving its original text has been a priority for the Muslim community not only to ensure the survival of the text as a whole, but also because the precise form of the words and the use of grammar have significance in understanding its message. This concern to maintain the integrity of original words explains why no translation of the Qur'an is acceptable to Muslims. Numerous translations exist in many languages, but they are regarded as paraphrases, approximations that place the reader a step further from the struggle to appreciate the significance of the Arabic word itself. The Qur'an is the enduring beginning and reference point; all schools of thought, all Muslim discourse of ideas, reform and change, are grounded in this one unitary text. It is the unity from which all diversity derives and by which it is validated. It was and is the basis of education in the narrow sense of religious learning, the education of those who studied what are called the religious sciences and Islamic law. But it was – and is – also the basis of education for those who went on to specialize in studying science, medicine and the arts. In a profound and extensive way Islam is the religion of the Book, the *Kitab*, the Qur'an.

The Qur'an describes itself as an instruction, a teaching and guidance. Its message is addressed to all of humanity; and in particular to 'people who think'. Again and again, it asks its readers to observe, reflect and question. Then it devotes considerable space to delineating the attributes of God. Throughout, the Qur'an stresses knowledge and reason as the valid ways to faith and God-consciousness. Surprisingly, it contains very few legal injunctions.

The Qur'an is composed of 114 chapters, or *surahs*, of varied length. Its structure often perplexes non-Muslims and has caused a great deal of controversy in

Western scholarly circles. Unlike the Bible, it is not structured as a linear narrative, nor are its verses arranged in chronological order according to the sequence in which they were revealed. It is often said that the long opening chapters are concerned with presenting the externals of faith – the details of how to live – while the short concluding chapters are concerned with the inner substance of faith, worship and spiritual verities. Yet even this broad distinction, which has been described as taking the reader on a journey from the 'what' and 'how' to the ultimate question, the 'why', is only an approximation of the way in which the Qur'an arranges its themes. Its subject matter includes events in the life of Prophet Muhammad and the circumstances of the community in which he lived; it introduces stories of previous Prophets; it uses metaphors, allegories and parables and returns to the same topic or theme a number of times. In this way, by instance and restatement, the Qur'an draws out, expands and adds layers of significance to elucidate its meaning and purpose. It is not so much episodic as an interrelated text concerned to make meaningful connections.

The Qur'an consciously declares itself in the circumstances of a particular history and its content is overtly concerned with historical events. But the Qur'an is not a narrative; rather a commentary on the meaning and implications of human history. It questions the past to illuminate and point to a deeper understanding of both spiritual and material truth. Its emphasis on history has had an immense effect on Muslim consciousness. From the outset Muslims have seen the historic circumstances of the Prophet's life and the social setting, time and place of Revelation as essential companion pieces that must be studied to aid understanding the Qur'an.

Muslims believe the Qur'an to be inviolable. The integrity of its text is preserved for all time. Its special structure, the interlocking character of each word and

Some verses from the Qur'an

God loves those who judge equitably. (5:42)

God loves the patient. (3:145)

And one of His signs is the creation of heaven and earth and the diversity of your languages and colors; surely there are signs in this for the learned. (30:22)

Even if you stretch out your hand against me to kill me, I shall not stretch out my hand to kill you. I fear Allah, the Lord of the World. (5:28)

Whosoever does a good deed, male or female, believing – those shall enter paradise, therein provided without reckoning. (40:40)

Take to forgiveness and enjoin good and turn aside from the ignorant. (7:199) ∎

verse, the nature and precision of its heightened language, the economy and subtlety of its style – all make the Qur'an 'inimitable'. Even the minutest change, a dot or a comma, renders the text out of sync. Whenever a verse of the Qur'an was revealed, the Prophet would recite the verse and teach it to his followers. The Prophet himself was unable to read or write as were many of his followers in what was largely an oral society. He was attended by a number of scribes or secretaries, such as Zayd ibn Thabit, who would write down the revealed verses. The Prophet would also indicate exactly where each verse belonged in relation to the others, and thus its place in the Qur'an. Just before his death, the Prophet recited the complete Qur'an to the Muslim community on a number of occasions. After his death, the written text of the Qur'an was given for safe-keeping to one of his wives, Hafsa. As the Muslim community rapidly expanded to new regions there was concern that inauthentic texts were beginning to circulate. Caliph Othman bin Affan, the third successor to Prophet

Calligraphy

The visual art most closely associated with the Qur'an is calligraphy. To the untrained eye what may appear as abstract patterns or elaborate decoration on wall hangings or as part of the fabric of buildings are often in fact Qur'anic texts. This one reads: *A Bismillah* – 'In the name of God, the Beneficent, the Merciful'.

Muhammad as leader of the Muslim community, established a committee to produce an official, authorized written Qur'an. Between the years 650-52 AD this committee, headed by Zayd ibn Thabit, gathered all the extant original materials, consulted with those who had regularly listened to the Prophet recite the Qur'an and produced the text that has been known and used by all Muslims subsequently. Copies of this official text were made and sent to all the major Muslim cities after a recall of all versions previously in circulation. Muslim confidence in the integrity, honesty and scrupulous attention to detail of this process is unshakable.

While the Qur'an is considered by Muslims to be uncreated, a divine gift, Prophet Muhammad is unquestionably human. Both in language and style, his words and sayings are entirely distinct from the Qur'an, and are never confused by Muslims. As the recipient of Revelation, the Prophet is the best guide on its meaning, the best example of its essence and spirit and of how the *din* of Islam (the teachings of religion as a way of life) should be applied and lived. The biography of Prophet Muhammad, known as *Sirah*, also provides information on the historic context in which the Qur'an appeared. The circumstances and conditions of the Prophet's life and the community in which he lived are used to understand the purpose and intention of the principles and regulations contained in the Qur'an. Thus, the *Sirah* is regarded as the second fundamental source of Islam after the Qur'an.

The *Sirah*

Prophet Muhammad was born in 569 AD in Mecca, a city surrounded by rugged mountains that form a chain parallel to the western coast of what is today Saudi Arabia. Mecca was situated on the caravan routes that from antiquity were part a global system of trading connections spanning the known world.

Southwards it was connected to the ports of the Red Sea and coasts of the peninsula linked to Africa and the trading world of the Indian Ocean; northward the trade routes were connected with the cities of Jordan, Palestine, Syria and the Mediterranean coast, the world of ancient Middle Eastern as well as Hellenic and Roman civilizations. The people of Mecca were traders and the city itself was an important trading center as well as a center of pilgrimage drawing people from the whole of pre-Islamic Arabia.

The Prophet's father, Abdullah, died around the time of his birth while on a commercial trip to Yathrib, the city that later became Medina. His mother, Amina, according to local custom, sent her son to be fostered by a wetnurse in the region of Taif. When he returned to his mother aged four years they journeyed to Yathrib where they stayed for two years. Amina died on their return journey to Mecca and Prophet Muhammad was taken in by his grandfather, Abd al-Muttalib, who lived only another two years. The eight-year-old was then placed in the care of his father's full brother, the merchant Abu Talib, helping tend the flocks of a neighbor as well as assisting in his uncle's cloth shop. At the age of nine, the boy accompanied his uncle on a trading expedition to Palestine.

By the age of 24, Prophet Muhammad was responsible for running the business of his aging uncle and had earned himself the surname al-Amin, the honest. Hearing of his reputation, a wealthy widow named Khadijah asked him to take a consignment of her goods to Palestine. He returned with double the expected returns. Khadijah then proposed marriage. It is generally said that not only was Khadijah the wealthier partner but also the elder one as she was 40 when the couple married in 595 AD. However, other reports put Khadijah's age as 28, a fact which might be corroborated by her bearing seven children after the marriage. Of these children, only the four daughters,

Zainab, Ruqaiya, Umm Kulthum and Fatimah survived to adulthood, three boys dying in infancy. On
his marriage Prophet Muhammad moved into his
wife's household. To lighten the burden on his uncle
Abu Talib the couple took in one of his sons, Ali, who
would later become the fourth leader of the Muslim
community. The Prophet continued to work as a trad-
er, traveling several times to Yemen and once to
Oman.

What drew pilgrims from all over Arabia to the
Prophet's birthplace Mecca was the *Ka'aba*, a shrine
originally built by Prophet Abraham for the worship
of the One God. By Prophet Muhammad's time the
Ka'aba had long become a polytheistic shrine housing
statues of 360 deities. In 605 AD the *Ka'aba* was damaged by fire and had to be rebuilt. The last phase of
renovation was to install a round black meteorite in
the wall of the building. There was considerable dispute among the citizens over which clan should have
the honor of setting the Black Stone in place. At this
point the Prophet arrived and was asked to settle the
dispute. His solution was to place the Black Stone on
a cloth. A representative of each clan would then hold
the cloth and together they would lift the Stone which
he then set in place.

For Prophet Muhammad the rebuilding of the
Ka'aba began a period of religious reflection. He
began to make regular retreats from the city to a cave
on nearby Mount Hira where he would spend a month
at a time in quiet contemplation. It was on his fifth
annual retreat, at the age of 40, during December 609,
that he first saw the Angel Gabriel. He was asleep in
the cave when the Angel appeared and commanded
him to 'Read'. Prophet Muhammad's response was to
say simply he could neither read nor write. Despite his
protestations, the Angel continued to command the
Prophet to 'Read!' Finally, the Prophet asked: 'What
shall I read?' The Angel replied:

> Read, with the name of Thy Lord, Who has created
> Who has created man of a drop of blood!
> Read, and thy Lord is most bounteous,
> Who has taught by pen:
> Who has taught man what he knew not!
> (The Qur'an: 96: 1-5).

This was the first revelation to be received by the Prophet, and he found the experience deeply unsettling. He returned home to confide in his wife Khadijah, who consoled and reassured him and accepted the validity of his experience. Khadijah is therefore considered the first person to embrace the new religion and become a Muslim. So begins what is called the Meccan Period, the early phase of Prophet Muhammad's life as the Messenger of Islam.

This formative period opens with his personal struggle to accept the idea of prophethood and initial tentative sharing of his experience with members of his family and closest friends. There were those, such as his friend Abu Bakr and nephew Ali, who accepted that Prophet Muhammad was now a Messenger of God and formed the kernel of a new body of believers. Equally, there were members of the Prophet's family, such as the wife of his uncle Abu Lahab, who were sceptical and soon openly derisive. It was three years after the event in the cave of Hira before a further instance of Revelation. The sequence and dating of each verse of the Qur'an has been meticulously compiled by Muslim scholars and the first halting steps of coming to terms with the enormity of the idea of Revelation features prominently in all biographies of the Prophet.

After the three-year hiatus, when according to al-Bukhari, one of the most authoritative early commentators and compiler of *hadith* (sayings of the Prophet), Prophet Muhammad had almost reached the point of despair, he was called on to proclaim the Message of Islam openly to the people of Mecca. The shift to publicly proclaiming a new religion to the entire community brought friction that developed into open animosity, especially with the powerful Quaraysh clan, and repression. The central message of Islam of the Oneness of God directly contradicts polytheism; and Prophet Muhammad's message and activities were seen as threatening and subversive to the vital interests of the community. The news of his activities spread rapidly across Arabia, again causing concern to the Meccan élite, headed by Abu Sufyan. Pressure was brought to bear on the gradually increasing number of Muslims to recant their new faith. As a member of the Banu Hashim, a prominent clan in Mecca, the Prophet was under the personal protection of the head of that clan, his uncle Abu Talib, despite the fact his uncle never embraced Islam. However, many of the new converts were easier targets. They were physically harassed, beaten, tortured and killed as the powerful of Mecca sought to stifle the new movement in their midst.

In 616 Prophet Muhammad became so concerned at the persecution of his followers he advised some of them to migrate to Abyssinia and seek refuge under the protection of its Christian ruler, the Negus. A group of 80 Muslims made the journey under the leadership of Ja'far ibn Abi Talib. They included the Prophet's daughter Ruqaiya and her husband Othman bin Affan, later the third Caliph or successor to Prophet Muhammad. In Abyssinia the refugees were permitted to practice their faith, and the Negus refused the two emissaries sent by the Quraysh clan to demand the Muslims be rejected as outlaws and returned.

The Prophet and his family remained in Mecca where they were subject to a boycott: nobody was to talk to them, sell to or buy from them or marry among them. Prophet Muhammad, the remaining Muslims and members of his clan moved to a secluded suburb where they were clandestinely supported by sympathetic relatives. The privations caused by this boycott further divided public opinion in Mecca. In 619, a group of citizens openly declared they would no longer support it; so the Prophet's clan was able to return to the city. The hardship and hunger they endured took their toll. In that year both Prophet Muhammad's wife Khadijah and his uncle Abu Talib died. Until her death Khadijah was the Prophet's only wife. After her death he re-married; in all he married 11 women. Many were widows whose husbands had died in the repression or battles of the early Muslim community. One, Safiyah, belonged to a Jewish tribe while his last marriage was to Maryam Qibtiyah who had been raised as an Egyptian Coptic Christian. Both women had converted to Islam before their marriage. All were given a free choice to accept or reject marriage to Prophet Muhammad. The wives of the Prophet became important and occasionally controversial figures in the Muslim community. They played a crucial role in reporting details of the custom, usage and opinions of the Prophet, the traditions which shaped the development of Islamic civilization.

With the death of Abu Talib, leadership of the Banu Hashim clan passed to Abu Lahab, a determined opponent of the Prophet's activities. The Prophet now considered the possibilities of emigrating, making an exploratory visit to Taif, where he had relatives. Shortly after his return he had the vision known as the *Miraj*, literally the ascension, the subject of the Night Journey (chapter 17 of the Qur'an). In this vision Prophet Muhammad was transported from Mecca to Jerusalem and then ascended to heaven into the Divine Presence. During this episode the clear lineaments of the *din* of Islam, religion as a way of life, were set. Some commentators see it as analogous to the Commandments given to Moses. After this event the pattern of five daily prayers as the way of worship was established.

The persecution in Mecca and the search for a new refuge continued. During the pilgrimage of 621 some members of the Khazraj group from the city of Yathrib converted to Islam and agreed to return the following year with an answer on the question of asylum for the Prophet. The following year 500 people from Yathrib attended the pilgrimage – of these, 74, including two women, were Muslims. They sought out the Prophet to declare their conversion to Islam and pledged a pact of allegiance, *bai'a*, to protect the Prophet and invited him and his followers to settle in Yathrib. Soon the *Hijra*, the migration from Mecca, began with small groups of Muslims leaving their native city. The Meccans were enraged at the prospect of the further spread of Islam and vowed to assassinate the Prophet who went into hiding to evade his pursuers.

His departure from Mecca is taken as the start of a new era and the beginning of the calculation of the Muslim calendar, expressed as AH from the Latin *Anno Hegirae*: in the year of the *Hijra*. The new calendar was actually introduced some 17 years after this event, which corresponds to 16 July 622 AD in the Julian calendar. It was instituted by the second Caliph, Umar ibn al-Khattab to provide consistency in dating of correspondence across the expanding Muslim empire.

The *Hijra* marks a major change in the preaching and institutionalizing of Islam as a way of life and living together. The Prophet was acknowledged as the leader of a newly renamed city, Medina. The city had a diverse population composed of a number of groups: the *Ansar*, the Helpers, were natives of Yathrib who extended practical support and aid to the *Muhajars*, the Migrants who had left behind their homes and had their property confiscated by the Meccan authorities. Medina was a heterodox city of Muslims, polytheists as well as Jews. The Prophet convened a general meeting of all citizens and a written agreement was drawn up defining the mutual relations of the various groups. Thus Medina became a political territorial entity of confederated groups: a

Some sayings of Prophet Muhammad

The world is green and beautiful and God has appointed you his trustee over it.

Little, but sufficient, is better than the abundant and the alluring.

The search for knowledge is a sacred duty imposed upon every Muslim.

God is gentle and loves gentleness in all things.

Pay the worker before his sweat dries.

He is not a believer who eats his fill while his neighbor remains hungry by his side.

As you are, so you will have rulers over you.

The special character of Islam is modesty. ∎

city-state with a written constitution. It was under threat from the hostility of the Meccans while having to integrate and build a new system covering the whole gamut of civic affairs for its citizens, Muslim and non-Muslim. It is in this context that the 10 years of the Medinan Period unfolds.

The center of community life in Medina was the Prophet's Mosque, where he actually lived. The community would gather at the mosque to discuss their affairs and reach agreement by consensus. From the outset mosques have always been understood as having dual functions, both religious worship and civil, especially social welfare duties. Reports give examples of men and women standing up at these assemblies and questioning the policy and decisions outlined, even those of the Prophet himself. There are examples of questions of marriage and divorce being settled by him, along with the panoply of individual and personal matters of concern to ordinary people coming to terms with the meaning of their new faith as a way of life. Collections of *hadith* (see next chapter), for example, usually have one whole section dealing with women who came to ask the Prophet questions on menstruation, childbirth and breastfeeding. It is in this period that the pattern of religious life was instituted, including the fast from dawn to dusk during the month of Ramadan and the paying of *zakat*, the obligatory 'poor due'.

The Medinan Period also includes the open warfare between Mecca and the new Muslim community. In particular the Prophet participated in three battles. There is an overriding tendency in biography, commentary and general histories, both Muslim and non-Muslim, to concentrate on the battles. Indeed, some Muslim biographies devote the bulk of the *Sirah* to the battles. Yet, collectively they occupied less than a month of the Medinan Period.

The emergence of conflict between Mecca and Medina was hardly surprising. The establishment of Medina as a confederated city-state under the administration of Prophet Muhammad, and which covered territory lying across the routes used by the two annual Meccan trade caravans, clearly impacted on vital Meccan economic interests. The battles were decisive in determining the continued existence of the fledgling Islamic community and created the conditions for its rapid expansion. The first, the Battle of Badr, took place in 624. Badr is a small town about 85 miles southwest of Medina on the caravan route connecting Mecca to Damascus. Here a force of 950 Meccans, dispatched to protect a caravan, engaged 300 Muslims. In a fierce battle that lasted less than a day, 45 Meccans including their leader Abu Jahl and a number of other prominent citizens were killed and 14 Muslims lost their lives.

The following year, the Meccans mobilized a force of 3,000 for an assault on Medina. Prophet Muhammad mustered about 700 Muslims and a pitched battle took place near the hill of Uhad just north of Medina. Rather than part of a concerted, ongoing war, the Battle of Uhad has all the marks of a traditional revenge raid. After initially repelling the Meccan force, the Muslims were thrown into disarray by an attack from the rear. In the fighting the Prophet was wounded, adding to the confusion. Seventy Muslims were killed while the Meccans lost 20 men. Among the Muslims killed was Hamza, Prophet Muhammad's uncle whose body was mutilated by Hind, the wife of Abu Sufyan, in revenge for her father whom Hamza had killed at Badr. When the day's fighting ended, the attacking force returned to Mecca.

In 627 a Meccan army of 10,000 laid siege to Medina in what is known as the Battle of the Trench, so called after the defensive ditch Prophet Muhammad had dug to protect his city. Repeated attempts to cross the ditch failed and after two weeks the Meccan army, dispirited by bad weather, failing supplies and internal dissension, decided to withdraw. This attempt to overthrow the new community resulted in ten fatalities on both sides. It clearly dented the prestige of the Meccans and added to the growing confidence of the Muslim cause. In the aftermath of the Battle, the Prophet sent 500 gold coins to be distributed among the poor of Mecca where a famine was underway. He also sent a large quantity of dates to Abu Sufyan and asked in exchange to barter the stock of hides which Abu Sufyan could not export. The reports of these events make it clear that women accompanied and supported both sides in each of the battles.

In 628, the Prophet announced his intention to make a pilgrimage to the *Ka'aba* (the sacred focus of Islam; see chapter 2) in Mecca and arrived with a group of about 1,600 people. When he reached Hudaybiya on the outskirts, he sent an envoy requesting permission to enter Mecca in peace for a few days. This request was denied by the Meccans but an agreement, the Treaty of

Hudaybiya, was declared. The Prophet would be permitted to make the pilgrimage the following year and the parties agreed to remain neutral should either city be engaged in conflict with a third party.

The Meccans did not stick to their side of the bargain making several infringements of the Treaty. So, in 630 Prophet Muhammad gathered together a force some 10,000 strong and marched on Mecca. On his approach, the city immediately surrendered and he re-entered his birthplace without fighting. The city elders were brought to the Prophet and stood in front of him. These were the people who for 21 years had opposed and persecuted him, tortured and killed his followers, and eventually drove him out of the city. The Prophet asked 'What do you expect of me now?' Then he answered his own question: All your crimes are forgiven; 'there is no responsibility on you any more today. Go, you are liberated.' This magnanimity shook the Meccans and many then embraced Islam, including their leader Abu Sufyan. The *Ka'aba*, which contained numerous statues, was cleared of its idols and rededicated to the worship of One God. Prophet Muhammad returned to Medina and no Muslim force was left in Mecca.

The fall of Mecca quickened the spread of Islam across the whole of Arabia. Not all the people of Arabia become Muslims but the authority of Muslim government was recognized by all. Initial contacts were made with the powerful empires, Byzantine and Persian, on the borders of Arabia. The Prophet wrote to their leaders inviting them to Islam. Throughout the Medinan Period religious and civic affairs were concentrated in the person of Prophet Muhammad and he was now surrounded by a growing body of secretaries. In 632 the ailing Prophet made his farewell pilgrimage (*hajj*) to Mecca. It was during this pilgrimage, on the ninth day of the month of Dhul Hijjah in the year 11 AH that the final verse of the Qur'an was revealed:

> This day have I
> Perfected your religion
> For you, completed
> My favor upon you,
> And chosen for you
> Islam as your religion. (5:3)

The date remains the culmination of the hajj, the annual Muslim pilgrimage to Mecca. During his pilgrimage Prophet Muhammad delivered his final sermon, describing himself as the slave of God and His Messenger, addressing the crowd: 'I enjoin you, O slaves of God, to fear God, and I incite you to obey Him. And I begin with what is good.' What he commends to Muslims is a charter of social justice and equity dealing with actual concerns and tensions of a society in transition, moving from the ways of the 'time of ignorance' to a new set of moral and ethical precepts. It includes seminal phrases: 'Your wives have a right over you and you have a right over them'; 'The believers are only brethren'; 'Your Lord is one, and your ancestor is also one: all of you are descendants of Adam and Adam was made of clay'; 'No Arab has any superiority over a non-Arab'; 'Let the present communicate to the absent.' On completing his hajj the Prophet returned to Medina where he died peacefully a few months later.

The Prophet Muhammad is known to Muslims as The Seal of The Prophets. His death marks the completion of both the fundamental sources of Islam – the Qur'an and *Sirah* – and of all prophethood. From this point Muslim history becomes the struggle of a human community to interpret and implement the teachings of Islam in a changing society.

2 What is Islam?

As a religion, Islam is deceptively simple. Its creed consists of a two-part statement: 'There is no god but God; and Prophet Muhammad is the messenger of God'. Anyone who makes this declaration – known as the *shahadah*, meaning bearing witness – freely and sincerely is a Muslim.

THE *SHAHADAH* BEGINS by negating the existence of false deities and affirming belief in One, Omnipotent, Omniscient, Omnipresent and All Powerful God. God, or Allah, is the absolute Creator and Ruler of the Universe. He 'beggetteth not, nor is He begotten.' Unlike Christianity, Islam rejects the idea that God intervenes in history in human form. No intermediaries are needed and God alone is worthy of worship. Indeed, God has no gender; though, by convention, Muslims use the pronoun, He. He is thus unique and can only be known by finite, human minds through His attributes or names. In Islamic tradition, there are 99 Names of God, beginning with al-Awwal, the First, to al-Akhir, the Last. The most common attributes of God are contained in the statement Muslims utter every time they undertake an action: 'In the name of God, the Beneficent, the Merciful'. The Merciful and Compassionate God is the Forgiving, Nurturing and Sustaining Creator, the Loving, Helper, Giver and Guide from which all creation derives, to whom all creation belongs and ultimately returns.

From this uncompromisingly monotheistic premise, Islamic theology derives a number of logical conclusions. The relationship between God and His creation, men and women, is that of dependence. Every individual has a direct relationship with God; and constantly needs Allah's guidance and forgiveness. Since everyone is the same in the eyes of God, all men and women are equal. Every individual is endowed with free will and has the choice to do good or bad. Everyone is ultimately individually accountable to God for his or her actions and will be judged after death.

This implies our existence does not end with death; there is life after death of reward and punishment. We should thus behave in this life in such a manner that we may not suffer in life after death. And, this applies not just to individuals but society as a whole which should follow the path of justice and equity.

The Muslim conception of God is often criticized by Westerners as austere and severe. It is certainly true Islam has no notion of 'God the Father' and specifically proscribes the idea of 'God incarnate'. But such comments fail to capture how ordinary Muslims experience and understand the idea of God. For a Muslim, the Infinite – while awesome and all-powerful – is also an ever-present reality, as witnessed by the innumerable idioms of Muslim daily speech that invoke and refer to Allah. Travelers to the Middle East frequently encounter the phrase *Alhumdu lil Allah*: 'Praise be to

Why I am a Muslim

The strangest question I have ever been asked is: why are you Muslim? I find the question strange because I have never thought of a reason. My 'Muslimness' comes naturally to me; no other alternative has ever crossed my mind. I am Muslim because the only logical explanation of all the wonder in the universe and in ourselves is that a Creator exists. Every breath I take is a mercy from that Creator. To deny God, I would be denying myself and my life. Indeed, I see God's miracles everywhere, I can not but love, worship and obey Him. Through God's commands, revealed in the Qur'an and the examples of the Prophet Muhammad, I know exactly how to live my life. I am free to choose between peace and happiness by becoming a part of God's greater design, and the nightmare of rejecting my Creator's guidance. I am Muslim because I choose to be logical and far-sighted. I see the logic of Islam and am far-sighted enough to plan for the eternity that God has offered. ■

Marwa El-Naggar, an Egyptian woman in her 20s.

What is Islam?

Allah'. Indeed, Arabs never seem to tire of uttering this and other similar phrases.

They affirm the Muslim belief that God is nearer to a person than their jugular vein, a perceptible presence all-knowing and all-seeing, constantly aware of each individual, their thoughts, motivations and deeds. For Muslims, the essence of religion is human effort to remain conscious of God's presence. And that is exactly what most pious Muslims strive to do.

The second part of the *shahadah*, the declaration that Prophet Muhammad is the Messenger of God, signifies God is not only present in an abstract sense but is actually known through revelation. Revelation, the self-declaration of God to human society through the medium of human prophets makes religion an historic presence in human society. For Muslims, the Qur'an is the direct word of God, an enduring record of the specific Revelation made to the Prophet between the years 610 and 633AD. But the Qur'an is not the only instance of revelation nor is Prophet Muhammad the only Prophet acknowledged by Islam. The Qur'an specifically names 25 Prophets, including Abraham (Ibrahim in the Qur'an), Moses (Musa) and Jesus (Isa) and many others familiar from the Bible. Christians and Jews are 'the People of the Book' and both the Old and the New Testaments are regarded by Islam as revealed – although corrupted – texts. But the Qur'an also refers to many more unnamed Prophets and states no society has been without a messenger; Muslims are required to give equal respect to all Prophets.

Prophets are recipients of specific divine guidance on how to live. Conceptually, prophethood means knowledge of God is not only innate in human nature but also the foundation of human history. The first Prophet according to Islam was Adam, the first human. Furthermore, all prophets brought the same basic message of Islam, recognition and acceptance of God. While the specifics of particular revelations, the rules and precepts of observance and living, may differ and human society may deviate from or distort the message of divine guidance, for Islam at core the moral challenge of living a good life in consciousness of God is the same for all peoples whatever their religious affiliation. What distinguishes Prophet Muhammad is that he is considered the last, or Seal of the Prophets, the revelation he received being a complete and enduring form of God's message for all humanity.

Thus, the basic articles of faith in Islam are three:
- Belief in the Unity of God;
- Belief in the Prophethood of Prophet Muhammad and the Message of guidance he received;
- Belief in the life after death and accountability on the Day of Judgment.

The Pillars

The *shahadah* is considered as the first 'pillar' of Islam. It is used in the *azan* or call to prayer. Every day, in every Muslim society, the believers are ushered to the mosque with these words:

> God is the Most Great.
> I bear witness that there is no god but God.
> I bear witness that Muhammad is the messenger
>   of God.
> Come to prayer.
> Come to success.
> God is the Most Great.
> There is no god but God.

Prayer, or *salat*, is the second pillar of Islam. Muslims are required to pray five times a day; wherever possible in congregation. But prayer is always an individual act of worship, a way of acquiring God consciousness in one's daily life. The midday prayer on Friday is a compulsory congregational prayer, bringing the entire neighborhood together for worship and social interaction. People who may be negligent of their daily prayers make a special effort to attend the Friday prayers. Prayer consists of recitation of verses from the Qur'an within a ritual pattern of movements established by the Prophet Muhammad. In congregational prayers worshippers stand in straight lines facing the direction of Mecca and are led by an *Imam*. Anyone can be an Imam and lead a prayer but it helps if they have a rudimentary of knowledge of Islam!

The third pillar of Islam is fasting during the month of Ramadan. Fasting is a spiritual and physical discipline, a way of learning self-control and teaching an appreciation of the trials and tribulations of hunger. Ramadan, the 9th month of the Muslim year, is known as the blessed month. It was in this month Prophet Muhammad received his first revelation. During Ramadan Muslims are required to make extra efforts to spread love, peace, harmony and good will. As the Muslim year is a based on a lunar calendar, Ramadan moves through the seasons and the months of calendars based on the Solar year, beginning approximately 11 days earlier each year. During Ramadan, special but voluntary evening prayers – known as *tarawih* – are held where, over the course of the month, the whole of the Qur'an is read. During these prayers, the Imam has to be a *hafiz* – someone who has memorized the Qur'an by heart. Each day's fast begins just before dawn and ends at sunset; during the fast it is forbidden to eat, drink, smoke or have sex. People who are sick, young children, the very old and those who are traveling, menstruating and pregnant women are exempt from fasting. The end of the month of Ramadan is marked by the festival of Eid al-Fitr, during which the entire community comes together for a large, thanks-giving, congregational prayer.

Ramadan makes a marked change in daily routine and in some countries introduces a new way of life. In

Saudi Arabia and much of the Arabian peninsula, for example, people tend to sleep most of the day and work during the night: shops are closed between 11.00 am and 5.00 pm, the streets are deserted, and come back to life after sunset. While people are supposed to eat less during Ramadan, breaking the fast is an occasion for celebration and may lead to eating rather more than usual.

Zakat, often called the 'poor due' or 'religious tax', is the fourth pillar of Islam. The word *zakah* means to purify; the purification of one's income by giving a proportion to the poor and the needy and for general public welfare is a religious duty for every Muslim. *Zakat* is normally given annually – traditionally at the end of Ramadan – and has to be at least 2.5 per cent of annual income or 'appropriated wealth'. 'Appropriated wealth' excludes debts and liabilities, household effects (except jewelry) required for living; and land, buildings, and capital materials used in or for production; but includes almost everything by which one makes a profit. No-one is exempt from *zakat*: even the dead have *zakat* deducted from their estate before inheritance and legacies are disbursed.

Zakat can be collected by social or welfare organizations on behalf of the community or by the State itself. But it can only be spent for certain specified purposes including to assist the poor, the homeless, the bankrupt, the needy, for education or medical treatment for those who cannot afford to pay and public works that enhance the general welfare of a community. Nowadays, many Muslim countries like Pakistan, Malaysia and Iran have state institutions that collect and distribute *zakat*. In Britain and America, during the last two decades, numerous non-governmental organizations – with names like 'Islamic Relief', 'Muslim Aid' and 'Muslim Hands' – have emerged for collecting and distributing *zakat* funds to refugees, victims of war and natural disasters.

The fifth and final pillar of Islam is hajj – the

The Islamic Year

Month	Festival
Muharram	Shia Muslims celebrate the martyrdom of Imam Hussain. The 10th is Ashura, a voluntary day of fasting.
Safar	
Rabi al-Awal	The 12th is Eid Milad un-Nabi, or the birthday of the Prophet Muhammad
Rabi al-Thani	
Jumada al-Ula	
Jumada al-Thani	
Rajab	The 27th is Lalat-ul Miraj, or the Night of the Miraj, the Prophet's Ascension to Heaven
Shaban	
Ramadan	The month of obligatory fasting. The 27th is the 'Night of the Power', the celebration of the first revelation to the Prophet Muhammad
Shawwal	The 1st is Eid al-Fitr, the celebration of the end of the Ramadan fast.
Dhu al-Qadah	
Dhul Hijjah	The month of the hajj, which occurs during the 9th and 12th days. The 9th is the Day of Arafat; and the 10th Eid al-Adha, when Muslims all over the world join the pilgrims in celebrating the ethical and humanitarian concerns of Islam. ■

pilgrimage to Mecca. Every Muslim who is physically able and can afford to undertake the journey is required to perform the hajj at least once in their lifetime. It is considered the supreme spiritual experience of a Muslim's life, a journey undertaken for individual self-renewal inspired by piety and devotion to God. It is performed during the month of Dhul Hijjah, two months after Ramadan; and like Ramadan it moves through the solar year covering the four seasons during a 30-year period. It falls on the 9th, 10th, 11th and 12th days of the month and like prayer follows a pattern established by Prophet Muhammad.

The word 'hajj' means effort – and the hajj requires a great deal of physical and mental effort. The pilgrims – on average over two million each year – travel in a vast company and are required to perform certain rituals at prescribed times. They begin by discarding their normal attire and entering the state of *ihram*. For men, the *ihram* consists of two simple, unsewn, white sheets of cloth (frequently two large towels); women wear plain, usually white, loose, full-length dress with a head-scarf. Once in *ihram*, the pilgrims have to follow strict rules of conduct: they cannot do anything dishonest or arrogant, show aggression or use abusive words, or shout at anyone in anger. They must show respect towards nature: even an insect should not be harmed. They cannot cut their hair or fingernails and must abstain from sex. Indeed, all material pleasures have to be abandoned; even the use of scented soap is not allowed.

After donning *ihram*, the pilgrims go straight to the Sacred Mosque in Mecca, the location of the *Ka'aba*, the stone shrine covered with a black cloth. For Muslims, it is the prime focus of Islam: they turn towards the *Ka'aba* when they pray; metaphorically, it symbolizes the unity and common sense of purpose and direction in life. The pilgrims walk round the *Ka'aba* seven times, a ritual known as the *tawaf.* Then, they perform the ritual of Sai, running between the two small hills of Safa and Marwah. This ritual commemorates the desperate search for water of Hagar, the wife of Prophet Abraham. Abandoned thirst-stricken in the heat and desolation near the *Ka'aba* along with her infant son, Ishmael, Hagar ran seven times up and down the hills in search of water. Then, the tradition has it, the spring of Zamzam gushed forth. The pilgrims re-enact this scene and end the ritual by drinking Zamzam water. Nowadays the entire Sai area is covered with a splendid structure and air-conditioned. Both the Sai and Zamzam are within the area of the Sacred Mosque. Spiritually, this ritual signifies the soul's desperate search for meaning and that which gives it true life.

The *tawaf* and Sai rituals comprise the 'lesser pilgrimage' or *umra* – which can be performed at any time during the year. The hajj requires additional rituals. On the 8th of Dhul Hijjah, the pilgrims travel to spend the night at nearby Muna. The 9th is the main day when the pilgrims descend to the plains of Arafat. Here, the entire congregation of some two million people offers the noon prayer as a single unit. After the collective prayer, they stand together under the burning sun to pray individually for forgiveness. The prayer and the ritual of standing is the essence of hajj. It is here that pilgrims experience an unparalleled sense of a brotherhood and sisterhood; but their overriding experience is personal: 'It is I and my Lord; and the noblest hours of my life.'

At the end of the Day of Arafat pilgrims make a dash to Muzdalifah, an open plain sheltered by parched hills between Arafat and Muna. Here they spend a night under the open sky. The next day they return to Muna, staying for three days during which they perform the ritual of Stoning, throwing three pebbles at each of the three stone pillars symbolizing the Devil. Tradition has it the Devil tried to tempt Prophet Abraham and his family at these spots. Remembering the incident, the pilgrims promise to cast out their own devil within. Finally, the pilgrims take off their ihram, have a bath, sacrifice an animal for the benefit of the poor (although some simply give money to charity) and close the hajj with celebration. Muslims throughout the world join the pilgrims in celebration of Eid al-Adha, the feast of sacrifice.

Until quite recently, the environment of hajj –

Mecca, the surrounding areas of Muna, Muzdalifah and Arafat – had remained largely unchanged from the times of the Prophet. But from 1970s onwards the entire region was extensively re-developed. Virtually all the historic cultural property was destroyed – even the hills, so steeped in history, were flattened. So, despite its sacred nature, and its central place in Muslim tradition, the city of Mecca appears to have no relation to Islamic history. It resembles Houston!

Tradition

The hajj provides a good example of Islam's emphasis on tradition. It invokes the historical narratives of Prophet Abraham, the founder of the monotheistic faiths, to whom Islam traces its origins. Like all religions, Islam aspires to maintain continuity with its original vision. Tradition is the soil from which the tree of Islam takes its nourishment to grow and flower. As a Persian proverb says, 'as long as the roots of the plant are in the water there is still hope'. For Muslims, tradition is like water – something that sustains and rejuvenates them. Pious Muslims everywhere thus strive to live within the traditions of Islam.

Islamic tradition was shaped in the process by which the practice of Prophet Muhammad came to be accepted as normative for the Muslim community. The words and actions of the Prophet became oral and written reports and came to be known as Traditions, which became a major branch of study soon after the Prophet's death. The reports were meticulously collected, critiqued and rejected or accepted as authentic; and became the basis for shaping Muslim values. These records are known as the *sunnah*; literally, the example of the Prophet. The sayings are referred to as *hadith*. Together, *sunnah* and *hadith* constitute the Traditions. These Traditions have been used in a variety of ways by the Muslim community, from law and scholarship to popular sayings, parables and homilies that sprinkle ordinary discussion.

The Traditions have kept the example and personality of the Prophet alive in Muslim consciousness. They provide Muslims with a rounded sense of a real human being and how he interacted with his followers. What is familiar to Muslims from reading *hadith* is a person of profound spirituality and humility with unfailing compassion and concern for fellow human beings. A man with a gentle sense of humor who is tolerant, forgiving and sympathetic of the failings and foibles of his fellow citizens, concerned for the dignity of each individual and utterly committed to improving the material as well as the spiritual condition of their lives.

The Traditions became the basis for the elaboration of Islamic legal principles. As noted, the Qur'an itself contains very few specific legal injunctions. Therefore from the outset both the Qur'an and how the Prophet determined matters, especially in his role as leader of the community, became a basis for developing Islamic Law, or *sharia*. Subsequent rulers of the Muslim community would request opinions from those learned in the Traditions to help them determine policy, a process in which politics, vested interests and differences of outlook played their part. Literally, the word sharia means 'the path or the road leading to water'. In its religious use, it has come to mean 'the highway of good life': that is, religious values expressed in concrete terms to shape and direct the lives of believers. In this way, the sharia is the path not only leading to

---

Authentic *hadith* collections

There are six collections of *hadith* regarded as most authoritative, often called canonical. These are: *Sahih Bukhari*, collected by Muhammad bin Ismail often called Imam Bukhari; the *Sahih Muslim*, of Muslim bin al-Hajjaj; the *Sunan Abu Dawud*, of Sulaiman bin Ash'ath, known as Abu Dawud; the *Sunan Ibn Majah* of Muhammad bin Yazid ; the *Jami' At-Tirmidhi* of Muhammad bin Isa; and the *Sunan An-Nasa'i* of Ahmad bin Shu'aib. All of these collectors of *hadith* lived and died between the 8th and 9th centuries. ∎

God; but the path shown by God through the Qur'an and the example of the Traditions of the Prophet. Collectively, the sharia provides a legal framework for family relations, crime and punishment, inheritance, trade and commerce, the organization and operation of communal affairs and relations between communities and states.

The Qur'an and the Traditions of the Prophet are not the only source of Islamic Law. Over the years, the custom and practice of early Muslim communities also became an integral part of the sharia. Legal consensus (*ijma*) of classical jurists acquired the force of sharia law and became binding on later communities. Slowly, a huge body of traditional jurisprudence, known as *fiqh*, became indistinguishable from the original sharia. *Fiqh* was largely a product of human efforts to understand and comprehend the message of the Qur'an and the Traditions. It evolved on the basis of the Islamic concept of *ijtihad* or systematic original thinking. But during the 14th century, religious scholars closed 'the gates of *ijtihad*' – and both sharia and *fiqh* became trapped in the traditions of the early Muslim communities. Contemporary Islam therefore tries systematically to replicate the customs and tradition of the classical period. How this system operates today is examined in chapter 8.

Fiqh, however, is not a monolithic body of traditional jurisprudence. Right from the beginning, there were strong differences of opinion between the classical jurists leading to five distinct Schools of Thought – or *madhabs* – named after the most eminent jurists of the period: Imam Malik, Imam Shafi'i, Imam Abu Hanafi, Imam Ahmad ibn Hanbali and Imam Jafar al-Sadiq.

The Maliki School, which was based in Medina, is the oldest and most deeply immersed in Arab traditions. It is now dominant in most countries of Muslim Africa. But the largest and most important School of the classical period is the Shafi'i which evolved in

Baghdad, the capital of the Abbasid Caliphate (652-1258). More sophisticated than the austere Maliki tradition, it gave more emphasis to free will and *ijma*, or consensus, of the community. The Hanafi School, considered to be more rationalist, developed as a reaction against the narrow traditionalism of Maliki Arabs. Imam Hanafi relied more on legal reasoning and precedents than on *hadith* in developing his thought. He also developed court procedures and rules of evidence and cautioned against extreme punishments. The Hanafi School is followed in Egypt, Turkey and much of Southeast Asia. The Hanbali is undoubtedly the most puritanical of all Schools of Thought. Imam Hanbali rejected the use of legal reasoning as well as *ijma*, and insisted that sharia be based exclusively on literal interpretation of the Qur'an. Saudi Arabia is the only Muslim country where the Hanbali creed is the state religion. The Jafari School, dominant largely in Iran and Iraq, is followed principally by Shi'a Muslims. Imam Jafar believed only direct descendents of the Prophet Muhammad have the right to interpret the sharia.

The overall emphasis of *fiqh* is on worldly life. But the classical period also saw the parallel evolution of a totally different tradition focused on the mystical content of the Qur'an and Traditions of the Prophet. The mystical tradition of Islam is called *Sufism* and is based on the concept of *tariqah*, the path of union with God. The word *Sufi* comes from the Arabic *suf* meaning wool; it refers to the undyed wool garments that early mystics of Islam, eschewing luxuries of dress and shelter and preferring an ascetic life of simplicity and poverty, used to wear. An alternative name for Sufism, used mostly in Muslim circles, is *tasawwuf*, again from the same root word, it denotes 'the practice of wearing the woolen robe' and hence the act of devoting oneself to mystical life. One of the first Sufis was the great women saint Rabia Basri, who developed the doctrine of 'disinterested love of God' which became both the basic motif of her life and a central tenet of Sufism.

In general, Sufis work to overcome the appetites and desires of the human body and thus purify the heart in preparation for union with God. The final goal is to become so close to God that human consciousness becomes totally absorbed in consciousness of God. This final state is known as *fana*: the annihilation of one's self and its dissolution in the love of God. In Islamic history, the most celebrated Sufi to achieve this goal is the Persian mystic, al-Hallaj, who in a state of *fana* declared: 'I am Truth'. Another central tenet of Sufism is the notion of Wahdat al-wajud, or 'unity of all being', associated with the name of the great Andalusian Sufi, Muhyi al-Din ibn Arabi. He frequently used a prayer which begins: 'Enter me, O Lord, into the deep of the Ocean of Thine Infinite Oneness'. Within Sufi mysticism, as in *fiqh*, there are different interpretations and approaches. There is devotional mysticism as well as intellectual and philosophical mysticism. Authority in Sufism belongs to the Sheikh, often considered the Perfect Master, who guides his followers in their mystical quest. There are many Sufi Orders, each with its own specific esoteric practices, each tracing its lineage to a great Sufi of the classical age with whose name the order is normally associated. The chain of transmission, or the *silsilah*, connects the Sufi masters of the present day with the grand masters and then to the Prophet Muhammad himself in a master-to-master line. Amongst the well-known Sufi Orders are the *Qadiriyyah*, founded by the Indian Sufi Abd al-Qadir Jilani, the *Chishti* Order founded by Abd al-Qadir's contemporary Muin ad-Din Chishti, the *Shadhiliyyah* order established by the North African Sufi Abu-Hasan ash-Shadhili and the *Maluvi* order associated by the great Persian/Turkish mystical poet, Jalal al-Din Rumi.

Throughout its history, Sufism has been in simmering conflict with orthodox, *fiqh*-based, Islam.

Sometimes, this conflict has boiled over: the orthodox had al-Hallaj executed for uttering and ascribing a central attribute of God – Truth – to himself.

Worldview

The religion and tradition of Islam, as well as its culture and civilization, are connected by the worldview of Islam. This worldview is shaped by a set of ideas, the concepts set forth in the Qur'an, the Traditions of the Prophet and embedded in their teaching and examples. It is these religious concepts and their associated norms and values that shaped the civilization of Islam in history and provide a coherent outlook across its diversity. Indeed, it is the understanding, interpretation, the actual and potential meaning given to these concepts, past and present, that gives Islamic civilization its particular character.

The fundamental concept of the Islamic worldview is *tawhid*, normally translated as 'the unity of God'. Islam is concerned not just with belief in one God but also the oneness of God and hence the unity of His creation. So, by extension this signifies the unity of humankind and the unity of people and nature. *Tawhid* is the significance behind that most familiar of Muslim expressions: *Allahu Akbar*, God is Great. It means nothing except God is eternal; everything other than God is limited and finite and belongs to God alone. Within this all-embracing unity creation is a trust from God, and men and women – equal in the sight of God whatever their color or creed – are *khalifah* or trustees of God. Therefore, human beings are not the absolute owner of existence, neither their own, that of other creatures nor the natural environment. People are temporary and transient users of this trust, *amanah*, therefore each individual and each community are responsible and accountable for how this trust is used. A steward or trustee should husband and nurture the resources entrusted to them and ensure they are handed to future users, subsequent generations, in the best possible condition. The idea of *khalifah* establishes humankind's place in the order of creation. It also sees that place as a relationship in time, within the succession of history, as well as in relation to what is beyond time, the return of each individual to God for judgment in the Hereafter.

Tawhid, or the unity of the Creator, gives significance and order to creation. Implicit in the created order are signs, known in Arabic as *ayah*, that help humanity to understand His creation. The *ayahs* of the Creator can be understood, and the responsibility of trusteeship fulfilled, through three other fundamental Islamic concepts: *ilm* (knowledge), *adl* (distributive social justice) and *ijtihad* (sustained intellectual reasoning). The thought and action of the *khalifah* are based not on blind faith but on knowledge and sustained intellectual effort; and the major function of all the ideas and actions of the trustee are to promote all-round justice.

Ilm, or knowledge, is a cardinal concept of Islam. Almost one third of the Qur'an is devoted to extolling the virtues of knowledge. Prophet Muhammad consistently urged it on his followers: 'seek knowledge from the cradle to the grave'; 'to spend more time in learning is better than spending more time in prayer'; 'knowledge is like the lost camel of a Muslim, take hold of it whenever you come across it', he is reported to have said. Not surprisingly the pursuit of knowledge and learning is considered to be the sacred duty of all Muslims, females as well as males. *Ijtihad* relates specifically to knowledge in religious matters. It functions to focus attention on the challenge of changing circumstances and the struggle to comprehend the meaning of religion in application to contemporary life.

Like *ilm, adl* too is a consistent theme running through the Qur'an, the sayings of the Prophet and reverberating in Muslim discourses throughout history. Its meaning as distributive justice is most clearly seen in one of the five pillars of Islam: *zakat*, whose

Monotheistic faiths

Islam regards itself as a continuation of Judaism and Christianity. The three monotheistic faiths share common threads. The Christian Bible includes the Judaic Old Testament in addition to the teachings of Jesus. The Qur'an refers to events in both the Old and New Testaments in addition to the prophetic career of Prophet Muhammad.

All three faiths share a common ancestor in Abraham, or Ibrahim. Details of his prophetic career are central to the most basic aspects of Muslim worship, from turning to the *Ka'aba* when they pray to the details of performing the hajj, the pilgrimage to Mecca.

While the New Testament builds upon the Old Testament, Christianity and Judaism are distinctly different faiths each with their own traditions of worship and practice. The same is true of Islam. The Qur'an presents the story of Prophet Adam and his wife, Hawa in Muslim tradition. But the detail and import are distinct. In the Qur'anic story both Adam and Eve were tempted, both erred equally, repented and both were forgiven. So for Muslims all human beings, male and female, begin life sinless, equally capable of error and reform.

One chapter of the Qur'an is entitled Mariam, named for Mary the mother of Jesus (Isa). Muslims accept the virgin birth of Jesus, his prophetic mission and crucifixion, but not his death on the cross or resurrection. And while Jesus, like all Prophets, is honored by Muslims he is considered human and not divine.

The encounter between Moses (Musa) and Pharaoh also features in the Qur'an. Pharaoh is a symbol of the arrogance, corruption and tyranny of earthly power. The decay and downfall of Empires is a recurrent Qur'anic theme used to emphasize human potential for error by turning away from God consciousness.

Similar narratives, differently told and interpreted, link Islam, Christianity and Judaism. But a more significant and neglected point is that these shared narratives point to common moral and ethical values and perceptions that stand just behind the different language of explication and interpretation of the three monotheistic faiths. ∎

function is providing a constant supply of funds for the needy. But there are a host of other concepts associated with *adl*. *Riba* is specifically the prohibition of interest but conceptually it is a powerful general principle working against the accumulation of superfluous riches in the hands of a few by providing the means and opportunity for those in need to better their circumstances. *Mudaraba*, for example, means sharing and participation founded on the proposition that all human activity includes risk; what is unavoidable and common to all should be equitably shared by all.

Furthermore, Islamic rules of inheritance – whose calculation gave rise to algebra – require that one's wealth should be apportioned in fixed proportions among one's immediate family members and then distributed amongst a broader range of relatives to ensure that wealth and resources are not concentrated in fewer and fewer hands.

Distributive justice

Distributive justice not only operates to secure the circulation of resources through society it seeks to ensure human dignity by creating the means and opportunity for achieving self-reliance. The pursuit of justice may require one to engage in jihad or righteous struggle to bring forth justice. Jihad begins with oneself; indeed, morally transcending the limitations of one's human failings and frailty is its highest form. Much of Sufism is devoted to personal jihad – the suppression of one's ego. Jihad extends to seeking justice with one's wealth, economic jihad, and one's knowledge, intellectual jihad. The final stage of jihad is armed struggle of the Muslim community as a whole against an unjust ruler. We will consider how this concept operates in today's world in chapter 8.

Both *adl* and *ilm* are to be sought on the basis of *ijma* (consensus), *shura* (consultation) and *istislah* (public interest). The Islamic worldview is deeply consensus-orientated: it seeks to bring the Muslim community together on the basis of general, wide ranging agreements. How a community should determine and organize itself to perform its tasks and fulfill its purpose as the trustee of God is delineated in the concept of *shura*. *Shura* is a procedure of consultation in which all members of the community have the right to participate and be heard. It also means decisions arrived at by consensus, the participatory engagement of citizens should result in their informed consent and acceptance of collective decisions. *Shura* provides an operative model for putting mutual responsibility into action.

The objective of communal decision-making is *istislah*, the public interest, the common good. Consultation and debate clearly require the freedom to express opinions, to criticize and question, to call officials to account. It is a prerequisite of the familiar phrase that sums up the purpose and defining character of the Muslim community: Islam: promoting what is right and forbidding what is wrong. What is right and wholesome, what promotes knowledge and justice, public interest and consensus, is considered *halal* (praiseworthy); outside this framework, where lies dissension, injustice and ignorance, and hence danger, is the *haram* (blameworthy) territory. *Halal* and *haram* are the axes upon which all concepts and elements of the Islamic worldview are assessed and operate. Thus halal food, now a common feature in Western societies is not merely a method of slaughtering meat. It should mean an entire process from production of food by sensitive ecologically sound methods through a chain of processing and marketing to consumption that is beneficial to the environment, human health and provides just returns to those employed at each stage of the process.

The Islamic term for community is *ummah*, specifically it identifies the global community of believers, Muslims, those who are faithful to the religion, Tradition and the worldview of Islam. All Muslims wherever they live, whether in majority states or as minority communities, are constituent parts of and belong to the *ummah*. The *ummah*, as Prophet Muhammad said, is like a human body: if one part hurts the whole body feels the pain. 'But one is not born into it by blind chance; one is elected and joins

Major world religions

Islam is considered the fastest growing religion in the world. Muslims consititute a fifth of humanity. Most are under 25.

TOTAL WORLD POPULATION
6.1 billion
MAJOR RELIGIONS
Christianity 2 billion
Islam 1.3 billion
Hinduism 900 million
Buddhism 360 million

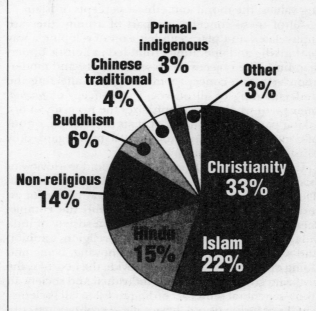

Primal-indigenous 3%

Chinese traditional 4%

Other 3%

Buddhism 6%

Non-religious 14%

Christianity 33%

Hindu 15%

Islam 22%

- Around 85 per cent of Muslims belong to the majority Sunni sect. The minority Shi'a Muslims are concentrated in Iran and Iraq.
- Less than 20 per cent of Muslims are Arabs. Almost half of the world's Muslims live in South and Southeast Asia.

Statistical, Economic and Social Research and Training Center for Islamic Countries (SESRTCIC), Ankara, Turkey; National Geographic, January 2002.

it as a rational being. The *ummah* is not a community-by-nature, but a community-by-decision, a "society"[.1] The *ummah* constantly seeks *islah,* meaning reform or setting right, the ongoing search for practical and sustainable ways to improve the condition of human life, individually and for the community as a whole. *Islah* is a reformative rather than revolutionary concept. Each individual as well as human society is potentially perfectible, but also prone to error, to being far from perfect. Reform is, therefore, a continual necessity that must take account of actual circumstances and real human needs. Setting things right requires continuous amendment by increments that work to move individuals and society nearer to achieving the enduring values, the moral and ethical percepts of Islam.

All of these concepts are part of a unity, they are interrelated and place emphasis on developing a way of thinking and operating grounded in holistic understanding. The objective is to seek balance and moderation with one concept tempering and affecting the understanding of all others. The concept of *tawhid,* oneness or wholeness, emphasizes the necessity of not taking particular elements or texts in isolation, or out of context. It is in this sense that Islam is regarded by Muslims as the Middle Way.

Collectively, the religion, tradition and worldview of Islam constitute the *din*: Islam's description of itself. The term *din* translates as an entire way of life for an individual as a member of society with the complementary meaning of a way of life for a society of individuals. It also contains the idea that religion, tradition and worldview shapes the way of knowing, being and doing of any society, that they provide the bedrock, the civilizing conscience of both individual and society. In its most general sense, according to Islam, all societies, whether Muslim or not, have a *din,* a civilizational core of principles from which its characteristic way of life and attitudes to life are derived. Explicitly, Islam as religion and worldview is an understanding of what it is to be human and the nature and organization of human existence. The term *din* emphasizes that all that exists shares a basic unity and partakes of a common sacredness, all is interconnected. From the perspective of Islam nothing is or can be entirely secular, in the sense of solely of this present world.

1 R al-Faruqi, *Tawheed: Its Implication for Thought and Life* (International Institute of Islamic Thought, Washington, 1982, p 139).

3 The Rightly Guided Caliphs

After the Prophet Muhammad, no-one could inherit the mantle of prophethood. But his four closest companions who took over the leadership of the Muslim community came to be known as al-Khulafa ar rashidun, or the 'Rightly Guided Caliphs'. The term 'Rightly Guided' signifies their actions are accepted by all Muslims as closest to the Prophet's example. After him, their words and actions are the most authoritative source on Muslim behavior.

THE DEATH OF the Prophet in 632 AD made the question of who should lead the Muslim community a matter of urgent discussion and debate. As usual, people gathered at the Prophet's Mosque in Medina. A number of prominent persons suggested that Abu Bakr, the closest associate and friend of Prophet Muhammad, should be asked to take over the political leadership of the community. The matter was settled by the unanimous election of Abu Bakr.

Abu Bakr

The speech Abu Bakr made on his election as the First Caliph of Islam has reverberated as an ideal in Muslim consciousness ever since: 'O people, I have been chosen by you as your leader, although I am no better than any one of you. If I do good, give me your support. If I do any wrong, set me right... The weak among you are the powerful in my eyes, as long as I do not get them their dues. The powerful among you are weak in my eyes, as long as I do not take away from them what is due to others... Obey me as long as I obey Allah and His messenger. If I disobey Allah and His messenger, you are free to disobey me.'

Abu Bakr was, like the Prophet, a merchant from Mecca. After his election he continued to go to the market to trade cloth. He was assured by Umar, soon to be his successor, that it was no longer necessary for him to pursue his trade and that the public treasury would provide him with a 'middling pension.' His stipend included one garment for winter, one for summer, and a daily allowance of lamb for food.

Two years younger than the Prophet, Abu Bakr served as Caliph or leader for just over two years; he died in 634. He had to deal with the many groups across Arabia who regarded their allegiance as given personally to Prophet Muhammad. He moved swiftly to reassert unity, seeking to make the bonds of common religion predominate over kinship. This included tackling economic revolts by groups who refused to pay *zakat*. The second aspect of his caliphate was expansion beyond Arabia. Expeditions were launched both to Syria and Palestine, then part of the Byzantine Empire, and Iraq, part of the Persian Empire. In 634 a Byzantine (Eastern Roman Empire) Christian force was defeated at the Battle of Ajnadain, 30 miles south west of Jerusalem, the remnant of their army falling back on the heavily fortified city. Most of the Palestinian cities submitted to the Muslim forces. On the Persian front inroads had been made into Iraq and an as yet inconclusive campaign against Persian forces was under way.

In 634 the ailing Abu Bakr consulted with senior Companions of the Prophet and nominated Umar ibn al-Khattab to be his successor. Their approval was readily granted and Umar became the Second Caliph of Islam.

Umar

Umar, Caliph from 634-44, was the first to adopt the title of Amir al-Mu'minin, Commander of the Faithful, which was retained by all later Caliphs. At the time of his accession Muslim forces were laying siege to Damascus, which surrendered in 635. In 637/8 Jerusalem was on the point of surrender, but its citizens insisted they would capitulate only to the Caliph himself. Umar traveled from Medina and the

The Rightly Guided Caliphs

Jerusalemites were amazed to see their new ruler arrive barefoot, poorly dressed, after a journey on which he had taken turns riding his camel with the one servant who accompanied him. Umar proclaimed that those who submitted to Muslim rule would have their lives, property and places of worship protected. This became the accepted precedent that laid the foundation for the heterodox nature of the new empire. Muslim forces were also engaged in Iraq. By 640 the campaign against the Persians concluded with the collapse of the Sassanid dynasty, most of their territory coming under Muslim rule. The coastal cities of Syria and Palestine, supported by forces from Alexandria in Egypt, were taken the following year. The victorious Muslim commander, Amr ibn al-As, then moved on to invade Egypt which was conquered by 642.

This vast territory needed a system of administration. Umar was largely responsible for establishing the form and character of this system. He introduced a highly developed fiscal system in which the public treasury raised revenue through personal and property taxation. The *kharaj* was a tax calculated according to the productivity of the land; the *jizya*, a personal tax paid by non-Muslims. During Umar's time Muslim forces were not permitted to become landowners in the newly acquired territory. Muslims, of course, were required to pay *zakat*. This distinction is the basis of what later came to be known as the *dhimmi* status, from *ahl ad dhimmah*, the category of 'protected people'. It is a matter of considerable controversy between Muslim and non-Muslim commentators. The controversy is whether non-Muslims were second-class citizens. Muslim scholars argued that as non-Muslims were exempt from military service, the *jizya* was largely a tax in lieu of military service. At the outset the various *dhimmi* communities were granted a degree of autonomy and their religious leadership was responsible for the collection and payment of their taxes to the administration.

Umar standardized the disbursement of state income. The customary practice of dividing the spoils was replaced by a *diwan* or registration of the Arab Muslims who were paid a proportionate pension, even down to slaves and children. He thus established that all citizens had a claim on the resources of the State. That those in need, whether Muslim or non-Muslim, had a right to assistance by state funds was a basic Qur'anic proposition. He organized the territory into a series of provinces and appointed a Governor for each. Living a simple even austere life himself, Umar was concerned at the potential consequences for Muslim forces occupying the wealthy and grandiose cities of the Middle East.

In 637, after his commanders sacked the Persian capital, Ctesiphon on the banks of the Tigris, some 20 miles southeast of where Baghdad would be founded in 763, he ordered a military camp to be made outside the town. Kufa, the site of this camp, developed into a city. It became famous as a center for the study of Arabic grammar and the distinctive geometric script of writing Arabic known as *Kufic* derives its name from this new city. Establishing cities became a pattern. When Muslim forces conquered Egypt in 641-2 they founded the city of Fustat, which continued to be the capital until 973 when it moved to Cairo (founded in 969). Muslim territorial advance proceeded with the building of new cities; Muslim civilization was an urban culture, a culture of the *medina*, the generic term for a city.

In 644 Umar was murdered by Feroz Abu Lu'Lu'ah, a disgruntled Persian servant of the Governor of Basra. The servant's complaint over taxation had been dismissed and in retaliation he stabbed Umar while he was gathering worshippers for morning prayers in the mosque of Medina. Fatally wounded, Umar appointed an Electoral Council of seven Companions of the Prophet to choose his successor. He ordered the Council to consult the chiefs of all the clans as well as prominent members of the Medina community and reach a decision within three days. The Council chose Othman bin Affan, then nearly 70 years old.

Othman

Othman had been doubly Prophet Muhammad's son in law. He had married Ruqaiya and after her death Umm Kulthum; neither daughter survived the Prophet. It is during the 12 years of Othman's Caliphate that tensions within the Muslim community came to the fore, organized along principles that over time came to identify different schools of thought, different factions and trends within the Islamic community.

Territorial expansion was consolidated during Othman's Caliphate. Attempts by Byzantium to recapture Egypt were repulsed. Byzantine power however still continued to pose a threat because of its sea-power. In response a Muslim navy, founded in 649, was developed. The shipyards of Egypt and Syria were operated in a collaborative effort between the Muslim forces and the indigenous Christian seamen. In the year of its founding a naval attack was launched on Cyprus. In 653 Cyprus was again attacked and Rhodes was also captured. In 655 the Byzantine navy suffered a disastrous defeat at the hands of Muslim sea-power. With Egypt secure, advances were made further across North Africa. In the east, around 650, Muslim forces pressed forward into Khursan, the easternmost region of the Persian Empire, advancing into what is today Afghanistan.

Othman's single greatest achievement was the production of an authorized written Qur'an, completed by 652. But he was accused of nepotism in appointing members of his own clan as provincial governors and to key administrative posts. While Othman himself led a simple life there was growing concern the enormous riches generated by conquest were having a

corrupting effect on the administration. Some argued that the riches gathered should all be spent on charity. There was resentment at the despotism of the Umayyad officials, members of the aristocratic Umayya clan of Mecca, to which Othman himself belonged. The widely dispersed armies became a seedbed of discontent and sedition. There were revolts in Kufa, Basra and Fustat. Muhammad, son of the first Caliph Abu Bakr, led a group of insurgents from Egypt and besieged the Caliph in his house in Medina. Breaking into the house they murdered Othman as he sat reading the Qur'an.

Othman left the question of his successor completely open. The rebels put pressure on Ali, the cousin of the Prophet, to become the next caliph. Despite the fact that Ali was ready to swear allegiance to other contenders he was persuaded to become the Fourth Caliph of Islam.

Ali

Ali ibn Abi Talib was elected Caliph in 656. He had married the Prophet's daughter, Fatimah, who died a few months after her father in 632 or early 633; the couple's children were the only direct descendants of the Prophet. The five years of Ali's Caliphate were marked by internal conflict. There had been those who from the death of the Prophet maintained Ali should have been his successor. Others, including Umar, were said to have been fearful of establishing a dynastic principal. Horror at the murder of Othman and then Ali's failure to punish the culprits also divided the Companions of the Prophet.

Two notable members of this group, with the support of the Prophet's widow Aishah, led an open revolt. It was defeated in the Battle of the Camel near Basra in Iraq (656), so called because the fiercest fighting took place around the camel ridden by Aishah. Aishah was captured and taken back to Medina where she renounced politics and continued to live in the precincts of the Prophet's Mosque. Ali then made his capital at Kufa; Medina was never again to be the center of government. The decision to engage in battle with fellow Companions alienated sections of the community.

Ali's accession was again contested, this time by Mu'awiya, the powerful Governor of Syria and a relative of Othman, who sought to maintain the interests of the Umayyad clan. Mu'awiya had governed Syria for 20 years and built up a large and loyal army. The rival claimants to the Caliphate met in a protracted battle at Siffin in Iraq (657). When Ali appeared on the point of victory he was forced by his army to agree to arbitration based on Qur'anic law. The armies returned to base, while two arbitrators, one selected by each side, met to deliberate the matter early in 658.

What divided the community were questions about the meaning of authority and legitimacy, the nature and meaning of leadership, how God's Will was to be understood as working within human society, especially its institutions of leadership. These matters of dispute raised other questions concerning the nature and actions of the community, whether it was fulfilling its moral and ethical duties, and how it would rely on God's Word, what it meant to be a Godly community. The questions were political, philosophical and theological.

The issues raised were by no means settled. The arbitrators decided both claimants to the Caliphate should stand down and a new election be held. This solution was no solution and only increased the bitterness between the factions. Some who had supported Ali then seceded and became known as the *Kharijites* (secessionists). They considered that Ali had diminished the Caliphate by agreeing to arbitration. The Kharijites went on to develop a radical political and theological position. The Muslim community had the right to depose or even assassinate a caliph deemed guilty of a grave sin, political or other, they argued. Furthermore, they suggested such grave sin called into question the status of the sinner as a true Muslim who therefore could be regarded as an infidel (*kufr*) and deserving of death. The Muslim community, they asserted, had the right to select whomever it wished as leader, whoever dealt with the people according to the precepts of justice and injustice was the rightful Imam, or Caliph. Ali moved swiftly to suppress the group in a bloody massacre at Nahrawan in 658. The Muslim world or Empire was effectively split. Mu'awiya continued to govern independently in Syria where, in 660, he proclaimed himself Caliph in defiance of Ali.

The Kharijites were not eradicated; indeed their ideas recur in many guises throughout Muslim history. In 661 they planned to assassinate the three most prominent leaders of the community: Amr, Governor of Egypt, Mu'awiya, Governor of Syria, and Ali. They succeeded only in the case of Ali, who in early 661 was murdered as he entered the mosque at Kufa for morning prayers. He was buried in a spot some miles from Kufa, where the town of Najaf later developed as a major pilgrimage center for those who adhered to his party, the Shi'at Ali, more commonly known as the Shi'a.

The death of Ali was an abrupt rupture in Muslim history. The ferment of this period stimulated a variety of trends of thought as well as the growth of factions that continued to divide the Muslim community, and do so today. There had been four Rightly Guided Caliphs; each had acceded by a different means. They had established many precedents that all Muslims accept as authoritative, but not on the question of leadership itself. And this question was leading the Muslim community towards the tragedy of Kerbala – one of the seminal events of the formative phase of Islamic history.

Kerbala

The Muslim community was now divided into three groups. The majority wanted political leaders to be elected or selected according the principles established by Abu Bakr and Umar. A minority favored hereditary rule by the Prophet's family. And an even smaller, secular minded minority, with political ambition and military might, sought simply to usurp authority. The politically ambitious won.

On his father's death, Ali's son Hasan was declared the legitimate Caliph. He was persuaded by Mu'awiya, who had already declared himself Caliph, not to plunge the community into further conflict. Hasan abdicated and retired from politics, living in Medina where he died in 669, allegedly poisoned. As the sole ruler, Mu'awiya then moved to re-establish the Empire and moved the capital to Damascus, his powerbase. Internal friction had been accompanied by continued hostilities with the Byzantine Empire. As civil war was suppressed, often ruthlessly, renewed attention was turned to external problems and expansion of the Empire resumed after a 10-year hiatus. Exploratory raids were made from Egypt across North Africa. The garrison town of Qairouan, in modern Tunisia, was founded in 670: later it developed into city and became a leading center of education. In the same year the first Muslim assault on the Byzantine capital, Constantinople (now Istanbul), was made. Successive attacks were made over the centuries, but the city did not finally fall into Muslim hands until the Ottoman conquest in 1453.

In 679 Mu'awiya nominated his son Yezid his heir apparent to succeed to the Caliphate. So it was the Umayyads in the person of Mu'awiya, the son of Abu Sufyan for so long leader of the opposition to Prophet Muhammad, who first put into practice the principle of dynastic succession. When Mu'awiya died the following year his son was acclaimed Caliph in Damascus. Many questioned Yezid's fitness to rule because of his dubious character, reopening all the varied political, spiritual and doctrinal questions about leadership. The questions were not confined solely to supporters of Ali, but the focus of alternative leadership fell on Hussain, the last surviving son of Ali, grandson of the Prophet.

Hussain took up arms against Yezid. At Kerbala, a short distance from Baghdad, Hussain and his 600 followers were besieged by an Umayyad army of 6,000. After fruitless negotiations lasting six days, during which his small force was trapped without access to water, Hussain finally rode out to meet the opposing army and was killed. Only two of his children survived the massacre that followed. The traumatic event of Kerbala established the Shi'a as the second major sect of Islam.

The Shi'a

After Kerbala the elaboration of Shi'a doctrine developed and diverged from that of the Sunnis. The term Sunni, derives from *Sunnah*, and is often translated as orthodox Muslims – these are the majority who supported the idea of an election or selection after the

murder of Ali. In contrast, the Shi'a believe in hereditary spiritual leadership known as *Imamate*. They hold
that Ali had a special spiritual function alongside the
Prophet which gave him an absolute right to succeed to
spiritual leadership, a right inherited by his sons. The
Imam is recipient of spiritual and political pre-emi-
nence by virtue of possessing special grace, miraculous
power and special knowledge. Shi'ism has developed
its own schools of thought, elaborate philosophy and
mystical tradition as well as schools of law.

There are numerous subdivisions within Shi'ism,
distinguished by the number of Imams each subdivi-
sion recognizes: the Fivers, known as *Zaydis*; the
Seveners, more familiar as the *Isma'ilis* whose leader is
the Aga Khan. Twelve-Imam Shi'ism became the official religion of Iran when the Safavid dynasty came to
power in 1501. After 500 years Iranian Shi'ism has
built up the most organized and developed body of
theory and practice. Iranian Shi'ism permits a much
stronger tradition of authoritative interpretation by
religious scholars, known as *mujtahids*, from among
whom individuals who have attained a certain degree
of knowledge are recognized by the community as
ayatollahs. This has permitted both an ongoing
process of *ijtihad*, reasoned struggle to reach contemporary interpretations of Islamic principle, and
greater flexibility in Shi'a thinking. Each ayatollah has
his own followers. When ayatollahs differ in their
interpretations and teaching, these differences are
binding only on those who have chosen to follow
them.

Shi'ism has remained a minority branch of Muslim
civilization accounting for only about 10 per cent of
Muslims. It was viewed with hostility by Umayyad and
later Abbasid rulers (descendents of one of Prophet
Muhammad's uncles, Abbas) who saw it as a potential
threat. But it is accepted as within the framework of
Islam by Sunni Muslims because of the acceptance of
the same basic principles and precepts. The concept

of consensus, keeping the community united and avoiding *bida*, innovation – that is, divergence from the example and practice of the Prophet – is central to the Sunni outlook. For the Sunni an imam is the term applied to the person who leads the congregational prayer, and therefore the term for an official of each mosque. Occasionally, it is an honorific for an especially eminent scholar, as in the case of Imam Bukhari, the compiler of one of the major collections of *hadith*. The issue of hereditary leadership, whether in empires, nation states or spiritual matters, is a debatable topic and not an accepted principle among Sunni thinkers.

The details of Hussain's death at Kerbala are re-enacted every year in the *Ta'iziyyah*, the Shi'a martyrdom play. The day of Kerbala, the 10th day of the month of Muharram, is known as *Ashura*. It was originally instituted as a day of fasting by Prophet Muhammad. Among the Shi'a it is a day of mourning and commemoration when certain groups parade the streets mortifying themselves with self-inflicted wounds as an expression of guilt for having abandoned Imam Hussain in his hour of need. Kerbala is the principal site of Shi'a pilgrimage. Many Shi'a place their heads on a tablet of Kerbala clay when they pray.

Under the Umayyads, Islam moved into an expansionary phase.

4 Expansion and empires

The rapid rise of Islam throughout the world has perplexed historians. The common belief is that Islam expanded through conquest. But trade and Sufi movements played an equally important part in its spread.

THE UMAYYAD DYNASTY ruled from 661-750. Their rule was despotic and unpopular right from the beginning. However, a great deal of the history of the Umayyads was written by their vanquishers, the Abbasids (749-1258) which may well contribute to the bad press they receive. The rebellion against Umayyad rule began in Khurasan in eastern Persia in 747, when Abu Muslim, a lieutenant of the Abbasid clan unfurled his banner reading: 'Leave is given to those who fight because they were wronged' (The Quran: 22:39).

The Abbasids moved the capital from Damascus to the newly created city of Baghdad in 762. Science, philosophy, medicine and education flourished under the Abbasids, who synthesized Persian learning with Greek heritage to fashion a unique Muslim culture. The Baghdad of Harun al-Rashid, who ruled from 786-809, is not only the setting of *The Thousand and One Nights*, the vision of a rich and splendid epoch, it is considered to be the Golden Age of Islam scholarship. The Abbasids were overthrown by the Mongol invasion of 1258: the Mongols ransacked Baghdad and burnt down its famous libraries. While the Abbasids claimed the Caliphate, the Muslim world was in fact no longer one empire. A network of regional empires had emerged, some making rival claims to the Caliphate while others offered it only nominal allegiance.

By the middle of the 8th century, Umayyad rule had already extended Muslim presence across the whole of North Africa. Territorial expansion of Muslim rule is one part of the creation of what is today called the Muslim world. The spread of Islam as the religion of the majority of inhabitants is a separate process that was seldom as complete; minority religions and communities continued to exist. 'Empire' is a loaded term in modern parlance. In history it is a varied, often negative but always complex development. However, the rise of a new system of political and territorial control often exploits pre-existing divisions and dissension.

What has been true of modern colonial empires is equally represented in the rise of Muslim Empires. For example, Muslim rule was welcomed in the heartlands of the Middle East where the oppressive regimes of the Byzantines and Persians created a population willing and ready to accept and co-operate with Muslim control.

On the other hand, the expansion of Muslim rule in North Africa met initial resistance from the indigenous Berber population, though they eventually adopted Islam and then spearheaded further expansion of Muslim territory. By 665 Muslim forces were using the Byzantine naval base at Jaloula, by 700 a naval base was established in Tunisia where 100 Egyptian families expert in boat-building were resettled. In 711, the Berber Tariq ibn Ziyad, commanding a large Muslim fleet and an army of 10,000, landed in the Bay of Algeciras in southern Spain. This force defeated the Visigoth King Rodrigo and moved on to capture Seville, Cordoba and in 713 Toledo. By 720 they had conquered all of the Visigoth territories to the north and south of the Pyrenees, the land the Muslims called al-Andalus. Muslim incursions into Europe were not confined to Spain. They extended into southern France: Narbonne, Nimes, Carcassone through Provence and the Rhone Basin. An incursion into France through Aquitaine was halted near Poitiers by the Battle of Tours in 732. This battle is seen by European historians as the highwater mark of the Muslim advance, a seminal event in European history even though it did not end the Muslim presence elsewhere in Europe. Al-Andalus, Muslim Spain, however, never encompassed the whole of the Iberian Peninsula and over the centuries was gradually eroded before the last Muslim sultanate, Granada, fell to the Spanish in 1492.

The Abbasid rule did not extend as far as Spain, where an Umayyad dynasty in exile was established. Other dynasties were established in North Africa. An Ismaili Shi'a dynasty, the Fatamid, emerged in 909 and ruled Egypt and parts of Palestine and Syria till 1171. They were replaced by the Sunni Ayyubid dynasty founded by Salahuddin al-Ayyubi. Better known to Europe as Saladin, he extended his rule from Egypt to Palestine and Syria from which he ousted the European enclaves established by the (Christian) Crusades (see chapter 6).

Another dynasty emerged in North Africa known as the Almoravids. Their name is derived from the Arabic al-Murabitun, meaning those who stand together for the defense of religion; the name and the dynasty originated as a religious revival movement. The Almoravids established their rule over a territory extending from Spain to the bend of the Niger River in West Africa. Muslim centers of learning in Spain were thus linked by the connective tissue of trans-Saharan trade to the university city of Timbuktu, in present-day Mali.

Umayyad expansion consolidated its hold on Persia and continued into the Caucasus, eastern Anatolia and Central Asia. From the province of Khurasan in eastern Persia they moved eastward along the trade routes to China establishing themselves, by 715, in Bukhara, Samarkand and Khwarizm, the modern Khiva in Uzbekistan. These cities of Central Asia were not only important centers of trade but also centers of learning that produced noted Muslim scholars. Imam Bukhari derives his name from the city of his birth,

Bukhara. The Turkic peoples of the steppes of Central Asia were renowned as soldiers and played a major part in the history of Muslim civilization. They also produced one of the most paradoxical institutions of Muslim civilization: the Mamluk dynasty. Literally the term Mamluk means 'one owned by another', a slave. They became a powerful fighting force employed throughout Muslim lands and went on to establish their own rule in Egypt in 1254. It was Mamluk forces that halted the advance of the Mongol hordes who sacked Baghdad. Mamluks continued to rule Egypt until 1517 when they were overthrown by the Ottomans, by which time they had become a landowning class.

The Ottomans emerged from Anatolia, taking their name from Osman, the founder of their dynasty, who was born in 1280. In 1301 an Ottoman force defeated the Byzantines at Nicea and began expanding into Byzantine territory in Eastern Europe. In 1369 they conquered Adrianople, the modern Edirne, on the European mainland. It became their capital and that meant the beleaguered city of Constantinople was surrounded. From their base in Europe the Ottomans advanced into Macedonia and Bulgaria. Their victory at the Battle of Kosovo in 1389 established their position in the Balkans. In 1453 Mehmet II, known as The Conqueror, finally took Constantinople – an event that sent shockwaves across Europe. Mehmet II went on to Bosnia, swept on through Greece and launched raids against Italy that had the Pope preparing to flee Rome – the threat subsided only with the Mehmet's death. Under Suleiman I, known as The Magnificent, Ottoman forces took Belgrade in 1521, overthrew Hungarian resistance at the Battle of Mohacs in 1526 and in 1529 arrived at the gates of Vienna. In this general advance they had captured Rhodes and established their sea-power throughout the Mediterranean. The era of Suleiman the Magnificent, 1521-1566, was the pinnacle of Ottoman victory in Europe. Under

Expansion and empires

Ottoman rule the Orthodox Church continued to operate while Islam gradually spread among the population of the Balkans.

Islam spread to Persia during the 7th century. The Abbasid Caliphs were impressed by the sophistication of Persian culture and adopted much of the protocol of the ancient Sassanid rulers. Persia was fought over and absorbed into the shifting pattern of empires established in the wake of the Mongol invasion. Stability was brought by the Safavid dynasty that ruled Persia from 1501-1732. The Safavid ruler Shah Abbas I made peace with the Ottomans, creating two great spheres of influence in the Muslim World. The Safavids became a major force extending the influence of Persian language and culture to territories to the east and into India.

In the west Ottoman supremacy continued to grow. It was the last dynasty to lay claim to the Caliphate. Sultan Selim I was ceded the title of Caliph after conquering Cairo, home of the last remnant of the Abbasid dynasty, in 1517. Their use of this title was viewed with considerable concern by European powers, especially by Britain which feared the emotive hold of the concept on the Muslim peoples it ruled, especially in the Indian subcontinent. British officials, backed by a battery of Orientalist scholars devoted great efforts to arguing for the illegitimacy of Ottoman claims to the Caliphate. The Ottoman Caliphate was ended by Turkish modernizer Kemal Attaturk in 1924.

The complex pattern of dynasties and the varying territories over which they ruled is only one part of the history of the Muslim world. Another way to approach the complex of geography and culture that is Muslim civilization is to follow the spread of Islam as a religion. The markets of the great cities of the Middle East were the hub of long distance trading routes extending over all the known world. Along these arteries of human contact, Islam spread

Major Muslim dynasties

The Umayyad	661-750
The Abbasids in Baghdad	749-258
The Abbasids in Cairo	1261-1517
The Spanish Umayyad	756-1031
Various Mamluk dynasties in Spain	1010-1205
Almoravids and other dynasties in Spanish city states	1090-1492
The Idrisids of Morocco	789-926
The Rustamids of Algeria	777-909
The Aghlabids of Algeria and Sicily	800-909
The Murabitun of North Africa and Spain	1056-1147
The Sharifs of Morocco	1511-??
The Ayyubids of Egypt, Syria and Yemen	1169-1462
The Mamluks of Egypt and Syria	1250-1517
The Safavids of Persia	867-1495
The Seljuqs of Iraq and Persia	1038-1194
The Ismaili Assassins of Alamut	1090-1256
The Seljuqs of Anatolia	1077-1307
The Safavids of Persia	1501-1732
The Ghaznavids of Afghanistan and India	977-1186
The Ghurids of Afghanistan and India	1000-1215
The Delhi Sultans	1206-1555
The Mughal Emperors	1526-1858
The Ottomans	1281-1924

through the agency of Muslim traders, peacefully and organically to many regions of the globe. Traders were often followed by Sufi mystics who established their own network of mystic circles. Where Islam was established new polities, states and regional dynasties were added to and became integrated with that complex whole referred to as the Muslim world.

China

As Umayyad power was moving eastward, the T'ang Dynasty in China was expanding its territory westward. The two forces met in the only direct confrontation

between Muslim civilization and China, the Battle of
Talas River, in today's Kyrgyzstan, in 751. The Muslim
forces emerged victorious. The Battle coincided with
the fall of the Umayyads and the establishment of the
Abbasid dynasty, whose main priority then became
securing their position in the Middle East. There was
no military impetus to move eastward into China. The
Battle of Talas however had a seminal impact on the
development of Muslim civilization, one more important than dynasties and the control of territory.
Among the Chinese captured in the battle were arti-
sans who knew the technology of paper manufacture.
This technology was avidly embraced by the Muslims.
Samarkand became a noted center of paper-making
and export. The industry was established in 793 in
Baghdad, which became famous for its large publications industry.

Though Muslim forces made no further territorial
expansion, Islam spread along the trade roads into
China. The westernmost province of today's China,
Xinxiang, is almost entirely Muslim. The land routes
through Central Asia were not the only means by
which the Muslim world and China remained in con-
tact throughout their history. The sea routes of the
Indian Ocean also brought Muslim traders to China.
By the 9th century it is estimated there were 100,000
Arab merchants in the southern Chinese seaport of
Canton (now Ghuangzhou) alone. Under the Sung
Dynasty (960-1279) the office of Director of Shipping
was always held by a Muslim. Apart from trade,
Muslim scholars were also openly welcomed in China;
there was an exchange of ideas in science and technology between the civilizations. Under the Ming
Dynasty (1368-1644) Islam was gradually integrated
into Chinese life to produce a distinctive culture out-
wardly Chinese but adhering to Islam. In the early
part of the 15th century, when Ming China began to
launch its own series of trade missions to the West visiting ports in Southeast Asia and India, the enterprise

was under command of the Chinese Muslim Admiral, Cheng Ho.

India

The Umayyad expansion into Central Asia took Muslim forces to Afghanistan and in 712 they invaded Sindh, establishing themselves throughout the region to the west of the Indus River in what is today Pakistan. In 994 the Ghaznavids, a Turkic people whose name derives from the city of Ghazna which eventually became their capital, established a regional empire that extended from the eastern areas of today's Iran through Afghanistan and modern-day Pakistan. It was Mahmud of Ghazni who in 1000 launched Muslim expansion into northern India. In this initial phase Muslim forces were predominantly engaged in seasonal raiding into India, though in some localities they established more settled rule. Muslim political authority in North India was not consolidated until 1206 with the foundation of the Delhi Sultanate.

The history of Islam in the Indian subcontinent is complex. Trade across the Indian Ocean brought Muslims to the ports of the Malabar Coast on the west of India, where Islam had begun to spread by the end of the 700s. This was a region outside the orbit of Muslim-ruled territory in the northern Gangetic Plain. The Hindu-ruled South Indian kingdom of Vijayanagar which developed after 1340, for example, came to rely on Muslim soldiers as the backbone of its army. Sufi mystics found resonance with Hindu mysticism and Islam spread rapidly through mystical groups.

Cultural interaction also produced a cross fertilization of knowledge in science, technology, arts and crafts, literature and philosophy. This process was well underway before the rise of the Mughal Empire in 15th century. Muslims from many parts of the world traveled to and settled in India. The great 14th century Muslim traveler Ibn Battuta served as a judge in Delhi, as well as in the Maldive islands on journeys that took him to China. Muslim civilization was a creative conduit through which Indian ideas traveled outward and India received ideas and contacts with the rest of the world.

The Mughal Empire represents the last great fluorescence of Muslim culture in the Indian subcontinent. It was founded by Babur, 1483-1530, a descendant of Timur on his father's side and Jenghiz Khan on his mother's, who became ruler of Ferghana in Central Asia at the age of 11 and conquered Samarkand at the age of 14. He lost both possessions before setting off for Afghanistan where he seized Kabul and Qandahar before overthrowing the Sultanate of Delhi and establishing his rule in India. His descendants expanded Mughal rule over much of India. The last Mughal ruler, who by then had little real power, was deposed by the British in 1858. Today Muslims make up about 12 per cent of India's population. This places India high in the table of countries with the world's largest Muslim populations.

Southeast Asia

Islam spread to Southeast Asia almost exclusively through trade and scholarly contacts. The Malay world – the islands of Indonesia and peninsula Malaysia – was the place where the various branches of the extensive Indian Ocean trade met. Traders came in search not only of spices but also tin, precious metals and the other produce of this rich and varied region. The Indianized states of Majapahit and Sri Vijaya on Java were centers of Hindu and Buddhist learning long before the coming of Islam. The regular monsoon winds that brought traders to this region meant they had to remain for a period of months before a change in wind direction enabled them to make their return journey. It is through this pattern of regular, often extended interaction that Muslim

Largest national Muslim populations

Country	Number of Muslims
Indonesia	170,310,000
Pakistan	136,000,000
Bangladesh	106,050,000
India	103,000,000
Turkey	62,410,000
Iran	60,790,000
Egypt	53,730,000
Nigeria	47,720,000
China	37,108,100

Sizeable Muslim communities

There are also sizeable Muslim communities in the following countries.

The US has an estimated 5.7 million Muslims – roughly equal to its Jewish population
France has an estimated 3 million
Germany has an estimated 2.5 million
The UK has an estimated 1.5 million
Canada has an estimated 0.5 million
Australia has an estimimated 200,000

traders and travelers introduced Islam to the Malays. By 1000, Muslim trading ports begin to emerge and by 1200 a Malay Muslim state was in existence in Aceh on the northern tip of the island of Sumatra. A succession of Muslim Malay states rose to prominence in succeeding centuries.

Africa

In the lifetime of Prophet Muhammad, as we saw, there was abundant contact between Arabia and the Horn of Africa. The Yemen had from earliest times been connected to Somalia, just as the Nile had connected Egypt to the Sudan since ancient times. Both these ancient connections provided means for Islam to spread organically through East Africa. After 900 Islam began to spread down the eastern coast of the continent into the region referred to as al-Zanj. It led to the establishment of a series of black African states in the coastal regions of Kenya, Tanzania – the name derived from the fusion of Tanganyika with the Muslim island of Zanzibar – as far south as Sofala in modern Mozambique.

These coastal trading states were in contact with the interior of Africa, from which they acquired such products as gold, ivory and slaves and to which they traded the produce of the whole Indian Ocean trading world. The trade in slaves was a feature of the ancient world that became a common practice in Muslim territory. As an institution little good can be said of slavery. However, there are significant differences between slavery within the ancient and Muslim world, where slaves were persons with minimal rights, and the chattel slavery, where they were purely property, shipped across the Atlantic to service the plantations of the Caribbean and the Americas. In no part of the ancient or Muslim world is a perpetual underclass of slaves or the descendants of former slaves found. The continued existence of slavery in certain Muslim countries in Africa, such as Mauritania, is less an anomaly than a disgrace.

The trans-Saharan trade routes linking the Mediterranean coast of North Africa with the riverine goldfields of West Africa below the great bend of the Niger river had also been in existence from ancient times. This was another artery along which Islam spread by organic means once the Berber and Tuareg traders who used these routes had embraced Islam. Trans-Saharan trade dealt not only in gold but also salt, hides and numerous other products. A series of black African states had been in existence since about the 5th century across the West African Sudan, the grassland region between the Sahara and the coastal equatorial forest region that derives its name from the Arabic *bilad al sudan* 'the land of the blacks'. The Dya'ogo dynasty of the Kingdom of Tekur in Senegal embraced Islam in 850. The gradual spread of the faith across this region became integrated into the life of the Empire of Ghana that existed on either side of the Niger river (not to be confused with today's Ghana). Muslims were widely employed in its administration.

Across the West African Sudan successive empires arose by fusing together and exerting central authority over differing stretches of territory composed of a network of cities and smaller regional polities. After the overthrow of Ghana, the Mali Empire founded in 1235, began its rise to prominence. At its height its rule extended along the Niger from the coast of Senegal to beyond the curve of the river where the major trading cities of Timbuktu and Goa were located, and on into the Saharan salt-producing areas. Its most glorious ruler, Mansa Musa, made the pilgrimage to Mecca in 1334. The Mali Empire began to dissolve under the rising influence of one of its vassals, Songhay which rose to prominence in the 1400s.

The great trading city of Timbuktu was founded around 1000. It was incorporated into successive regional empires but it was principally a city governed by its scholars. The city's most important institution was the Sankore mosque, which like so many great mosques across the Muslim world was also a university. Leo Africanus, the Muslim Moorish writer who was kidnapped by pirates and adopted by Pope Leo X had visited Timbuktu 1510-1513. The book he wrote while incarcerated in the Vatican after his abduction became Europe's principal source of information about the interior of Africa until the mid-19th century. Leo Africanus wrote of Timbuktu: 'Here there are many scholars, judges, priests and other learned men that are well maintained at the king's cost. Various manuscripts and written books are brought here out of Barbarie and sold for more money than any other merchandise.' Learning laid the basis for the civilizing influence of Islam, as described in the next chapter.

5 Civilization and learning

Islam produced a civilization with achievements in thought and learning, scientific development and philosophical sophistication that has few equals. Its enduring strengths were its civil society, institutions, and a way of living that defined the identity of Muslim people.

THROUGHOUT MUSLIM LANDS, dynasties produced noted rulers who, on occasion, were admirable, respected, learned and wise. Equally, they produced many a despot and tyrant who were ruthless and gave ample reason for all the political, spiritual and doctrinal questions about leadership to remain clearly in the minds of those they ruled.

However, from the period of the Rightly Guided Caliphs, scholars and thinkers were able to provide a framework of law and institutions within which civil society could operate and Muslim civilization could evolve. Study of the Qur'an and *Sunnah* for precept and precedent was the basis of the development of government, administration and the system of law. It also provided the model of domestic and family life, economic organization, and the modes of interpersonal behavior that shaped communities and even influenced the physical environment and ecological patterns in which they lived. The thought of Abu Hanifa, one of the founders of the Schools of Thought, provides a useful insight into the way of thinking that established the foundations of Muslim civilization. Abu Hanifa issued a statement of principles known as *Fiqh al-Akbar.*

> We do not consider anyone to be an infidel on account of sin; nor do we deny his faith.
> We enjoin what is just and prohibit what is evil.
> What reaches you could not possibly have missed you; and what misses you could not possibly have reached you.

We disavow none of the Companions of the
Messenger of God; nor do we adhere to any
of them exclusively.
We leave the question of Uthman and Ali to God,
who knows the secret of hidden things.
Insight in matters of religion is better than insight
in matters of knowledge and law.
Difference of opinion in the Community is a token
of Divine mercy.

After the bitter factionalism surrounding the end of
the era of the Rightly Guided Caliphs this endorse-
ment of legitimate differences of opinion set an
important marker. This, and similar declarations, also
clearly established the proposition that there were
moral and ethical limits within which thought, speculation and belief operated. Abu Hanifa declined to
serve as an Umayyad judge. This too was a precedent
for many religious scholars who kept themselves at
arm's length from authority. By maintaining their
independence scholars became a repository of critical
reflection on the leadership of Muslim society, custo-
dians of the ideals of Islamic justice in the face of
tyranny and despotism.

Classical Muslim scholars were obsessed with the
concept of knowledge, which they defined and redefined literally thousands of times, producing elaborate
classifications. They saw knowledge and education as
the bedrock of Muslim civilization. Education became
institutionalized in the *madrassa*. Literally meaning
'place of study' the actual *madrassa* was more a resid-
ence for students, the instruction normally taking
place in the mosques to which the *madrassas* were
attached. Wherever Islam spread mosques were built
and building *madrassas* was the function of rulers who
provided a pension for the students, this being a recognized use of *zakat* funds. These schools were also
sponsored by merchant and craft guilds and set up as
private endowments by individuals.

Civilization and learning

The specific function of the *madrassa* was higher education. Students were expected already to have mastered the fundamentals of the Qur'an and *Sunnah* and committed the whole of the Qur'an to memory. In its fully developed form, established by the 10th century, the course of study included logic, rhetoric and law; traditional systems of mathematics; grammar, literature and history; the calculation of prayer times; and Qur'anic exegesis and recitation. In some institutions medicine and agronomy were also taught. The *madrassa* student would receive a certificate, an *ijaza*, which served as a record of their course of study and qualified them to teach the specified works they had learned. In parallel with the development of the *madrassa*, institutions known as *jamia* or universities also emerged, offering courses organized in different *kuliya* or faculties. The teachers in the universities were known as professors – those who professed original knowledge – and sat on 'chairs', the students sitting on the ground below them in circles. The oldest university in the world still in operation is the Al-Azhar University in Cairo, Egypt, founded in 970.

The system of education that spread throughout the Muslim world provided scholars with a recognized intellectual passport. The personal history of innumerable Muslim scholars includes moving from the domain of one ruler to another and finding employment as a *qadi*, or judge. The 14th-century Tunisian Ibn Khaldun, often called the founder of sociology and famed for his studies in history, lived in turbulent times that forced him to move between Tunisia, Morocco and Spain. When he decided to perform the hajj he stopped en route in Egypt and served for a time as Grand *Qadi* of Cairo. During his employment he was dismissed and reinstated five times, not an unusual fate: the holder of the post regularly came into conflict with the wishes of the ruler. The hajj, the pilgrimage to Mecca, was a common reason for travel, and provided a meeting place for scholars from all parts of the Muslim world.

Early intellectual and scientific developments were stimulated specifically by the practice of Islam. For example, the question of how to calculate shares in inheritance, as required by the Qur'an, was an ethical ideal that had to be made into an operative system and led to the development of algebra. How to establish the precise date of the beginning of the fasting month of Ramadan by calculating the phases of the Moon determining the Muslim lunar calendar was another necessary inquiry. Another was calculating the direction of Mecca, called the *Qiblah*, to which Muslims turn during prayers, from any place on earth. Each of these problems led to innovations in mathematics, astronomy and trigonometry that laid the foundations of the intellectual achievements of Muslim civilization. 'Algebra' is an Arabic word, and the foundations of algebra were laid by al-Khawarizmi in the 9th century; his name is the derivation of 'algorithm'. He also wrote the first manual on the Indian system of reckoning, around AD 875. The concept of zero was first developed in India and then integrated into the mathematics of the Muslim world. Building on the work of al-Khawarizmi, the first book including an explanation of decimal fractions was written by Abu'l Hasan al-Uqlidisi in 952-3. The problems of the *Qibla* and sighting of the moon led the famous 10th-century astronomer al-Battani to develop the cosine formula and to the development of the planetary model of Nasir al-Din al-Tusi in the 13th century. Al-Tusi developed a special mathematical formula known as the *Tusi* couple which later enabled Renaissance scientist Copernicus to place the sun at the center of the solar system. Copernicus also relied on the work of 14th-century astronomer Ibn al-Shatir who made major advances in the calculations of orbits of planetary bodies.

While Muslim intellectual tradition derived its impulses from the fundamentals of Islam, it was actually founded in the context of the learning of many civilizations. The centers of classical learning of the Hellenized Middle East, Persia, India and China were known to Muslims not only through territorial expansion but also by trading contacts. Peoples from each of these civilizations, with knowledge of their languages, culture and history became Muslims. As Muslims they acquired a common language, Arabic, that enabled knowledge from non-Muslim traditions to circulate across the length and breadth of the Muslim world. Furthermore, Muslim civilization remained heterodox, a patchwork of multicultural societies where Christian, Jewish, Hindu and Chinese peoples lived side by side with Muslims, maintaining their own traditions of scholarship in their own languages as well as adopting Arabic.

A great enterprise to translate the heritage of the classical civilizations began towards the end of the 7th century. The Umayyad prince Khalid ibn Yazid, who died in 704, is credited with sponsoring the translation of medical, mathematical and astronomical works into Arabic. The first translations of Greek philosophical works, including those of Aristotle, are attributed to Abdullah ibn al-Muqaffa, who died in 759, or possibly his son Muhammad. The translations were probably made from Persian editions of Aristotle's works. The Abbasid Caliph al-Ma'mun placed the translation of Greek and foreign works in philosophy, science and medicine on an official footing by founding the Bayt al-Hikmah, the House of Wisdom, in Baghdad in 830.

The Bayt al-Hikmah sent missions to Byzantium to collect Greek manuscripts. It also housed a library, a successor to the Khizamạt al-Hikmah, the library of wisdom, founded by Harun al-Rashid, 786-809. Public libraries, free and open to all citizens, became a common feature of the great cities of the Muslim world. The Khazain al-Qusu in Cairo, for example, contained 1.6 million manuscripts in 40 purpose-built rooms.

At its zenith, Muslim civilization supported a truly monumental book publication and selling industry. One of the most famous booksellers was ibn al-Nadim who died in 995. In 987, he published the *Fihrist*, a catalogue, which sought to provide an annotated bibliography of all the books available in his shop, running to many thousands of entries (see box). Each entry noted the number of pages in the text so that purchasers could be sure they were not sold an abridged version. The *Fihrist* was more than a bibliography: it included a section on the alphabets of 14 different peoples with a preface on the distinctive scripts used by different languages. The topic headings of the entries give an overview of the literary wealth of Muslim civilization. They included the holy scriptures of Muslims, Jews and Christians; books on the religious doctrines of the Hindus, Buddhists and Chinese among other non-monotheistic traditions; grammar and philosophy; history, biography, genealogy and related studies; poetry; scholastic theology, *kalam*; law and traditions; philosophy of ancient sciences; legends, fables, magic and conjuring; alchemy; and sexual manuals.

The bookshops were often pleasant places where purchasers could examine books, order titles they desired that would be copied by the scribes working for the bookseller, as well as meeting places where purchasers could enjoy conversation and refreshments.

Education was a recognized application of the funds of the state treasury, the Bayt ul-Mal. Another important application was for health services. The study of medicine and the development of a health system was a further major development of Muslim civilization. Free hospitals were the basis of this system: the first was founded in Baghdad in 809, and soon no Muslim city was without one.

What distinguishes these institutions is that they were hospitals as we would understand the term today. They provided free medical care to anyone who needed it,

Al-Nadim on the catalogue of his book-shop

This is a catalogue of the books of all peoples, Arab and foreign, existing in the languages of the Arabs, as well as of their own scripts, dealing with various sciences, with accounts of those who composed them and the categories of their authors, together with their relationships and records of their times of birth, length of life, and times of death, and also the localities of their cities, their virtues and faults, from the beginning of the formation of each science to this our own time, which is the year 377 *hijrah* (987/88). ■

whatever their faith or origin. Patients were assigned to different wards according to the nature of their illness. They were teaching hospitals, places where students learnt clinical practice.

Medical education, as well as the training of pharmacists, was regulated and supervised by the state. The basic set of surgical instruments, that would be familiar to today's surgeons, was developed within this system. It is illustrated in the medical encyclopedia written by Aub al-Qasim al-Zahrawi (c 936-1013). The first treatise on smallpox and measles was written by Abu Bakr al-Razi (c 864-925), perhaps the greatest clinical doctor of Muslim civilization. Inoculation against smallpox became a common practice in Muslim lands. The Canon of Medicine written by Ibn Sina (980-1037) became a standard text for the next 800 years, not merely in the Muslim realm but throughout Europe.

While state funds were invested in education and health there was another major institution common throughout the Muslim world that supported these activities and many other charitable undertakings: *waqf*, which literally means a standing or stopping. A *waqf* is a trust, commonly land or houses, assigned in perpetuity to the state, the income generated from the property to be used for the public good. The *waqf* were administered by a separate government ministry, and the proceeds could fund mosques, schools, hospitals, orphanages and a host of other projects. Many research projects, as well as individual scientists and scholars, were supported by *waqfs*.

The state was also responsible for regulating the operation of markets, through the institution of *al-hisbah*, which ensured that weights and measures were properly maintained. Trade was the lifeblood of Muslim civilization as well as its connective tissue, aided by the introduction of a standardized currency. The prohibition of interest, *riba*, in the Qur'an, and its insistence on written contracts to ensure equity and justice made commerce and economic affairs a recognized department of Islamic law. The ethos of equitably sharing risk affected forms of contractual arrangements across the whole range of productive activity from sharecropping to establishing business enterprises. The operation of these principles throughout Muslim lands facilitated the development of economic activity and financial transactions over enormous distances. Cashing a check in a different country, far from being a modern innovation, is derived from the normal practice of the Muslim World, just as the word itself, check, is derived from Arabic.

The Bayt al-Hikmah founded in Baghdad was not a place but the model for an institution that was widely replicated. This development was not only important for its role in promoting translations, it also promoted an effective science policy, the development of experimental science as well as providing a forum where scientists met. Attached to the Bayt al-Hikmah were two astronomical observatories, one in Baghdad the other in Damascus. Soon a network of observatories spread throughout the Muslim lands. The most famous observatory was in Maragha where al-Tusi established an influential school of astronomers. The various Houses of Wisdom served as a meeting place for scholars, scientists, doctors, astronomers and

Some Muslim discoveries and inventions

Algebra
Algebraic variable symbols
Analytical geometry
Animal Rights charter
Astronomical observatories
Astronomical tables
Binomial theorem
Camera obscura
Carrying capacity of cities
Decimal notation
Experimental method
Glass making
'Golden Mean' in architecture
Gynecology
Hospital
Asylum for mentally ill
Laws of reflection and
  refraction
Logarithm
Mechanical clock
Number theory
Ophthalmology
Paint

Pendulum
Planetary orbits
Public lending library
Pulmonary circulation
Sociology
Solutions to higher-order
  equations
Specific gravity
Spherical geometry
Surgery
Surgical instruments
The guitar
The law of conservation of
  mass
The novel
The rotation of Earth on its
  axis
Treatments for meningitis,
  smallpox and numerous
  other diseases
Trigonometry
University

mathematicians. Each had its own library served by librarians and copyists. Lecturers were provided to teach all scientific subjects and their facilities were free and open to the public who were provided with ink, pen and paper.

Both chemistry and physics were established as experimental sciences by Muslim civilization. Chemistry – the word comes from the Arabic *al-Kimya* – was established by the 8th-century scientist, Jabir bin Hayyan. The works of Jabir (Geber in Latin) and his contemporaries, al-Razi and al-Kindi were full of technical knowledge to which modern industrial chemistry and chemical engineering owe a great deal. Physics was established by the 10th-century scientist Ibn al-Haytham whose work on optics is now considered to have made a major contribution. He correctly described rays of light traveling from an object towards the eye – the reverse of the standard opinion of ancient Greek scholars. He was also the first person to devise a *camera obscura* (a dark room or box into which light is passed through a double convex lens, forming an image of external objects on paper, glass and so on). In his *Book of the Balance of Wisdom*, al-Khazini (d 1121) wrote on mechanics, hydrostatics and physics. The book included a theory of gravity, identified as a central force directed towards the center of the Universe (ie the Earth) some centuries before scientist Isaac Newton (1642–1727) encountered his falling apple.

Observation and experiment were the basis of science, but the natural outcome of this very 'modern' approach was the practical application of learning and experiment to meeting the actual technological needs of society. The books of Muslim scientists show they made improvements in many aspects of agriculture, irrigation and the manufacture and refinement of numerous products and, through publication, stimulated further creative responses in technological development. Writing in the 9th century, the Banu Musa brothers produced their *Book of Ingenious*

Ibn al-Haytham on science

Truth is sought for its own sake. Finding the truth is difficult and the road to it is rough. For the truths are plunged in obscurity... It is natural for everyone to regard scientists favorably. God however has not preserved the scientist from error and has not safeguarded science from shortcomings and faults. If this had been the case, scientists would not have disagreed upon any point of science, and their opinions upon any question concerning the truth of things would not have diverged... A person studying science with a view to knowing the truth ought to turn himself into a hostile critic of everything that he studies... He should criticize it from every point of view and in all its aspects. And while thus engaged in criticism he should also be suspicious of himself. ■

From Ibn al-Haytham's *Critique of Ptolemy*, early 11th century.

Devices. Out of the hundred devices included in the book, seventy-five were of their own design. When al-Jazari, writing in the 12th century, published his influential *Compendium of the Theory and Practice of the Mechanical Arts* he made it clear he was not content merely to describe former designs. He praised the work of the Banu Musa brothers, but produced his own designs rather than merely following their ideas. Glass, ceramics, textiles and dyes, paper and ink manufacture and a diverse range of instrument-making as well as the development of water- and wind-power, oil-distillation and mining technology were among the subjects that benefited from the attentions of Muslim scientists.

Agriculture became a science in its own right, *ilm al-filaha*, and had an enormous impact on the life of the Muslim World. The interconnections of the Muslim sphere led to the diffusion of a whole range of new crops such as rice, sugar, cotton, hard wheat, eggplant/aubergine and watermelons from Spain to Transoxiana. Scientists studied soil conditions, climate and irrigation as well as the development of agricultural tools, crop storage and preservation, producing innovations that overturned the agricultural practice of the ancient world. The Muslim agricultural revolution introduced new crop rotation and growing seasons. The technology of seeking water and water utilization were vastly expanded as was the land available for cultivation. By the 11th century Spanish agronomists were carrying out research and experimentation in the royal botanical gardens in Toledo and Seville. Agricultural manuals were widely published containing detailed studies of appropriate manures for different soils and crops.

Science and technology as well as Islamic precepts also had a profound effect on the built environment in which Muslim peoples lived. Muslim civilization advanced by building new cities and the glories of Islamic architecture from Cordoba to Istanbul, Agra to Samarkand are a visible legacy. But the impact extended much beyond the investment in grand buildings and concerned ideas about town planning based on carrying capacity, zoning of industrial and productive activities to avoid pollution of water sources, and provision of social amenities and services to the urban population. Study was made of the use of light and environmental conditions to provide natural heating and cooling of buildings. *Harams*, inviolable areas outside towns and cities, near watercourses and other areas were established where development was prohibited. A second concept concerning areas where development and exploitation were prohibited, *hima*, was developed solely for the conservation of wildlife and forests.

The moral and ethical precepts of Islam were an active ingredient in the approach to all subjects, including science. Ibn Sina for example wrote of poisons but regarded experimentation with such substances as unethical. Ethics also lent a distinctive style to Muslim works. The normal form of a book would begin with a reprise of the opinions of the leading authorities on a subject before the critique and addition of the opinions of the writer. The exposition of ideas was cast in phraseology and terms of reference making explicit reference to Islam and giving prominence to intellectual humility, what was known and humanly possible to know was circumscribed by human ignorance.

The most characteristic figure of Muslim scholarship was the polymath, the sophisticated scholar whose interests and expertise ranged over a diversity of fields. Jabir bin Hayyan, for example, not only established chemistry, he also wrote on religion and philosophy, medicine and astronomy. The mathematician al-Khawarizmi was also an astronomer and geographer who corrected in detail Ptolemy's map of the world and made original contributions related to clocks, sundials and astrolabes. The 9th-century scholar al-Kindi is renowned as the father of Islamic philosophy yet he was also a mathematician, physicist, physician, and geographer who wrote a treatise on music. Al-Farabi, the 9th/10th century commentator on Plato and author of *The Perfect State*, was an encyclopedist who contributed to the fields of philosophy, logic, sociology, medicine and music. The 9th-century geographer al-Masudi (d 957) was also a physicist and historian. Omar Khayyam is noted as a poet; yet his major achievement was in mathematics where he was the first to solve equations with cubic roots.

Perhaps the greatest polymath of all was al-Biruni, who during the 10th and 11th centuries wrote 180 works of which 40 have survived. He was equally well-versed in mathematics, astronomical, physical and natural sciences, was an accomplished linguist, a distinguished geographer and historian, and a competent instrument maker who made a geared mechanical calendar. He could measure the specific gravity of certain metals correct to three decimal places and wrote a monumental study on India, its people, culture and history. His approach to learning bore the essential outlook of Muslim scholarship, being founded on careful observation and experiment, respecting the culture and customs of other people, and always emphasizing his humility.

The intellectual climate of Muslim culture produced an extensive literary culture of poetry and *belles lettres* as well as popular entertainment. Ibn Tufail (d 1185), a noted philosopher in his own right, as well as serving as Vizier at the Almohad court of Granada, wrote the first novel as we understand it today. *Hayy ibn Yakzan*, the story of a spontaneously generated individual who learns to recognize God through reason, was later translated into Latin and provided the inspiration for Daniel Defoe's *Robinson Crusoe*.

Where did it all go? The decline of Muslim civilization has perplexed both Muslims and non-Muslims alike. Conventional Western histories presume the

The 'Brethren of Purity' on Animal Rights

So it was not long before men had captured a number of animals and were keeping them for their own use and making them work for them. And they began killing some of them so they could cook and eat them. Occasionally some men would go out to hunt the wild animals who lived in the woods and forests, or would trap them so they could have their meat for food and their skin for clothing; sometimes they even hunted animals just for the pleasure and excitement of chasing after them and killing them.

The animals quickly realized how changed their lives had become since the arrival of men on their island. They talked to each other and compared the peaceful freedom in which they had been living with the harsh and cruel way man was now treating them.

From 'The Dispute between Animals and Man', one of the *Epistles of the Brethren of Purity*, published in the 10th century; translated as *The Island of Animals* by Denys Johnson-Davies, Quartet Book's, London, 1994. ■

inevitability of decline and write it backwards into the history of the non-Western world just as the inevitable rise and supremacy of Western civilization is assumed and projected forward. But the decline of Muslim civilization was as complex as its rise. Certainly, Islam contributed to its decline by losing the spirit of inquiry, and internal decay. However, the hostility of the West to Islam as well as colonialism also played its part in the downfall of Muslim civilization, as we see in the next chapter.

6 Islam and the West

The history of hostility and open conflict between Islam and the Western world is long and complicated. It gave rise to Orientalism, the specific way of describing, representing and controlling Islam. But there is also an equally long but hidden history of cooperation and coexistence.

RIGHT FROM ITS inception, Islam presented the Christian world with a 'problem' of three distinct dimensions. What was the purpose of the new revelation to an Arabian Prophet over 600 years after the crucifixion and resurrection of God's own son? This theological dimension had no counterpart in Islam. Christianity presented no problem to Islam as this contained within itself recognition of Christianity. Right from the days of Umar, the second Caliph, Muslims kept churches open and provided all the necessary guarantees for the survival of Christianity and its institutions. The strong military presence of Muslims on the borders of Europe produced the political dimension of the issue. Finally, the scholarly achievements of the Muslim civilization, particularly after the Abbasids, presented the intellectual dimension.

Europe responded to the problem of Islam with the Crusades, a series of religious wars lasting almost 200 years, from the end of the 11th to the 13th centuries. Towards the end of the 11th century, the Seljuqs of Asia Minor, who had already taken Jerusalem in 1071, were threatening the Byzantine Empire. Emperor Alexus I dispatched an envoy to Pope Urban II seeking military assistance. The result was the sermon preached by Urban at the Church Council of Clermont in November 1095. We do not know what Urban actually said, but we do know that his words struck chords with his audience. 'It is reasonably plain that he proclaimed that by undertaking an armed pilgrimage to Jerusalem the participants would not only bring succor to their Christian brethren in the East but would also acquire spiritual merit and earn themselves a place in paradise. Notions about pilgrimage, holy war, the threat to Christendom and the numinous sanctity of Jerusalem were not new: what the Pope did was to tie them all together in such a fashion as to make them irresistible to the unsophisticated piety of the Western European knighthood'.[1] Thus, knights as well as peasants, monks as well as children, began their march towards Jerusalem.

The First Crusade lasted four years (1095-99). Initially, Crusades were led by French and German peasants who began by massacring European Jews en route to Jerusalem but were easily defeated by the Muslims. The second force, consisting of four large European armies led by Godfrey of Bouillon captured Jerusalem in 1099. Thousands of Muslims and Jews were slaughtered; a Latin Kingdom of Jerusalem was established. The success of the First Crusade also brought political and economic interests to the fore. The Crusades then combined the idea of religious wars with wars of conquest. The Second Crusade (1147-48) led by Louis VII of France and Conrad III of Germany was aimed at the capture of Damascus. It failed. But it galvanized the Muslims who under Salahuddin al-Ayyubi ('Saladin') recaptured Jerusalem in 1187. In contrast to the Crusaders, Salahuddin treated the Christian inhabitants of the city with respect and dignity. The Third Crusade (1189-92) was led by the Holy Roman Emperor Frederick I and Richard I, the Lionheart, of England: that too failed. But the Crusades continued right up to the Eighth Crusade in 1270 and even included a Children's Crusade (1212) in which most of the children died en route to Jerusalem while the survivors were sold into slavery.

The Crusades played an important part in creating a European image of Islam and Muslims that has persisted to this day. The purpose of carefully constructed stereotypes based almost exclusively on hatred and self-imposed ignorance of Islam was to propagate and maintain the crusading spirit. Incredible stories about the Prophet Muhammad became popular throughout Europe. He was a magician who destroyed the Church in Africa and the East. He attracted new converts to his religion by promising them religious promiscuity. He died during one of his fits among a herd of pigs. Muslims, on the whole, were bloodthirsty, amoral and licentious. A whole genre of biography, epic poems and passion plays, known as *chansons de geste* (verses or songs of 'heroic' deeds) evolved to portray Islam and Muslims as the darker side of Europe. *The Song of Roland*, a French epic poem popular throughout the Middle Ages and one of the oldest of the *chansons de geste*, describes Muslims as pagans who worship a trinity of gods. It popularized the term 'Mahound' which was used by scholars and storytellers alike to describe the Prophet Muhammad as 'devil incarnate'. *The Song of Roland* begins:

> The king our Emperor Carlemaine,
> Hath been for seven full years in Spain.
> From highland to sea hath he won the land;
> City was none might his arm withstand;
> Keep and castle alike went down
> Save Saragossa, the mountain town.
> The King Marsilius holds the place,
> Who loveth not God, nor seeks His grace:
> He prays to Apollin, and serves Mahound;
> But he saved him not from the fate he found.[2]

Underlying the poem is the unspoken assumption that the world of 'Saracens' is a mirror-image of Christendom, structured in exactly the same way but inverted in every moral sense. Thus a valorous Saracen would have been an ideal *chevalier* (knight) had he been a Christian. When the hero Roland dies he offers his soul freely to the archangels. But when the Saracen Marsilius dies his soul has to be wrestled out of him by 'lively devils'. Such imagery sealed the perception of Islam as an ungodly and violent creed in the European consciousness.

The Crusades were the early precursors of colonialism. In Spain, for example, frontier warfare waged by the Christian kingdoms against the Moorish sultanates aimed to clear the land of its non-Christian inhabitants. Newly conquered territory became available for settlement by influxes of Christian colonists who often brought with them a new system of land use. The previous inhabitants who did not remove from the newly acquired territory were expected to convert to Christianity, the only recognized means to become full citizens of the newly enlarged Spanish territory. This ideology was not only exported to the New World, where it became the model for European settler colonies in the Americas, but became the cornerstone of the emerging European empires.

Colonialism

The process of European colonialism began in the Muslim world with the movement known as the *Reconquista*, the rolling back of Muslim territorial control in Portugal and Spain. It begins as an ideological movement explicitly understood by Europe as a clash of civilizations. The *Reconquista* was an alternate form of Crusade, equally backed by Papal decree along with the European military excursions aimed at wresting the Holy Land from Muslim control.

Knights from all across Europe came to the frontier wars in Portugal and Spain. Portugal completed its *Reconquista* in 1249, when Faro in the Algarve was taken. Among those who participated in the Portuguese *Reconquista* was John of Gaunt of England (who had initially set out to join a crusade to the Holy Land) thus creating the long-standing link with Portugal that eventually provided England with possession of Mumbai (formerly Bombay) in India. Mumbai was part of the dowry the Portuguese princess Catherine Braganza brought to her marriage to Charles II of England.

The Portuguese appetite for expansion then became insatiable. During the 14th century, the kings of Portugal sought no less than five Papal bulls (decrees) of Crusade for plans to conquer Morocco and Granada. Extending the logic which began with Urban II, these bulls provided justification for the overarching ideology of European expansion. The Bull *Dum Diversas* of 1452 granted to King Alfonso of Portugal set out the terms used by all European monarchs who authorized speculative voyages of exploration. *Dum Diversas* was the warrant 'to invade, search out, capture, vanquish and subdue all Saracens and pagans... and other enemies of Christ' whose property could be taken and their persons 'reduced to perpetual slavery'. It was written by Pope Nicholas V who was at the same time concerned with trying to establish a rapprochement with Eastern Orthodox Christianity (Byzantium) so that together they could renew the eastern Crusade against the expansionary Ottoman Empire. The following year, 1453, Constantinople fell to the Ottomans. Nicholas failed to stir Europe to another eastern crusade. The immediate beneficiary of the crusading impulse of a fearful Europe was Spain in its campaign against the last remaining Muslim sultanate, Granada.

In 1492 Granada fell to the victorious forces of Ferdinand and Isabella, the Most Catholic Monarchs of Spain. Weeks later they gave royal warrant to the Italian explorer Columbus for his voyage across the Atlantic. The day after Columbus set sail from Spain was the date by which all Jews were expelled from Spain, their property and lands having been confiscated. In 1502 the same fate befell Spain's remaining Muslim population. The Bull *Inter Cetera* granted to Ferdinand and Isabella in 1493 by Pope Alexander VI continued the terms of *Dum Diversas* by expressing the Pope's desire that 'all barbarous nations be overthrown'. It was a precursor to the negotiations that a month later produced the Treaty of Tordesillas by which the Pope divided the rights to exploration and acquisition of all newfound territory around the globe between Spain and Portugal.

The pace and form of colonialism differed from colony to colony and among the different European nations. Contending for colonial possessions and dominance in the trade it generated was the extension of European rivalries onto a global stage. The history of colonialism is most often written and viewed through the gaze of these European preoccupations leaving out the ramifications and impact on the colonized. The eastward expansion of Europe into lands of the Muslim world overwrites and obscures a long and crucial period when there was no clear inevitability to the rise of Europe. Europe achieved its footholds in the Muslim world not because of superior technology and enterprise, as is commonly believed, but in large measure as a result of knowledge acquired from Muslim civilization. European powers retained their footholds because they were tolerated as small-scale new arrivals within the diversity of a complex and long-established trading world.

Portugal arrived in India and promptly declared the Indian Ocean a closed sea where all trade would be policed by its armed galleons, a singular new development in the Indian Ocean. It was an effective offensive threat since Portuguese vessels designed for Atlantic waters rode higher in the water than Asian ships, so their guns could bear down on native ships. Portugal moved quickly to establish a string of strategic defensive enclaves and decreed that all shipping had to proceed to these ports to be licensed to trade: unlicensed ships were liable to attack. Goa in India became the Portuguese headquarters but its next major objective was possession of Melaka on the west coast of the Malaysian peninsula, the principal port of the spice trade, which was conquered in 1511. Melaka was the center of a trade network and its conquest was considered essential for controlling the trade routes of the Muslim world.

Portugal and Spain were soon joined by England, the Dutch and France, as well as other smaller powers such as Denmark and Sweden, in contesting for trade and territorial footholds. The English and Dutch East India Companies – John Company and *Jan Compagnie* – were formally established in 1600 and 1602 respectively. In Asia, Portuguese and Spanish dominance was challenged and eventually supplanted by England which became the dominant colonial power from the Persian Gulf through the Indian subcontinent to Malaysia, as well as in parts of Africa. Holland took that role across the Indonesian archipelago, and France was dominant in North and West Africa, as well as Indo-China. Bestirred by its opening to Europe from the late 17th century, Russia also began a colonial expansion from the Caucasus through Central Asia.

The varied movements of European colonialism had a gradual and diverse impact on the Muslim world. The ideology of colonialism that grew out of the crusading ethos was rooted in the perception of Muslim civilization as barbaric, tyrannical, inimical to Western civilization and implacably hostile. Despite the fact that, objectively, Europe was at least no more sophisticated, learned or technologically endowed than the Muslim world, the notion of Muslim civilization as decadent, mired in superstition, a faded glory and with a particular problem in its treatment of women became a recurrent theme in European literature of the 16th and 17th centuries. Muslim power as a direct and real threat to Europe, in the shape of Ottoman expansion in the Balkans and up to the gates of Vienna was exercised as the foundations of European empires were established among Muslim

peoples in Africa and Asia. The productive and technological potential of Asia was not overtaken by
Europe until the Industrial Revolution when the pro-
tectionist policies of European domestic economies
were allied to purposeful colonial destruction of the
industrial capacity of Asia and its single-minded conversion into production of primary goods to service
European industry.

India, Indonesia, Malaysia, Central Asia, Mauritania
and Senegal were areas where early trading footholds
gradually developed into full-blown colonies. Algeria
and Tunisia were invaded and reduced to formal
colonies. Morocco, while never fully a formal colony
was the scene of successive interventions by various
European powers and American interests before
becoming a formal French 'protectorate'. The interi-
or of Africa had long suffered the destabilizing ramifications of European activities on its coasts – the slave
trade – but escaped full-scale colonial intervention
until after the 1880s Berlin Conference that settled
the 'Scramble for Africa'.

In this, the continent was divided into areas for colonization by specific European powers, the zones having been established by 'scientific' and missionary
expeditions undertaken by their nationals. The 'scientific' interest in the 'search' for the source of the
Nile became a precursor to British colonial possession
in East Africa, while French success in the 'search' for
Timbuktu opened the way for French possessions in
West Africa. From Senegal, where they had been
ensconced since 1638, the French expanded across
the predominantly Muslim savannah zone into Mali,
Burkina Faso, Niger and Chad. They also formalized
possession of colonies in the Horn of Africa, in
French Somaliland and Mogadishu.

Britain expanded from the Nigerian coast into the
Muslim north of what is modern Nigeria, and formalized its East African colonies including Sudan, Kenya
and Tanganyika, Zanzibar, and part of Somalia.

Britain also became the dominant power in Egypt, where it sought to protect its interests in the Suez Canal route to India. This also explains the increasing British presence during the 19th century in Yemen, Oman and the Persian Gulf States. By the end of the 19th century only Afghanistan, Safavid Persia and the Ottoman Empire were technically independent of colonial control. However, many regions nominally part of the Ottoman Empire and Persia were subject to considerable European influence and intervention in their internal affairs.

Colonialism from the beginning of the 15th century to the First World War introduced new divisions in the Muslim world, divisions of language, economic dislocation and new forms of economic development geared to primary resource extraction. It affected civil administration, social affairs, education and had a devastating effect on intellectual life. How colonialism worked to disrupt indigenous economy and society varied, but consistently worked to comparable ends.

In the economic sphere, for example, a pattern was established that still persists to this day. In Indonesia the Dutch used brutal means to establish a monopoly over spice production on plantations they owned and operated by slave labor. This included destruction of all the spice-bearing trees of Halemera island in the Maluku (Moluccas) island group to force the local population to seek employment on Dutch-owned and operated plantations. The introduction of plantations dedicated to cash crops became a general European pattern of enterprise across the colonized world involving cotton, coffee and eventually rubber.

When the late 19th-century rubber boom took off, Malay smallholders in peninsular Malaysia were the most efficient producers. They were systematically prevented from entering the market in competition with British-owned large-scale plantations worked by imported Tamil laborers. In Algeria, the French invasion led to the best agricultural land being assigned to French peasant colonists, the *pieds noirs*. In Egypt, the Mamluk authorities tried to revitalize their economy through investment in new cash crops, building up the local infrastructure such as irrigation and railways while asserting their power in seeking greater autonomy from the Ottoman Empire. These undertakings were enthusiastically funded by European banks, building up a serious debt burden. A considerable part of the debt resulted from the building of the Suez Canal, and the concessions that formed part of that project. Reliance on cotton production, the dominant cash crop, meant the economy was dependent on the fluctuating world market price tied, in particular, to the needs of the British textile industry.

The resulting debt crisis led to Britain buying the largest shareholding in the Suez Canal. It also led to European oversight of the Egyptian economy. While Egypt fulfilled all its obligations in repaying its rescheduled debt, foreign intervention in its economy and society steadily increased, leading to local opposition and unrest. The turmoil included British and French support for undermining the democratic institutions that had had been introduced as part Egypt's reform process, fuelling further unrest. In 1882 Britain invaded Egypt, defeated the rebel force and backed a series of puppet regimes that meant Egypt was officially independent while the real power was held by a British agent and consul-general backed by British troops.

Colonial powers also worked consciously to destroy the intellectual and educational structure of the Muslim world. Universities and colleges were systematically closed; Islamic medicine was outlawed; and Islamic science was declared to be nothing more than superstition and dogma. In Indonesia, the Dutch banned Muslims from pursuing higher education; a ban that lasted till the 1950s. In Algeria and Tunisia, the French introduced the death penalty for the practice of Islamic medicine, leading to the execution of many *hakims*, Muslim doctors. In India, the British established a new system of education to create 'go-betweens' for the rulers and the ruled. As Lord Macaulay wrote in the famous Minute of Indian Education in 1835: 'We must at present do our best to form a class who may be interpreters between us and the millions whom we govern; as class of persons, Indians in blood and colour, but English in taste, in opinion, in morals, and in intellect'. [3] And so it went on.

The increasing impact of colonial intervention meant administering the lives of the indigenous Muslim population by European legal codes and norms. Throughout the colonized Muslim world, Islamic law remained in operation only in limited spheres of personal and family law. This bifurcation had consequences for the education and operation of Muslim *ulema*, the religious scholars, and worked to reinforce the conservational paradigm that was making itself felt as European intervention began. Islam became an effective rallying point for many resistance movements that opposed colonial encroachment.

The need to defend Islam was most effective as a call to support publicly accepted received authority, unquestioned tradition. External pressure reinforced and empowered the ossification of tradition. The more Islam was marginalized to operate only in the sphere of personal and family law the less impetus there was to apply the pressing questions of contemporary life to the scrutiny of the Islamic worldview. The subtle redefinition of Muslim education to the study of religion in a narrow sense, that had initially been more apparent than real, gradually became very real and highly apparent as the division between a modern sector created under the dominance of European power and a traditional sector that was everywhere marginalized. Internal trends in Muslim society worked to increase the distinctions between

traditional and modern as they redefined and solidi-
fied what was meant and taught as traditional Islam.

Orientalism

Colonialism gave a new lease of life to the essential
features of the medieval representation of Islam and
Muslims. During the period known in Europe as the
Age of Discovery, representation of Islam acquired a
coherent structure and became an integral part of
European scholarship across a new range of disci-
plines such as anthropology and political science. The
tradition and scholarship by which Western civilization represents and perceives Islam and Muslims
came to be known as Orientalism.

The term was made popular by the noted
Palestinian academic Edward Said, but it existed long
before the publication of his book *Orientalism* in 1978.
Within the literary conventions of 18th and 19th century colonialism, Said found a consistent set of ideas,
a cultural imperialist code by which the West
described, investigated and presented its view of the
East as fact, a function of the nature of the Oriental
who is knowable through neutral, objective scholarship. Said described Orientalism as an overarching
style of thought, with a history going back to antiquity, based on the ontological and epistemological distinction between the 'Orient' and the 'Occident'. It
was a particular 'Western style for dominating,
restructuring, and having authority over the Orient'.
Orientalism was a 'corporate enterprise' that used a
'system of representation framed by a whole set of
forces that brought the Orient into Western learning,
Western consciousness, and later, Western Empires';
'a way of coming to terms with the Orient that is based
on the Orient's special place in European Western
experience'.[4]

Said's concept of Orientalism is not a description of
its origins: as we have seen, these go much further
back in history. What substantiates Said's concept is a

coherent history of the transmission of a repertoire of ideas that has been documented by many writers. One can begin with the polemics of John of Damascus (c748 AD), a Christian scholar who was a friend of the Umayyad Caliph Yezid, who declared Islam to be a pagan cult and described Prophet Muhammad as a corrupt and licentious man. Then move forward to the production of propaganda and popular literature created to stimulate, explain and justify the Crusades. And next, move forward to the vast body of literature produced during the colonial period by scholars, travelers, and writers – known collectively as the Orientalists – that systematically represents Muslims as militant, barbaric fanatics, corrupt, effete sensualists, decisively inferior to the West; and Muslim lands a haven for sexual adventurers. Included amongst the Orientalists were the most respectable and noted figures of the Western civilization covering almost every field of human endeavor.

The scholars who specialized in Islam, and hence played a major part in giving intellectual respectability to racist ideas about Muslims, included Englishman Edward Pocock, the first occupant of the Chair of Arabic in Oxford and Simon Oakley, the 18th-century historian and author of *History of Saracens*. There was also George Searle, one of the earliest English translators of the Qur'an. The dominant theme of their works was hatred and open abuse of Islam. The first Chair of Arabic at Cambridge was established in 1632 and was occupied by William Bedwell. As a biographer of Bedwell has noted, 'The gratuitous venom which Bedwell expends on Islam at every opportunity, even in his dictionary, is striking in its intensity. A manifest exhibition of his attitude can be seen in the title *Mohammedis Imposturae* in the first edition, and *Mahomet Unmasked* in the second, with the recurrent title, "a Discovery of the manifold forgeries, falsehood and horrible impieties of the blasphemous seducer Mohammad: with a demonstration of the insufficiencies of his law, contained in the cursed Alkoran'".

But such venom was not limited to scholars of Islam. Many of the *philosophes*, the founders of the Enlightenment – including Voltaire, Montesquieu, Volney and Pascal – demonstrated the same trait. And, not to be outdone, philosophers such as Hegel, von Ranke, Ernest Renan and Oswald Spengler worked hard to show that Islam was totally devoid of thought and learning. Even Karl Marx had some disparaging and plainly racist things to say about Muslims. And adventurers like Richard Burton, the famous translator of *Arabian Nights*, Charles Doughty, author of *Travels in Arabia Deserta*, and E W Lane, who wrote *Modern Egypt* in 1834, added extra layers of exotica to the representation of Islam in the West. They described a treasure-house of magic and occult, astrology and alchemy, hemp and opium, snake-charmers, jugglers, public dancers, superstitions, homosexual dens, women ready to satisfy every sexual urge, supernatural beliefs and bizarre incidents that defied imagination. While a string of noted painters, from Jean-Auguste Dominique Ingres, Henri Regnault to Eugene Delacroix, developed a genre of Orientalist painting that placed barbaric Muslim men and sensuous, inviting and submissive Muslim women on the canvas. Colonial administrators like Lord Cromer of Egypt and T E Lawrence, aka 'Lawrence of Arabia' who in reality was a spy for the British, turned these images and representations into policies.

Orientalism was thus a wide-ranging enterprise concerned with almost every aspect of life. It served both as a justification of colonialism – why the Muslim rulers and population of that region were illegitimate and unfit occupants and possessors of the place – as well as a strategy to manage and control colonial subjects. It was not something that was based solely on ignorance; rather, as British scholar Norman Daniels has suggested, it was 'knowledgeable ignorance',

Orientalism on film

Lives of the Bengal Lancers (1935)
Northwest Frontier (1959)
Khartoum (1966)
Midnight Express (1978)
Jewel of the Nile (1985)
Iron Eagle (1985)
Delta Force (1986)
The Sheltering Sky (1990)
True Lies (1994)
Executive Decision (1996)
The Siege (1998)
Rules of Engagement (2000)

defining a thing as something it could not possibly be, when the means to know it differently were available. Orientalism acquired its authority by making Muslims incomprehensible yet predictable.

But Orientalism is not something that only existed in the past. It continues to this day; alive now as it ever was during the days of the crusaders and colonialists. Its basic codes and structures can be found in learned books as well the popular press. It finds its outlets in plasterboard movie villains as well as strategic political thinking. We can see Orientalism in action in films like *Executive Decision* and *Rules of Engagement* which present Muslims not just as terrorists but totally devoid of any kind of humanity. We can read Orientalism in the coverage by right-wing newspapers of such issues as 'refugee problems'; and in novels like Salman Rushdie's *The Satanic Verses* which caused such an uproar amongst Muslims when it was published in 1989. But most of all the concept inhibits, constrains and provides an edge of fear and discomfort in the relations between ordinary people, the non-Muslim and Muslim populations of Western nations. Racism and discrimination in towns and cities across Britain, Europe and North America exists not only in the attitudes and actions of an obnoxious extreme fringe, they can be implicit in the commonplace attitudes and information of well-meaning and well-intentioned nice, sensible people. The demonization of the Arab and Muslim community after the atrocities of 11 September 2001 in the US had all the hallmarks of Orientalist stereotypes.

Happily the relationship between Islam and the West is not only one of conflict, antagonism and distrust. There is also an equally distinguished history of collaboration.

Collaboration

The contacts between Muslims and Europeans during the Crusades were not all hostile. Many crusaders returned from the Muslim lands intellectually enriched and loaded with manuscripts. During the first renaissance in the 12th and 13th centuries, the time of philosophers St Thomas Aquinas and Roger Bacon, the transfer of knowledge, literature and culture was solely in one direction: from Islam to Europe. It was in this period that European students began to go to Muslim seats of learning to acquire higher education – just as Muslim students nowadays come to Europe and the US to pursue their higher studies. At the same time, Europe began a major initiative for translation of Arabic thought and learning into Latin and other European languages.

Right up to the end of the 15th century, translation from Arabic was the main intellectual task in Europe. Muslim thinkers including ibn Rushd, ibn Sina and al-Haytham, who had their names Latinized, became integral parts of the rise of knowledge and technological progress in European life. Thus, it was from Islam that Europe learned the very idea of reason and how to reason; Greek philosophy, experimental method, and much of its mathematics; and how to establish universities, set up public libraries and run hospitals. The crowning glory of Europe, liberal humanism, also comes from Islam. In short, Islam taught Europe the true meaning of civic culture and civilization.

The most shining example of collaboration is Muslim Spain. By any definition, Muslim Spain was a genuinely multicultural society; and the rise of individuals to a position of power and prestige depended largely on their learning and professional skills. Not surprisingly, it was a magnet for thinkers, scholars and learned people of Europe who came to study in Cordoba, Granada and Seville in droves. Muslim Spain was not only home to some of the greatest names of Islamic civilization it was also the place where Jews enjoyed their finest intellectual flowering since the dispersal from Palestine.

One of the foremost Jewish philosophers, Moshe ben Maimon, or Maimonides as he is generally known, was born in Cordoba in 1135. He codified Jewish doctrine in his *Mishneh Torah*; and his *Guide to the Perplexed*, written in Arabic, occupies a place in Judaism similar to the works of Thomas Aquinas in Catholicism. Andalusian Muslims did not consider Maimonides a 'Jewish' scholar. He was an integral part of the intellectual scene of Muslim Spain and, as such, was seen as a natural part of the Muslim community. The Jewish scholar Bahya ibn Pakuda, who lived in the 11th century, was deeply influenced by Sufi thought: his *Guide to the Duties of the Heart*, also written in Arabic, was an outcome of this encounter. The work became famous throughout the Jewish Diaspora. His contemporary, Solomon ben Judah ibn Gabirol, poet and neo-Platonic philosopher, also drank deep from the Sufi fountains of thought. His famous hymn, *Keter Malkhut* (Royal Crown), which concludes with a confession of sin that has been adopted for the Jewish Yom Kippur (Day of Atonement) service, contains deep echoes of ibn Arabi. The term used by the Spanish to describe the 'living side by side' of Jews, Christians and Muslims is *convivencia*: an experiment in collaboration that lasted over 800 hundred years.

Much of this history of collaboration and enrichment has been deliberately suppressed by Europe.

W Montgomery Watt, a noted Orientalist of the 20th century, suggested this was largely due to a 'feeling of inferiority' on the part of Europe. The suppression of the extent to which Islam shaped and influenced Europe as well as 'the distortion of the image of Islam among Europeans was necessary to compensate them for this sense of inferiority'.[5] It is high time this history was retold, recovered for the benefit of both the West and Muslim civilization.

Islam and the West

1 Richard Fletcher, *The Cross and the Crescent*, Allan Lane, 2003, p 78.
2 Translation by John O'Hagan; available on the Internet Medieval Sourcebook   http://www.fordham.edu/halsall/basis/roland-ohag.html
3 Michael Edwards, *Raj*, Pan Books, London, 1969, p 151. **4** E Said, *Orientalism*, Routledge and Kegan Paul, London, 1978, p 1, 3, 41-42.
5 W M Watt, *The Influence of Islam on Medieval Europe*, Edinburgh University Press, 1972, p 82.

7 Reform movements

The decline of Muslim civilization and the onslaught of European colonialism led to self-examination amongst Muslims, and the emergence of a host of revivalist and reformist movements.

COLONIALISM WAS RESISTED throughout the Muslim world. The 1857 'mutiny' in India, for example, was largely led by Muslims – the names of Tippu Sultan and Haider Ali, who led numerous campaigns against the British, are particularly associated with this history of resistance. In Indonesia, there were periodic rebellions against the Dutch. In northern Africa, the French were confronted with a strong resistance movement that culminated in the brutal Algerian war of independence (1954-62), portrayed in the famous 1965 French film *Battle of Algiers*. But along with resistance movements, colonialism also generated a host of reform movements concerned with the internal reform of Islam. These movements wrestled with the ideas of modernity and tradition and sought to revitalize Muslim society.

One of the earliest attempts to address the internal decay of Islam was led by Muhammad ibn Abd al-Wahhab (1703-1787). Apart from uniting the warring peoples of the Arabian Peninsula he preached a return to the basic purity of Islam. His writings argued against all forms of superstition and in particular devotional cults venerating saints which he regarded as placing intermediaries between the believer and God. He stressed strict observance of the religious duties of Islam. One might argue that ibn Wahhab was the Muslim equivalent of the spirit and temper of John Calvin in Europe's Reformation, and both became the guiding lights of states formed around their religious outlook.

Ibn Wahhab found a sympathetic follower in Emir Muhammad ibn Saud of the Nejd region of Arabia, centered near the present-day city of Riyadh in Saudi Arabia. The alliance of doctrine and political power was cemented by the marriage of ibn Wahhab to the daughter of ibn Saud and advanced by the introduction of firearms into desert warfare. Puritanical insistence on strict religious observance among their followers was matched by their willingness to regard opponents as heretics and apostates. This enabled them to declare jihad against fellow Muslims, which would otherwise have been impossible. The expansion of Wahhabi territory after the death of ibn Wahhab brought conflict with Ottoman authorities and Egypt in the early decades of the 19th century. Ibn Saud established the Kingdom of Saudi Arabia where *Wahhabism* is the dominant – indeed the sole – creed.

A contemporary of ibn Wahhab was Shah Wali Allah (1703-1763), the Sufi scholar active in India. Shah Wali Allah promoted a reformed and more assertive Islam. His writings drew upon all fields of Islamic study and sought to rethink the entire system of Islam in a spirit of objectivity. His emphasis on social justice combined with popular mysticism won him an enormous following. In West Africa, Usman dan Fodio (d 1817) began a reform movement dedicated to increasing knowledge of Islam, replacing superstition and tackling the corruption within Hausa society. The author of numerous works on Islam as well as poetry, Usman dan Fodio began a movement to bring social justice to ordinary people and was noted for his liberal attitude to the role of women in society and his dedication to improving female education.

His growing following was seen as a threat by the rulers of the Hausa states and led first to persecution of his followers and then open warfare. By 1809 Usman dan Fodio and his followers had established the Sokoto Caliphate exercising its authority over all the Hausa states after a war couched in the language of jihad. The ideas and example of Usman dan Fodio extended beyond the Hausa states and was part of a revival and reform movement all across the West African Sudan affecting the Bornu states, Chad, Mali and the Senegambia region where it became the backbone of resistance to the expansion of British and French colonialism. It is possible that Usman dan Fodio's writings and example extended even to slave populations in Jamaica and played a role in the major slave revolt on the island.

The Algerian Muhammad Ali as-Sanusi (1791-1859) founded a further reform movement. It was an admixture of ideas of Wahhabism with the esoteric practice and organization of Sufi orders, a curious combination. The *Sanusiyyah* movement was a politico-religious organization that became dominant in Libya where it spearheaded resistance to European encroachment. As-Sanusi's grandson became King Muhammad Idris of Libya. Another reform leader who expounded his message through the organization of Sufi orders was Muhammad Ahmad ibn Sayyid Abd Allah (1844-1885) better known as the *Mahdi* of Sudan. Muhammad Ahmad declared himself the Mahdi, the Divinely guided leader predicted by *hadith* who would come at the end of time. The *dervish* order he founded had strong links with that of Usman dan Fodio. For a time the Mahdi and his followers managed to roll back British control in the Sudan by defeating General Gordon before suffering defeat by the revenging force led by Lord Kitchener in 1898.

Opposing colonial expansion produced localized resistance influenced by particular circumstances in different parts of the Muslim world. But the call to reform also had a pan-Islamic dimension, an appeal to all Muslims everywhere. This global dimension was founded on a call to return to the spirit of early Islam and a reinterpretation of the Qur'an and Sunnah in light of modern times. The leading names among these reformers are Jamal al Din al-Afghani (1838-97)

Reform movements

and Muhammad Abduh (1849-1905). Afghani has been called 'the wild man of genius'. Born in Afghanistan where he received his education in Islamic religious sciences, from the age of 18 he began his travels around the Muslim world becoming involved in a diverse variety of local movements of dissent. He urged Muslims to engage intellectually with the ideas that underpinned European power, the philosophy and learning that stood behind the political, technological and scientific might of Europe. Afghani joined forces with Abduh, the *mufti* or leader of Egypt, and together they established the *salafiyya* movement based on the idea of using the first Muslim generation, *al-salaf al-salih* (the venerable ancestors) as a model through which contemporary Muslims could re-examine their predicament. It became a systematic philosophy of Islamic reform, influencing generations of Arab Muslims.

The Muslim Brotherhood was another reform movement to come out of Egypt. It was founded in the 1920s by Hasan al-Banna, a schoolteacher, but its leading intellectual and theoretician was Syed Qutb. A literary critic, Qutb collaborated with Gamal Abdel Nasser, the socialist nationalist leader, in the revolution which deposed King Farouk and established Nasser as president of the new Egyptian Republic in 1952. But the two fell out when Nasser refused to introduce sharia law in Egypt. The Brotherhood tried to assassinate Nasser in 1954. Qutb was imprisoned and tortured; and emerged from prison radicalized. In his numerous books, and particularly his commentary on the Qur'an, *In the Shade of the Qur'an*, Qutb argued for a pure Islam uncontaminated with modern illusions. He also called for a jihad against Western and socialist interests as well as against corrupt Muslim rulers. The Brotherhood was outlawed and Syed Qutb was executed – forcing the followers of the Brotherhood to seek refuge in Saudi Arabia and the Sudan.

In India, the call for *ijtihad*, or systematic original thinking, to revitalize Islam made by Afghani and Abduh had tremendous impact on the poet and philosopher, Muhammad Iqbal. In his *Reconstruction of Religious Thought in Islam*, Iqbal argued for a total overhaul of Islamic thought. It was his vision of a separate state for the Muslims of India that eventually led to the creation of Pakistan. The ideas of the Muslim Brotherhood were echoed in India/Pakistan by *Jamaat-e-Islami*, founded in 1932 by Malauna Abu Ala Maududi, a journalist and reformer. *Jamaat-e-Islami* agitated for the sharia in Pakistan and advocated democratic rather than revolutionary reform.

Collectively, the *Jamaat-e-Islami*, the Muslim Brotherhood and the *salafiyya* movement exert tremendous influence throughout the Muslim world. Books by Maududi and Qutb are widely popular among diverse sections of Muslim societies.

8 Contemporary issues

Throughout the world, Muslim societies face a host of pressing issues. Many of these have an overtly political dimension, such as the struggle for a viable Palestinian state, civil war in the Sudan, and post-war reconstructions in Afghanistan and Iraq. There are also huge humanitarian challenges: most of the world's refugees are Muslims, victims of civil wars, political suppression and the 'war on terrorism'. But by far the greatest challenges facing Muslims are internal to Islam: the issues of democracy, women's rights, Islamic law and the rise and spread of fundamentalism. These have trapped Muslim societies in a cycle of despondency and violence.

WHEN MOST MUSLIM countries first obtained their independence in the 1950s, a great deal of hope was placed on economic development as a catalyst for democracy. But the 'development decades' that followed were based on the established patterns of European colonial dominance. Independence did not improve the economic plight of Muslim societies. Worse: the new rulers of Muslim states did not come either from the reform movements, which spearheaded the fight for independence, or from the traditional sector, the religious scholars, who conventionally commanded the respect and loyalty of the populace. The political leadership of the new Muslim states was in the hands of Westernized élites who acted as surrogates for the departing colonial powers. The modern, secular ruling élite marginalized the traditional sector from power and ruthlessly suppressed all forms of tradition. There was thus a constant conflict between the Westernized rulers and the hopes and aspiration of the vast majority of the citizens who were more traditionally inclined.

The jihad in Afghanistan against Soviet occupation gave a new lease of life to the more militant elements in

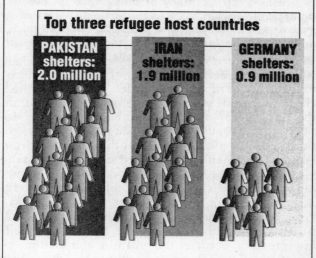

Refugees

The majority of the world's estimated 12 million refugees are Muslim. And most of them take refuge in other Muslim countries.

Top three refugee host countries

PAKISTAN shelters: 2.0 million

IRAN shelters: 1.9 million

GERMANY shelters: 0.9 million

the reform movements. The 1979 'Islamic revolution' in Iran provided traditional scholars with a success story and a taste for power. The militant *jihadis* who brought the Soviet empire to its knees, and who took up arms on behalf of their oppressed brothers in Chechnya, Palestine, Kashmir, Bosnia and other places, wanted to create an ideal Islamic state. The Taliban – literally student – regime in Afghanistan was an attempt to implement that vision. The fall of the Soviet Union brought a string of new nations into the fold of the Muslim world. So now there are some 57 Muslim countries; and an estimated 1.3 billion Muslims worldwide. But in almost every Muslim country, militant fundamentalists are making their presence felt and calling – indeed, in some cases openly fighting – for the establishment of an

'Islamic state'. They see 'the West' as an avowed enemy of Islam. Fundamentalist rage is directed as much against the West as against the modern and moderate elements within Muslim societies.

Fundamentalism

The 20th-century reform movements shared a common theme in stressing the need for a return to *ijtihad*, for sustained reasoned struggle to accommodate Islam with modernity. In contrast, the 21st-century fundamentalist movements are led by an entrenched class of religious scholars whose outlook is based on the fear of *bida*, or innovation. Fundamentalists do not want any change in how Islam was perceived and practiced in medieval times. But this does not mean Islamic fundamentalism is based on a classical religious narrative or Muslim tradition: in fact, it has no historical precedence. It is a concocted, modern dogma. There are two basic elements to this dogma. First, the fundamentalists confuse believing in the truth of Islam with possessing the Truth. Thus, their interpretation becomes the only true and valid interpretation; all others are *bida*, and people who follow such 'innovations' are not true Muslims.

By claiming their version of Islam as the absolute truth, they not only deny the manifest diversity and plurality of Islam, but also arrogate divine powers to themselves. Second, the idea of a modern nation-state is central to the vision of Islamic fundamentalism. Islam and state are one and same thing; one cannot reach its full potential without the other. Thus, all Muslim fundamentalists strive to establish an 'Islamic state', despite the fact Islam categorically rejects the idea of geographical boundaries and sees nationalism as anathema.

This fabricated dogma of Islam-as-State is a totalitarian enterprise. Virtually all Islamic states in contemporary times have been authoritarian and oppressive. Saudi Arabia, revolutionary Iran and the

Sudan provide good examples. Fundamentalist organizations themselves, as their names suggest, are minority movements that seek to exclude the majority from power: 'The Muslim Brotherhood', '*Hizbullah*' ('The Party of God'), *Gamaa-el-Islam* (the Egyptian 'Party of Islam'). The very nature of these insular movements, based as they are on the retrieval of an imagined 'pristine' beginning, leads them to engage with the world in terms of stark dichotomies: fundamentalism versus liberalism, tradition versus modernity, puritanism versus reform, Islam versus the West. Thus everything must be rejected; and everything must be based on the sharia, 'Islamic law'. It is 'Islamic law', fundamentalists argue, that makes an Islamic state Islamic.

Islamic law

Wherever the fundamentalists have acquired power, their first act has been to establish sharia, Islamic law. The sharia, as it is understood and practiced today, owes very little to the Qur'an; so it cannot really be taken, in Islamic terms, as Divine. The Qur'an, as we saw, has remarkably few rules and regulations: most of the Holy Book is devoted to elaborating the attributes of God and the virtues of reason. What goes under the rubric of sharia is mostly *fiqh*, classical jurisprudence, formulated in the Abbasid period when Muslim history was in its expansionist phase, and incorporates the logic of Muslim imperialism of the 8th and 9th centuries. Hence the black and white division of the world into 'the abode of Islam' and 'the abode of war'. This leads to the ruling on apostasy (religious rebellion) which, contrary to the unequivocal declaration of the Qur'an that 'there is no compulsion in religion', equates apostasy with treason against the state. Or the dictate that says non-Muslims should be humiliated and cannot give evidence in a Muslim court. What this means in reality is that when Muslim countries apply or impose sharia – the demand of

Muslims from Algeria to Pakistan to Nigeria – the contradictions inherent in the formulation and evolution of this jurisprudence come to the fore.

Moreover, the puritan fundamentalists are concerned largely with the crime and punishment part of sharia, or what is known as *hudud* laws. The word *hud* means limit; and *hudud* laws are the boundary or outer limit of the laws. A *hudud* punishment is the maximum and most extreme punishment that can be given for a particular crime. The sharia in the guise of the philosophy of Islamic jurisprudence, following the example of Prophet Muhammad, actually discourages the use of *hudud* punishments. Indeed, it insists such punishments can only given in a perfect and just society where economic opportunity for all and social equality are the established norms. So, the *hudud* punishments of cutting off the hands of a thief can only be given in a society where there is no need for anyone to steal and the state has provided all opportunity to make theft a superfluous activity of unmitigated malign intent.

However fundamentalists are only concerned with *hudud* punishments as demonstrable proof the state is enforcing the whole of Islam, not the parameters that define it; or with the notion of balance sharia demands. Their conception of purity means punishments have to be handed out exactly as they were formulated in the 8th century. Thus, the sharia is reduced to cutting off hands of thief, beheading culprits in public squares, and stoning adulterers to death. That is why, wherever Islamic law is imposed, Muslim societies acquire a medieval feel. We can see this in Saudi Arabia, the Afghanistan of the Taliban or Pakistan under General Zia. The fundamentalists' obsession with extreme punishments generates extreme societies.

Even though the sharia is touted as law, it can hardly be described as such. Law, by its very nature is dynamic and takes the moral evolution of humanity into full consideration. The argument within Muslim

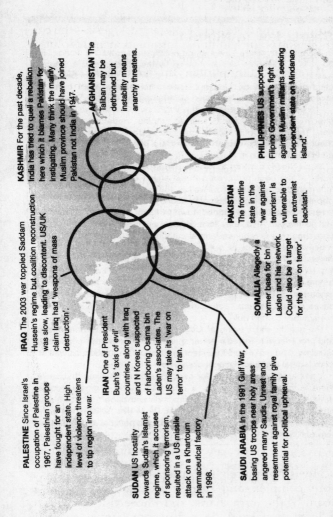

Fundamentalist hot spots

Sharia law in Nigeria

In March 2002 Amina Lawal made headlines around the world. The 30-year-old divorcee was sentenced by the Sharia Court in Bakori, Katsina State in Northern Nigeria to be stoned to death for bearing a child out of wedlock. Charges against her partner were dropped when he retracted his admission of fathering the child.

The case is one of a number in which Sharia Courts have sought to impose *hudud* punishments such as stoning, amputation or mutilation. The word *hudud* means limit and is derived from the Qur'an though the punishments themselves are products of the development of Islamic law in history.

Since Nigeria's return to civilian rule in 1999, eleven states in the north of the country have instituted sharia or Islamic law. It is an intensely charged political as well as communal issue in Africa's most populous and ethnically complex country.

However, sentences handed down by lower sharia courts are subject to appeal. Also, they face political pressure and constitutional challenge by the Nigerian federal authorities who argue that Muslim Nigerians should not be subject to harsher punishment than other Nigerians. The case of Safiya Husseini, sentenced to death by stoning for adultery, was quashed on appeal. Amina Lawal's case is before the Sharia Court of Appeal of Katsina State and has been adjourned a number of times. The appeals process means such cases remain pending, defendants are bailed and no punishments are actually carried out.

The quality and training of judges, representation for defendants and procedures followed in lower sharia courts draw criticism among Muslims, who make up 50 per cent of Nigeria's population, as well as from federal and international observers.

It has long been a cause for concern among Muslims that while there is popular pressure for a return to sharia, ordinary people remain ignorant of their rights, obligations and opportunity to question the procedures within the system. While this remains the case the issue will continue to test the limits of the political and legal system of Nigeria. ■

society is not merely for or against the sharia. It is a more complex and diverse cleavage over what is meant by the term sharia, and whose vision of it is to be institutionalized. As a conceptual term, sharia is intrinsic to Islam and therefore has a claim on the allegiance of all Muslims. For many Muslims it is a vague shorthand for their attachment to Islam as the source of their identity and their vision of social justice. This makes it an effective political slogan: to ask Muslims in general terms to oppose the sharia is akin to inviting them to vote for sin. But sharia as wielded by radical Islamic movements in many countries is an obscurantist (opposed to reform and enlightenment) body of rules and regulations, with little relevance to contemporary times.

When this reductive sharia acquires power it and its power-brokers lack the means and willingness to wrestle with contemporary dilemmas, they fall back on extracting the 'problem' of modernity from the equation by retreating to a supposedly pure, uncontaminated and truncated vision of civic existence. And its first victims tend to be women.

Women's rights

Those who formulated the legal rulings now popularly understood as sharia were largely men. While their intentions were good, and they clearly did not wish their opinions to be cast in stone, they were firmly rooted in their time. They had never known the Prophet and were directly influenced by cultural, intellectual and moral climates which were sometimes antithetical to the Islamic ethos. They thus moved away from the Qur'an's ethical codes for women's full spiritual, moral, social and intellectual autonomy and towards their culturally entrenched notions of women's subservience, objectivity, silence and seclusion.

Thus, the radical changes introduced by the Qur'an in 7th-century Arabian society were totally undone. The Qur'an provided women with explicit rights to inheritance, to property, the obligation to testify in a court of law, and the right to divorce. It made explicit prohibitions on the use of violence against female children and women as well as on duress in marriage and community affairs. Records of legal cases in the classical era of Muslim civilization provide evidence that these precepts were applied and upheld. Marriage in Islam is a civil contract. Historical evidence shows the great diversity of conditions women specified on entering marriage, up to and including the demand for sexual satisfaction, male failure to perform being a matter that could be pursued through the courts both as grounds for divorce and compensation. Property rights and rights to a share in inheritance made independently wealthy Muslim women, who were not obliged to share their wealth with their husbands.

In modern times an entire aid and investment organization has been established to attract funds from women in oil-rich states to support development projects in other parts of the Muslim world. Women were equally responsible for ensuring that all religious duties of the individual and society were fulfilled, in terms of punishment for social, criminal and moral infractions. They were also offered equal opportunities to attain the ultimate boon: paradise and proximity to Allah if they strove with all their means to 'establish what is good and forbid what is evil'. In contrast, the formulators of law could make women in law literally equivalent to material objects and possessions. When they considered women's agency, it was only in regard to service to men and family. Even in matters pertaining to women's exclusive biological make-up, the law focused on the convenience and inconveniences of men. The fundamentalists' sharia approach to women reduces the diversity of practice and interpretation in history to its most chauvinist, exclusivist and morally reprehensible tendencies.

Sharia-minded traditionalists, conservatives and fundamentalists treat women with contempt. For example, the testimony of women is considered – contrary to everything the Qur'an teaches – to be only worth half that of a man. Moreover, being a product of male perceptions, sharia law cannot distinguish between adultery, fornication and rape. As a result victims of rape and sexual abuse can find themselves charged with a crime and sentenced to be stoned to death – an aberrant law since the Qur'an does not sanction stoning to death for any crime whatsoever. Even though the Qur'an privileges women's testimony over men in cases of sexual offenses, in practice sharia courts choose to ignore them. In countries where sharia is the state law, women have worse than third-class status. In Saudi Arabia, for instance, they are not allowed to go out unless accompanied by a male. They may not drive, and have to wear a veil that by law must be black, despite the fact that black absorbs all the heat and is the least appropriate color to wear in a desert climate. (That's why men all wear white!).

In Pakistan and Nigeria, there have been a number of celebrated cases where women who were raped ended up charged with adultery – and, in some cases, sentenced to be stoned to death, although none of the sentences was actually carried out. Certain groups of fundamentalists, such as the Taliban who ruled Afghanistan and dominate the provinces of Northern Pakistan, even deny basic education to women. Statistics clearly show in general Muslim countries lag well behind comparable nations in female literacy and have worse than expected rates for the provision of health care to women and hence higher rates of perinatal and infant mortality.

The picture is bleakest for the weakest and most vulnerable women in Muslim societies, in general those who live in the poorest, most traditional and conservative enclaves. However, women's movements that express their aspirations for individual and social empowerment by appeal to Islam are to be found everywhere. There are women who regard Islam as emancipatory, and who use Islamic institutions and teaching as a resource to empower the poorest and most vulnerable of their sisters. Equally, there are Muslim women who endorse and support the conservative and obscurantist fundamentalist vision of the

Homosexuality

Most Muslims believe that the Qur'an outlaws homosexuality. In fact, the Qur'an is silent on the issue. The only reference it makes to homosexuality occurs when it relates the narrative of Sodom and Gomorrah where it describes the harsh punishment handed out to the people of Prophet Lot. Some Muslim scholars have suggested that this punishment was for 'doing everything excessively' rather than for homosexuality itself.

Classical Muslim jurists have tended to agree that sodomy is a sexual offense but differ in their punishments. According to Imam Abu Hanifa, homosexuality does not amount to adultery and therefore there is no punishment. But Imam Malik, who always takes an extreme view, insists that homosexuality is a capital crime and should be punished by stoning to death. This judgement is based solely on a couple of traditions of the Prophet; the authenticity of these traditions is doubted by some scholars. There is no evidence to suggest that Prophet Muhammad ever punished anyone for sodomy.

Homophobia and persecution of homosexuals is widespread in the Muslim world. Homosexuals have been executed in Saudi Arabia, Iran and Afghanistan, and capital punishment for homosexuality is on the statute books of some 10 Muslim states. In many countries, such as Malaysia and Indonesia, sodomy carries long prison sentences. In Turkey and Egypt homosexuality is not illegal. But Egypt was one of the five countries – which also included Pakistan, Libya, Saudi Arabia and Malaysia – which in April 2003 successfully derailed UN attempts to protect the rights of gays and lesbians. The move by the five countries was strongly supported by the Vatican.

Throughout the world, many Muslim groups, such as the scholars describing themselves as 'progressive Muslims' in the US and the Washington based network Al-Fatiha, are campaigning to reform Muslim attitudes to homosexuality. ∎

sharia and the radical political movements that espouse it. To see Muslim women only as helpless victims would be a mistake, one akin to the enormity of the most chauvinist male Muslim outlook. While the condition of Muslim women is not uniform across all Muslim nations and communities, or indeed between classes and sections of any one society the excessively patriarchical temper of Muslim societies is everywhere present as an impediment to democracy.

Democracy

There is nothing inherently inimical about Islam and democracy. Democracy, or indeed any specific concept, Western or non-Western, clashes with Islam only when it conceives itself as a doctrine of truth or violates one of the fundamental tenets of Islam. Only when democracy is wedded to atheistic humanism and lays claims to being the truth, or when secularism interprets itself as an epistemology or basic guiding philosophy, does it clash with the faith of Islam. As a mechanism for representative government, devoid of its ideological pretensions and trappings, democracy has no quarrel with Islam. Indeed, many concepts of the Islamic worldview, such as the notion of accountability and the injunction to consult (*shura*) the population, can be used to lay the foundations of democracy in Muslim societies and in modern complex societies can be argued to require democratic forms of organization and operation in order to function. But Muslim states, by and large, have chosen not to take this course.

Muslim thinkers have tended to reject democracy on the basis of two dubious arguments. First: the two are incompatible because Islam requires acceptance of unquestionable basic tenets and democracy insists on ceaseless debates and questions. As an example of the irreconcilable nature of the two, we have the frequently cited assertion that in Islam sovereignty belongs to God and in democracy sovereignty belongs to the people. This argument assumes Islam is a blind, unquestioning creed: an assumption contrary to the Qur'anic description of Islam. Moreover, it assumes politics is about relations between people and God, when the business of politics is one person's relation to another. But Western democracies are not perfect; many for example only belatedly came round to the idea that democracy and politics should include women. Democracies, like all other human cooperative endeavors, are also based on principles that are not open for questioning. On the other hand, religion is dependent on human consent, starting from its adoption and ending with its interpretation. Put succinctly, it is the people who determine religion, and not religion that makes the people. Democracy in a society where people are attached to their religious beliefs must reflect this fact.

The second argument is even more banal. It simply states that democracy is a Western construction and, as such, it has nothing to do with Islam and thus must be rejected.

There are deep divisions and animosities among and between various sections of society throughout the Muslim world. Most major political groups hate and fear each other so much they are happy to lose their own freedom to see their opponents defeated or shorn of their freedoms too. These divisions make it difficult to develop sustained democratic movements, since democracy cannot function without a broad consensus on certain basic issues. While an important aspect of democracy is uncertainty about the outcomes of the process, sufficient guarantees are needed that a change of government is not going to be a disaster for the losers. In Pakistan, for example, the leadership of the major losing party has ended up in prison or exile after every election.

The lack of consensus on basic issues has been further aggravated by open conflict between those seeking a more central role for religion in public life and those who oppose it. The growing support for fundamentalist groups, coupled with the capture of power by the Mullahs in Iran, Sudan and the now deposed Taliban in Afghanistan, has worsened the tensions and increased the worries of the dominant secular élite. Since the Algerian democratic experiment of 1988-1991 came within a whisker of putting fundamentalists in power through the ballot box, democracy has became a dirty word in Arab political ruling circles. The wave of democratization that swept the world after the fall of the Berlin Wall left the Muslim world untouched. There is not a single Arab state with even a modicum of democracy. Violations of human rights are common in despotic and authoritarian regimes, such as those in Saudi Arabia, Egypt and Iran. However, there are a few success stories. The democratic experiments in Indonesia, Bangladesh and Tunisia demonstrate that democracy can come to the Muslim world. In all these countries, a broad alliance of democratic forces, which does not exclude the fundamentalists or anyone else, has emerged to champion democratic reform.

9 Beyond the impasse

The spirit of Islam is seriously at odds with the contemporary practice of Islam. This much is obvious. Islam perceives itself as a liberating force; a dynamic social, cultural and intellectual worldview based on equality, justice and universal values. But in the hands of its most pious and puritan followers, it often turns out to be an oppressive and obscurantist enterprise, hell-bent on dragging society back to medieval times. Indeed, many observers can be forgiven for thinking Islam seems to have acquired a pathological strain.

MANY MUSLIMS BLAME the West for their current predicament. Indeed, the West has a great deal to answer for: colonialism, support of despotic regimes in the Muslim world, oppressive economic policies that have reduced many Muslim countries to dependency and abject poverty, and Orientalism, the representation of Islam and Muslims as the darker side of Europe and America. The list is as long as it is painful.

Blaming the West for their ills has almost become a part of Muslim faith. Orientalism, for example, has become a general scapegoat for everything. Among Muslims the existence of Orientalism has become the justification for every sense of grievance, a source of encouragement for nostalgic romanticism about the perfections of Muslim civilization in history and hence a recruiting agent for a wide variety of Islamic movements. It has generated a sense of exclusivity, of being apart and different, from the rest of humanity – a trend that has no precedent in either Islam as religion or Muslim history. Because Orientalism has been demonstrated to exist, then from the Muslim perspective by definition that which is offended against must be defended. That which is the subject of discrimination, prejudice, oppression and all manner of wrongs is thereby established as both innocent and good, no matter what its actual imperfections in practice.

However, Muslims cannot blame everything on the West. The internal problems of Islam are a product of their own failure to come to terms with modernity and interpret their faith in the light of contemporary demands. Whether it is the question of poverty or gender relations, democracy or globalization, the 21st century is full of challenges and new questions. These require new ways of knowing, doing and being for Muslims to understand – let alone to answer. Muslims are thus required to find fresh ways to keep their religion and tradition alive and relevant.

In particular, the tendency to fall back comfortably on age-old interpretations is now dangerously obsolete. This is not a new realization. Scholars and thinkers have been suggesting for well over a century that Muslims must make a serious attempt at *ijtihad*, at reasoned struggle and rethinking, to reform Islam. Ossified and frozen historic interpretations constantly drag Muslims back to medieval times; worse, to perceived and romanticized contexts that never existed in history. So the very ideas and concepts that are supposed to take Muslim societies towards humane values now actually take them in the opposite direction. From the subtle beauty of a perennial challenge to construct justice through mercy and compassion, we get ancient mechanistic formulae fixated on the extremes repeated by people convinced they have no duty to think for themselves because all questions have been answered for them by the classical jurists and religious scholars, far better men now long dead. And because everything carries the brand name of Islam, to question it, or argue against it, is tantamount to voting for sin.

This is why attempts to reform sharia law are seen as attacks on Islam itself. The guardians of the sharia, the religious scholars who were responsible for 'closing the gates of *ijtihad*' several centuries ago, have

been particularly clever in declaring sharia to be totally Divine and equating religion with law. By collapsing
law with religion, any effort to reform the law looks
like an attempt to change the religion. Moreover, by
appropriating all interpretative power in their own
hands, they deny agency to ordinary believers who
have nothing to do except blindly follow obscurantist
mullahs, clerics, who dominate Muslim societies and
circumscribe them with fanaticism and absurdly
reductive logic. To change the sharia, and hence
reform Islam, ordinary Muslims have to stand up to
powerfully entrenched clerics and interpretive communities who see any reform as a direct threat to their
monopoly on religious knowledge. By equating Islam
with the State, obscurantist religious forces are also
trying, and indeed have succeeded in many cases, to
add political power to their religious authority.

Unless Islam is reformed, authoritarianism, oppression of women and minorities, obscurantism and nos-
talgia for medieval times will continue to reign
supreme in the Muslim world. The way to a fresh, contemporary appreciation of Islam requires Muslims, as
individuals and communities, to reclaim agency. They
have to insist on their right and duty, as believers and
knowledgeable people, to interpret and reinterpret
the basic sources of Islam. They need to question what
now goes under the general rubric of sharia, to
declare that much of *fiqh* is now dangerously obsolete,
to stand up to the absurd notion of an Islam confined
by a geographically bound state. The very survival of
Islam as a viable, thriving worldview depends on these
radical transformations.

The West has the task of learning to think differently about Islam and Muslims. The Muslim world must
rethink Islam itself. It needs to learn how its values, its
moral and ethical impulses are not a separate order
but integral part of the common concerns of contemporary human dilemmas. Muslims want sustainable
development, human betterment, are concerned

about saving the Earth, where science is going, how to attain a just, equitable and inclusive social and political order where they live and are worried about the downside of globalization. To these common concerns they bring a particular way of seeing problems. They have to realize Islam does not provide ready-made answers to these concerns. Only by working together, with mutual respect, can Islam and the West transcend their history of conflict and suspicion and shape a viable future for all humanity.

Glossary

Adl: justice, more particularly, distributive justice in all its various manifestations: social, economic, political, environmental as well as intellectual and spiritual.

Din: Islam's description of itself. In its primary sense *din* means a return to man's inherent nature. In general, *din* not only includes the idea of religion as commonly understood, but also the notions of culture, civilization, tradition and worldview.

Fiqh: Islamic jurisprudence.

Hadith: sayings or traditions of the Prophet Muhammad.

Halal: lawful, good and beneficial.

Haram: unlawful, and socially, morally and spiritually harmful.

Hijra: the migration of the Prophet Muhammad from Mecca to Medina in the 12th year of his mission in June 622 CE/AD. It marks the beginning of the Islamic calendar (the years AH) which is thus referred to as *hijra* calendar.

Ijma: literally, agreeing upon, consensus of the community in general, and the learned in particular.

Ijtihad: systematic original thinking; exerting oneself to the utmost degree to reach comprehension and form an opinion.

Ilm: knowledge in all forms, and distributive knowledge in particular; it incorporates the notion of wisdom and justice.

Islam: peace, submission to God, religion of God, the natural inclination of man.

Jihad: literally, striving. Any earnest striving in the way of God, involving personal, financial, intellectual or physical effort, for righteousness and against oppression or wrong doing.

Sharia: literally means the path to a watering hole; it is the ethical, moral and legal code of Islam. Conventionally translated as 'Islamic Law'.

Sirah: the life or biography of the Prophet Muhammad.

Sunnah: literally, path or example. Applies particularly to the example of the Prophet Muhammad and includes what he said, actually did and agreed to.

Ulama: religious scholars.

Ummah: the ensemble of Muslim individuals and communities forming an entity of common culture with common goals and aspirations, as well as certain self-consciousness, but not necessarily a coincident common polity.

Waqf: pious, charitable foundation.

Zakat: the compulsory purifying tax on wealth; one of the five pillars of Islam.

Timeline

569-649
Prophet Muhammad born in Mecca (569)
Death of the Prophet Muhammad (632)
Abu Bakr becomes First Caliph (632)
Omar becomes Second Caliph (634)
Expansion to Syria
Expansion to Iraq
Capture of Jerusalem (638)
Introduction of the Hijra calendar
Expansion to Persia
Conquest of Egypt
Othman becomes Third Caliph (644)
Expansion into the Maghreb
Creation of Arab Navy
Capture of Cyprus

650-700

Compilation of the Qur'an (650-652)
Defeat of the Byzantines
Ali becomes Fourth Caliph (656)
Proclamation of Mu'awiya as Caliph in defiance of Ali (660)
Assassination of Caliph Ali (661)
Umayyad dynasty established in Damascus
Mu'awiya I becomes Caliph (661)
Indian numerals appear in Syria
Introduction of Arabic coinage
Yezid becomes Caliph (679)
The battle of Kerbala and massacre of Hussain and his party (689)

700-750

Invasion of Spain (711)
Expansion of Muslims into Indus Valley
Crossing of Muslims into France (718)
Battle of Tours (732)
Umayyad dynasty ends (749)

751-800

Introduction of paper industry in the Arab world
The publication industry established as a sophisticated enterprise
The great compliers of *hadith* publish their works: al-Bukhari, Muslim, Abu
Dawood, al-Tirmidhi, ibn Maja and al-Nasai
Abbasid dynasty founded
Al-Saffar becomes Caliph
Spanish Umayyads established in Cordoba (756)
Beginning of the Mutazilite philosophy (757)
Foundation of Baghdad (762)
Ibn Ishaq publishes the famous biography of the Prophet Muhammad
Death of Imam Hanifa

Timeline

Charlemagne's Invasion of Spain; Death of Roland (778)
Blue mosque of Cordoba founded, Harun al-Rashid becomes Caliph (786)
Idrisids are established in Morocco (788)
Islamic Jurisprudence (*fiqh*) codified with six 'Schools of Thought' established

800-850

Ibn Hisham publishes his biography of the Prophet Muhammad
Philosopher al-Kindi established as the first Muslim philosopher
The first public hospital established in Baghdad (809)
Jabir ibn Hayan establishes chemistry as an experimental science
Imam Shafi dies (820)
Sicily conquered (827)
al-Khwarizmi publishes *Algebra*
Bayt al-Hikmah (House of Wisdom), public library, is founded in Baghdad (832)
The translations of the works of Greece, Babylonia, Syria, Persia, India and Egypt reaches its peak
The Mutazalite (rational) School of philosophy founded
The Thousand and One Nights makes an early appearance

851-900

Al-Jahiz, the 'goggle-eyed' publishes *The Book of Animals*
Philosopher al-Farabi publishes *The Perfect State*
Hunyan ibn Ishaq, the renowned translator, publishes translation of Greek philosophy and other works
Mosque of ibn Tulun built in Cairo (878)
The Ulama established as a major force against the State
Philospher al-Razi
Musa Brothers publish their book of mechanical devices
Al-Battani publishes *On the Sciences of Stars*
Al-Fargani publishes his *Elements of Astronomy*

901-950

Death of Thabit ibn Qurrah, mathematician, philosopher
Historian al-Tabari and poet al-Mutanabbi born (915)
Death of Al-Hallaj (922)
Al-Razi, publishes first book on smallpox and measles
Poet Firdawsi born (934)
Mathematician Abu al-Wafa born (940)

951-1000

Geographer al-Masudi dies
al-Haytham publishes *Optics* containing the basic formulae of reflection and refraction
Fatimid dynasty established in Egypt (966)
Al-Azhar mosque built in Cairo (970)
Al-Baruni publishes *India and Determination of the Co-ordinates of the Cities*
Poet al-Maarri born (973)

Ghaznavid dynasty established in Afghanistan and northern India (977)
Philosopher and physician ibn Sina publishes *Canons of Medicine*, the standard text for the next 800 years; and many philosophic works
The publication of *Fihirst al-Nadim*, the Catalogue of books contained in the bookshop of al-Nadim (987)
Al-Azhar University, the first in the world, established in Cairo (988)
The Ghurids succeed the Ghaznavids in Afghanistan and northern India
Humanist Al-Masudi lays the foundation of human geography

1001-1100

Statesman, educator Nizam al-Mulk born
Poet Omar Khayyam solves equations of three degrees
Theologian, thinker al-Ghazali publishes *The Revival of Religious Sciences* and *The Incoherence of the Philosophers*
Geographer al-Idrisi born
'The Brethren of Purity' and other Encyclopedists publish various encyclo-pedias, including periodical part-works
Muslims travel as far as Vietnam where they establish communities

1101-1200

Al-Idrisi of Sicily publishes the first detailed map of the world
Philosopher, psychologist ibn Bajja publishes *Ilm al-Nafs*, and establishes psychology as a separate discipline
Philosopher, novelist ibn Tufail publishes *The Life of Hayy*
Ibn Rushd publishes *The Incoherence of the Incoherence* and other philo-sophic works
Salahuddin ('Saladin') captures Jerusalem (1187) and unites the Muslim world with Egypt as its center
Al-Hariri publishes his linguistic masterpiece, *The Assemblies*
Yaqut al-Hamawi publishes his Geographical Dictionary
Poet Nizami born

1201-1300

Fakhr al-Din Razi publishes his great *Encyclopedia of Science*
Mystic poet Jalal-al-Din Rumi publishes *The Mathnavi*
Biographer Abu Khallikan establishes philosophy of history as a distinct discipline
Farid al-Din Attar publishes *The Conference of the Birds*
The Nasrids established in Granada (1230)
Mongols sack Baghdad (1258); the city's 36 public libraries are burnt
Abbasid Caliphate ends (1258)
The Ottoman Empire founded (1281)
The Rise of the Mamluks in Egypt
Ibn Nafis accurately describes the circulation of the blood
Nasir al-Din al-Tusi completes his work *Memoir of the Science of Astronomy* (1261) at the Maragha observatory setting forward a compre-hensive structure of the universe; and develops the 'Tusi couple' enabling mathematical calculations to establish a heliocentric worldview
Islamic science and learning translated into European languages

Timeline

1301-1400

Ibn Khuldun establishes sociology and publishes *Introduction to History*
Ibn Battuta publishes his *Travels*
Islam established in Indonesia and Malayan Archipelago
Mali, Gao and Timbuktu become important Muslim centers
Poet Hafiz, master of the *ghazal*, publishes his poetry

1401-1500

Death of Jami, the last of the great Sufi poets
Islamic science and learning begins to be incorporated in Europe

1501-1600

Mughal dynasty established in India (1526)
Eclipse of Timbuktu as the Great City of Learning (1591)
Ottoman Architect Sinan builds the Blue Mosque complex in Istanbul

1601-1700

Taj Mahal completed in Agra, India (1654)
Islamic Humanism adopted in Europe

1701-1800

British colonization of India
Shah Waliullah establishes resistance against the British in India
Usman dan Fodio establishes the Sokoto Caliphate in Northern Nigeria
Muhammad bin Abdul Wahhab establishes the Wahhabi movement in Arabia, Syria and Iraq
Sayyid Muhammad bin Ali al-Sanusi establishes the Sanusiyyah movement in North Africa

1801-1900

'Indian Mutiny' (1857)
Jamal al-Din Al-Afghani, Muhammad Abduh and Rashid Rida establish the pan-Islamic movement
Sir Syed Ahmad Khan establishes the Muslim University of Aligrah, India (1875)

1901-2000

Kemal Ataturk ends Caliphate (1914)
Rise of Nationalism in the Muslim World
Poet and philosopher Muhammad Iqbal publishes *Complaint and Answer*
Pakistan created as the first 'Islamic state' (1947)
Organization of Islamic Conference (OIC) established (1969)
Emergence of OPEC (1972)
'Islamic revolution' in Iran (1979)

Bibliography

The Koran Interpreted by A J Arberry (Oxford University Press, 1964).

The Meaning of the Glorious Koran by M M Pickthall (various editions).

Introducing Islam by Ziauddin Sardar and Zafar Abbas Malik (Icon Books, 2002).

On Being a Muslim by Farid Esack (One World, 1999).

Revival and Reform in Islam by Fazlur Rahman (One World, 2000).

Women in the Qur'an by Amina Wadud (Oxford University Press, 1999).

'Believing Women' in Islam by Asma Barlas (University of Texas Press, 2002).

Orientalism by Ziauddin Sardar (Open University Press, 1999).

The Crusades Through Arab Eyes by Amin Maalouf (Al-Saqi, 1984).

Islamic Science and Engineering by Donald R Hill (Edinburgh University Press, 1993).

A History of Arab People by Albert Hourani (Faber and Faber, 1991).

The Venture of Islam Marshall Hodgson (Chicago University Press, 1974, 3 vols).

Contacts

AOTEAROA/NEW ZEALAND
International Muslim
Association of New Zealand
PO Box 3101, Wellington
Tel: + 644 387 4226
Email: iman@paradise.net.nz

AUSTRALIA
The Australian Federation of
Islamic Councils
PO Box 1185, Waterloo DC NSW
2017
Tel: + 61 2 9319 6733
Fax: + 61 2 9319 0159
Email: afichalal@bigpond.com

CANADA
Canadian Islamic Congress
Suite 424, 420 Erb St W
Waterloo N2L 6K6
Tel: + 1 519 746 1242
Email: cic@cicnow.com

Canadian Muslim Civil Liberties
Association
885 Progress Ave. UPH 14, Toronto
M1H 3G3
Tel: + 1 416 289 3871
Fax: + 1 416 289 0339

IRELAND
The Islamic Foundation of
Ireland
163 South Circular Road, Dublin 8
Tel: + 353 453 3242
Email: ifi@indigo.ie

UK
Muslim Council of Britain
PO Box 52
Wembley, Middlesex HA9 0XW
Tel: + 44 20 8903 9024
Email: admin@mcb.org.uk

The Islamic Foundation
Markfield Conference Centre
Ratby Lane, Markfield
Leicester LE67 9SY
Tel: + 44 1530 244 944
Email: info@islamic-
foundation.org.uk

US
Islamic Society of North
America
PO Box 38
Plainfields, IN 46168
Tel: + 1 317 839 8157
Email: info@isna.org

American Muslim Council
1212 New York Avenue
NW Suit 400, Washington DC
20005-6102
Tel: + 1 202 789 2262
Email: amc.dc@ix.netcomcom

The Council of American-
Islamic Relations
453 New Jersey Avenue SE,
Washington DC 20003-4034
Tel: + 1 202 488 8787
Email: webmaster@cair-net.org

Index

Index

Index

Index